MAN
OVERBOARD

Dan Buckley is a journalist, essayist and commentator. He is a columnist with the *Irish Examiner* newspaper and has had his work syndicated in Britain and the United States. A graduate in law, from the National University of Ireland, he lives in Cork with his wife and three children, who think that when he is not at home he is working hard in the office.

MAN
OVERBOARD

DAN BUCKLEY

MERLIN
PUBLISHING

First published in 2003 by
Merlin Publishing
16 Upper Pembroke Street
Dublin 2, Ireland
Tel: +353 1 676 4373
Fax: +353 1 676 4368
publishing@merlin.ie
www.merlin-publishing.com

ISBN 1-903582-53-9

A CIP catalogue record for this book is available from the
British Library.

10 9 8 7 6 5 4 3 2 1

Typeset by Gough Typesetting Services
Cover design by encoredesign
Printed and bound in Denmark, by Nørhaven Paperback A/S

Dedication

To Lorraine, with love

In memory of Donal Buckley (1921–2001) and Noel
O'Sullivan (1972–1999)

Acknowledgements

Thanks to PJ Gibbons, Gerard McCarthy, Brian Looney, Mick Keohane, Jim Buckley, Neil O'Sullivan, Bob Linehan, Pat Brosnan, TP O'Mahony, Conor Keane, Brian O'Connell, Eddie Lyons, Martin Ellis, Michael McAuliffe, Martin Howard and Dick Brazil for their friendship.

To my children Luke, Adrian and Fiona, and my mother, Imelda, for their love and wisdom.

To Linda Kenny for her encouragement.

To Aoife Barrett, my editor, for helping to turn an idea into a reality.

To Lorraine for everything.

Contents

	Introduction	ix
ONE	Home and Away	1
TWO	Football Fever	24
THREE	Father's Daze	40
FOUR	Family Values	59
FIVE	Brave New World	77
SIX	Growing Old Disgracefully	93
SEVEN	The Wrong Stuff	108
EIGHT	Celebrity Squares	123
NINE	DIY Disasters	140
TEN	The Mother of all Househusbands	155
ELEVEN	Eat Your Heart Out	175
TWELVE	The Body Beautiful	192

THIRTEEN   Cheers   208

FOURTEEN   Play Mates   225

FIFTEEN   Game of Love   243

SIXTEEN   Young and Old Fogies   259

SEVENTEEN   Toys for Big Boys   275

EIGHTEEN   Back to the Future   291

Introduction

Tammy Wynette was right when she declared: "Sometimes it's hard to be a woman." What she never sang about, and what is rarely mentioned in song or in story, is that it is often even harder to be a man, particularly in the 21st century. While women are said to Want It All, men are often expected to Do It All. Mostly they fail miserably.

For example the NEW MAN has to be:

1. A superstud in bed, even if he's knackered or if the only thing that makes his blood boil is the electricity bill.

2. Forceful, proactive, and often ruthless at work when he's a wimp at heart.

3. Kind, caring, gentle and mild with the kids even if they are driving him up the walls.

4. Great 'craic' with the lads down the pub.

5. DIY genius even if the only jigsaw he's ever tackled before had 1000 pieces.

6. Healthy – trying to keep his six-pack while drinking a six-pack (not an easy thing to do).

7. Great cook, great host. (I think I have got this one figured: get everyone pretty pissed with granny's eggnog and feed them amazing concoctions like black pudding and raspberries.)

8. Clever, thoughtful and an adept at *The Time's* cryptic crossword. (If in doubt, cheat.)

9. Reasonably good at housework and has to know where

the vacuum cleaner is, even if he rarely bothers. Must be able to make feeble attempt at ironing and appear contrite when he makes a hash of it.

10. Must be good in a crisis, like when the dog pees between the floorboards. (Kick his arse out the door and spray Dettol between the cracks.) If there is a loose floorboard, it can be fixed in a jiffy but don't do what I did – hammered a nail through the water pipe and flooded the kitchen and had to call a REAL MAN in to fix it.

11. Has to know the name of the subs on the Liverpool team – otherwise he's not really a sports fan.

12. Cannot put his arm around a buddy unless they are both pissed. (This is only in the western world – in North Africa and among the Eskimos men hold hands all the time without embarrassment.)

* * * * *

We don't do a lot of male bonding in the pub or even when a few of us get together for a weekly round of poker. But what the card game does that no pub has ever managed is to allow a bunch of guys talk to one another without slurring too much. We often discuss our innermost feelings (yes, girls, really). My buddies have, each of them, helped, guided, goaded and saved me through the years in my quest to be friend, lover, husband, father, brother, son and colleague. I have changed not alone their names but also their occupations, hobbies and interests. This is not to protect the innocent, but to protect me.

The following mixture of reflections, observations and home brewed philosophy, was inspired by all of them.

ONE
Home and Away

"Whose twist is it?"

"What do you mean?"

"I mean whose turn is it. You've got to learn the lingo."

"I think it's mine," said Dan, "but I've lost track. Are Clubs wild or what?"

Mick threw down his hand, exasperated. "Jesus, Dan, you're always the same. I know you're only learning to play but you have to concentrate if you want to stay on top of your game. Keep focused, or you'll never get anywhere. You have the attention span of a gnat. You always seem to have your mind on something else."

Mick was right, of course. I was always losing my concentration and I often despaired of ever improving. Mick had tried to teach me everything he knew about the game but no matter how hard I tried my mind tended to wander a bit. The other problem was that I didn't really have a killer instinct and would never make anything more than a very mediocre player, even if I could learn how to remember every hand played. I'll never forget the first thing he said to me when he agreed to teach me the basics: "Poker isn't a matter of life and death, Dan. It's more important than that." Even after a year of being a fully-fledged member of the poker school I still managed to get the hands confused. That's partly because I never seem to have much time to practice: three kids, a dog and

1

a goldfish take up a lot of time.

There are five of us in the school, all guys, and we usually meet every Wednesday night for a game. Some of the others have been playing together for years but I'm still the rookie. On this occasion, we were in my place seated around a small round table in the sitting room. Plato, our King Charles spaniel, was lying at my feet and the kids were watching TV in the living room. There was an easy air of home comfort about the place. It's a different venue each week but what the lads call "the married houses" are usually favoured. If we're really lucky we might get to play a couple of times a month at Mick's house. He's married to Laura, an American, and she makes a blueberry pie to kill for. She was once a beauty queen but now loves nothing better than to cook all day and wait hand and foot on her husband and kids. Mick, of course, isn't complaining.

I raised up both hands as a kind of mock surrender. "I'm sorry, guys. It's just that I can't decide whether I should simply see Jim's bet and call, or raise the bet." With an audible sigh, Mick lifted his enormous bulk from the table to come around and help me with my hand.

It was shaping up to be one of those nights. Five guys, five card poker, little enough in the pot but everyone but me playing like it was downtown LA and the game was seven card stud for high stakes.

Jim – the only divorcee among us – couldn't resist one of his usual bitchy comments. According to him, Mick has it all.

"It's incredible. Can you imagine in this day and age any guy getting away with things the way he does? Here's Mick, forty-one, 6'2" at least 22 stone and with a beer gut the size of Texas. He spends his time either playing

2

poker, trout fishing or drinking, and yet the lovely Laura thinks the sun shines out of his ass," Jim moaned.

"Maybe it does," said Martin with a laugh as he gazed over the top of his Dolce and Gabbana glasses and stroked his goatee beard. "His ass is certainly big enough."

Mick turned on Martin, obviously about to explode but just then an eight-year-old vision in blonde pigtails and a combat jacket shot out from behind an oversized pot plant brandishing a very realistic looking rifle. She was supposed to have gone to bed by now and I was supposed to have made sure she'd got there. Her mother had, very sensibly, skipped town in order to avoid five pairs of smelly feet around the kitchen table.

Looking like a cross between Annie Oakley and Heidi, she yelled: "Ok, Dad, I'm ready to kick some serious ass."

I stared in amazement at the murderous looking piece of machinery slung nonchalantly over her tiny shoulders.

"What the hell is that?" asked Gerry, in his usual polite manner. He seems to reserve his worst moments for kids, probably because he can't stand them.

Raising herself to her full four-foot nothing, Fiona pointed the gun directly at his big head. "Don't you know anything? It's my AK47."

It could have been a P45 for all I knew.

Gerry's jaw dropped. "Is she demented or what?"

I decided not to answer that one – she was armed after all. I know it's a cliché but it is nonetheless true: it's all the fault of television. I don't mind *The Rugrats* so much; I have become accustomed to *The Simpsons* but I reckon that watching one dysfunctional TV family is more than enough. I just never figured on programmes like the news or documentaries as sources of corruption. In fact,

I positively encourage the kids to watch the news in the hope of instilling them with a sense of wonder. I want the kids to at least have some idea about what's going on in the wider world. Clearly, I realised as I eyeballed Fiona, I should have monitored it more closely. How was I to know that the sight of huge naval ships on the high seas in various war-torn parts of the world would excite my very own battalion? How could I have guessed that those giant aircraft carriers could stir the blood and fire the imagination like no amount of watching *The Simpsons* could ever do? Who could have imagined that the sight of those armoured cars and guns would inspire war games on the home front? As a result, the style of the moment has changed to combats, fatigues and flak jackets, and the mood has obviously become combative.

"Look honey," said Gerry, "we're in the middle of a war of our own here and we don't need AK47s to win. It's called poker. Fighting a war is like playing poker. You just have to find your enemy's weak spot and let him have it. Don't they teach you anything useful in school?"

Fiona ignored him with a haughty air.

He then turned to me. "Isn't she supposed to be in bed or something? It's nearly nine o'clock and she's still running around the place. It's not good for kids to be up late."

It is, of course, typical of Gerry to rattle on about something he knows absolutely nothing about. He is always reminding us that he has no intention of having kids. But, then, he used to say the same thing about getting married. He was once a serial-shagger until, aged thirty-seven, to everyone's surprise, he settled down with Fionnuala, literally the girl next door. He used to go backpacking in the Andes during the summer; now he's

4

bought a house in the suburbs, drives a Ford Mondeo and has even taken up DIY. He'll probably take up knitting next. We're all counting the days until he and Fionnuala have twins. I can't wait until he has to drag himself out of bed for two o'clock feeds. He won't know what's hit him. He was the youngest in his family so, unlike myself, he never had the joy of looking after younger brothers and sisters. If he had, he might have learned that when it comes to the arduous and often dangerous task of minding kids you need an eagle eye, a sixth sense and the stamina of a racehorse.

Once, when I was fourteen, my babysitting services were offered, without consultation, to a young couple up the road who had twin boys. They had been badly in need of a night on the town – the parents, not the children. I had, of course, been duly informed that the kids were little angels and wouldn't be the least bit of bother. I should have guessed that this was mere tactical evasion, considering the haste with which the couple took their departure. They'd stopped only to impart fleeting kisses on their children along with a mumbled: "Be good."

The kids hadn't looked like twins. One had been a big bruiser with foxy hair and the other had been a stick insect with ears so big you could feel a draught whenever his head moved. But they'd been as one when it came to making life a misery for the minder. I don't remember exactly how all the fuss started, but it had something to do with the mystery of the missing toffees. They began by bickering and whingeing and trading insults and, before I knew it, Foxy had Big Ears by the throat while, at the same time, the slighter boy was attempting to implant a fork into the ample rear end of his bigger brother. "Cut that out," I'd barked, to no avail. It had soon become

5

apparent that no amount of shouting, cajoling or pleading was going to make the slightest difference. Physical intervention was called into play but it was a big mistake. They now had a common enemy and they played me like a fool. I had been prepared to let them have their little victory when I'd heard the cat screeching from the confines of the bin under the sink but I'd had to draw the line when I discovered my glasses hidden in the fridge. Different tactics had been called for and, as luck would have it, relief came in the form of a particularly scary ghost story that sent the little horrors to bed white-faced and shivering. Served them right, too.

Recalling my encounter with the terrible twins, I smirked at Gerry. "You know, Gerry, why don't you take Fiona to bed? It will be good practice for when you and Fionnuala have a big brood of your own."

He looked horrified, as I thought he would be at the notion of having anything to do with kids. I certainly could never imagine him being able to cope with those little childish disasters, like the time when Adrian, my Number Two Son, went AWOL and was finally found on the roof of the garage with arms outstretched, singing a nursery rhyme. He was a year and a half at the time and still in nappies. Not long after that episode I'd had the stupidity to bring the new all-singing, all-dancing video player back to the shop, in a state of high dudgeon. I had been quickly informed that Sony could hardly be held responsible for the fact that it didn't work, considering that within its bowels rested half a pack of digestive biscuits along with the baby Jesus from the crib that had been missing since Christmas. Lorraine, had had a few things to say to me when I'd taken the video player home. She'd said a lot more when she caught me using an antique silver fish fork to extricate the baby Jesus from his new manger. In any event, no amount of poking and prodding did any good. I'd even tried praying for a miracle, considering that The Man Above might take pity on The Baby Below but Jesus had refused to budge and the video had to be despatched to the dustbin.

Gerry wasn't the only one looking aghast when I suggested he put Fiona to bed. Martin didn't fancy the idea one bit because he liked to do it and Fiona loved his bedtime stories. Martin is great with kids. He is forty-two, a pilot, single and not the marrying kind, anyway. Martin is gay and, while he doesn't try to hide it, doesn't believe in shouting it from the rooftops, either. Being in the airline business, he spends a lot of time abroad and when he is drunk he loves to regale us all with tales of his one-night stands all over the world. Unlike Gerry he would make a great dad; he loves kids and they seem to adore him He often looks after Jim's son Cian, when Jim is away on business.

"I'll take her up," said Martin, as he lifted Fiona and the AK47 in one swoop. He ignored her pretend protest and started carrying her upstairs. "You take my turn, Dan. I'll be a few minutes."

I shouted out a placatory goodnight but got no reply.

I didn't bother taking Martin's turn as no-one else seemed interested in continuing to play until he came back. Instead, I uttered the magic words.

"Anyone for a beer?"

What a stupid question. Everyone wanted a beer, even my fourteen-year-old, Luke, who peeped his head around the door and shouted: "Make mine a Carlsberg." Seeing the look on my face, he quickly disappeared again.

When Martin returned ten minutes later we settled

down to continue playing.

"How's the little soldier?" asked Gerry. "Did she fall asleep with her AK47 under her pillow?"

Martin ignored him and sat down to play, but the game seemed to have lost momentum.

After another hour of lacklustre playing, we all decided to pack it in for the night and just lay about drinking. Martin had already chucked in his hand and had started scouring the newspaper horoscopes – his latest passion.

Everyday he scours whatever paper he can get his hands on to read 'Mystic Meg' or whoever and he takes it all very seriously. Whether he is asked to or not, he will read out everyone's horoscope like he is Moses announcing the Ten Commandments.

"You're Capricorn, aren't you?" he asks.

"Yes, you know that, you always ask and I am still a Capricorn, sign of the goat."

It didn't faze him one bit.

"Well, have I got news for you. According to Meg, you are about to '…enter a period of supreme enlightenment, perfect happiness and undiluted contentment.'"

"I'm not impressed."

"It could be worse. You could be a Libra and be facing ' …dark clouds on the horizon and troubled finances.'"

In any case, my horoscope couldn't be right I thought gloomily, only half-listening as Martin told Gerry, who is – big surprise – a Taurus, about life changing times ahead. Meg's crystal ball must have been a bit overcast because it obviously had not taken into account the advent of that most momentous, calamitous event that sweeps through the solar system annually. Most people murmur about it in hushed tones and only the bravest of the brave will dare to talk about it – The Annual Family Summer

Holiday. Unless you are one of life's planners, preparations for this do not start until schools close for the summer. When classrooms spill their contents, parents, minders and guardians of trainee delinquents, know exactly what they are letting themselves in for. It means that you are parentally obliged to organise something at least approaching a family holiday, even if it's only a mobile home perched on a wet and windy hilltop somewhere.

Every family needs to strike off for somewhere, anywhere, with more weather and less climate than home. The only problem is I should have sorted it out months ago but I am not one of life's planners. In fact, the one time I did take our holiday into my own hands, it was a disaster. Just ask the kids. They are still scarred by the memory of The Holiday That Never Was.

It had seemed like a good idea at the time. There I was in the office trawling through the 'Holiday Bargains' on the net when I should have been working. (Mick is right: I do have the attention span of a gnat.) I clicked on 'Family friendly' and up came 'Half price special to Lanzarote'. It had also defined 'family' as two adults and three children' which was unusual because usually tour operators assume there are only two kids in any family. I decided there and then to do the manly thing and book the lot. Lorraine wasn't exactly overjoyed when I'd arrived home later that day and announced: "It's all sorted. I have made an executive decision. We're going to Lanzarote. Everything is done and dusted. We leave on Saturday night at eleven o'clock."

The only trouble was when we had arrived at the airport on Saturday night, the place had looked strangely deserted, without the usual frantic crowds queueing at the check-in desks. It had turned out that the eleven o'clock flight had gone at eleven o'clock that morning. The scene of grief that followed still gives me nightmares. As we had driven home from the airport, I had felt four pairs of eyes aimed at my head. I had been about as popular as a wet week in Kerry, which is what we'd ended up with.

After that experience you'd think I would have known better. But, no, last weekend there I was again doing the rounds of the travel agents months later than any sane and organised dad. Ever the optimist, though, I'd still held onto my dream. We would all jet off into the wide blue wonder with a smile as wide as the Grand Canyon and not a care in the world. The destination would be warm but not too hot, sultry without being oppressively humid, exotic yet civilised, exclusive but not too remote. I had even thought of my Nana and taken into account her old dictum: "Who's going to pay for all this?" Why, the Lotto, of course. But just to be safe I had worked out that in the meantime my, sometimes, friendly bank manager would have to do. I was looking for something at a reasonable price so I wouldn't have to pretend that I was planning yet another home extension. Really, all I wanted was a family holiday in some nice hotspot by the beach with a swimming pool or two, half-board, with lots of kids' stuff going on.

As I had quickly discovered things in the holiday market have not changed for the better. There was a time when you could venture inside the door of your local travel agent and expect to be treated, if not like a long lost cousin, at least as a welcome customer with money to spend. The staff would be attentive and affable, helpful without being sickeningly deferential, and just on the right side of cheerfulness. You could browse through the

10

brochures at your leisure, ask any manner of stupid questions like: "Do the Turks really eat their young?"; "Is it really cold in Alaska?"; "Would I need to bring much rain gear with me to Gran Canaria?". The staff wouldn't bat a false eyelash.

Nowadays you have to wait and wait – marking time long enough for the climate to change. Then they will barely offer you the time of day, except to say: "You left it a bit late, didn't you? Nothing doing in this decade, I'm afraid."

When I'd finally got to the desk I could see the travel agent sizing me up. You didn't have to be a rocket scientist to see she'd had me figured for a born loser. It must come from years of dealing with no-hopers and eternal optimists who always leave everything to the last minute. She hadn't even bothered trying to disguise her disdain when I'd innocently enquired as to what might be available for July.

"Which July do you mean? Next year or the year after?"

Some questions don't need answering and that had been one of them. I hadn't been inclined to give her any more ammunition. She had still managed to throw me a sidewinder, though, with a question of her own, as I attempted to slink out the door.

"Is it still raining outside?"

That hadn't needed answering either.

Bloodied but unbowed, I had tried another agency and, as I'd waited for my turn again or death – whichever came soonest – I had begun to toy with the idea of choosing the destination alphabetically, as in B is for Bali, C is for the Canaries, G is for Greece, T is for Turkey. It was a way of passing the time. The place was packed solid – if

11

they'd allowed any more people in, they would have needed a lubricant. Eventually, the assistant had granted me an audience and I'd decided to share my novel approach.

"Of course, B is also for Brighton and Baltimore," she'd said with an evil titter, before going on to suggest that B was for Ibiza (I'd dared not contradict her), and that was all that might be available. "Nothing else, I'm afraid. I've gone through the rest, unless you fancy Z for Zanzibar."

I had left in a fury, harbouring dark thoughts of what F might stand for.

On the way home, in a moment of madness, I had even wondered about asking Mick for a loan of his mobile home for a week or two. Lorraine had not been exactly over the moon about the idea. "Are you kidding me? First of all, it's right in the middle of a bog and, secondly, it's a caravan, not a mobile home, and it isn't much bigger than a kitchen table. We'd be dug out of each other before the day was out. In any case your record as regards family holidays leaves a lot to be desired. I'll just have to sort it out myself!"

She'd spent the rest of the night stalking the web for last minute offers. I could tell she was far from happy from the body language and some subsequent dark mutterings about not being able to get anywhere except France and nothing being available even there until August.

I was still wondering about the mobile home idea as Mystic Martin ended the horoscopes and started counting his winnings. Mick, though, didn't look in a favour-granting mood as he carefully counted up the deck. He does this towards the end of every session and it drives us all mad. Does he really think anyone is going to run off with an eight of clubs?

12

Martin looked at the money. "It isn't much but I'll be in foreign lands next week and it will come in handy. I'm not working, just taking a few days of well-earned rest in Bali. It beats the hell out of Brittany, Dan."

It certainly did and we were all jealous as hell, especially Mick who had two weeks with five kids in a mobile home to look forward to. Even Gerry couldn't help but envy him.

"I lived there for a while after I left college. It's really beautiful. It will probably be years before I ever see it again. Fionnuala and I are going hill walking in Wales."

Any kind of holiday sounded good to me, considering I had made a botch of planning our own. Jim was in a similar predicament. "What with all the hassle over the divorce, I never got round to organising anything. I'll have to, though. I can't let Cian down."

Listening to a stressed out Jim it occurred to me that there's one thing you have to say about school holidays – at least it's a summer free from high anxiety. No more dashing about like a maniac in the morning constructing sandwiches, no more gulping down cold coffee and chewing the end of a rasher while simultaneously herding the kids into the car and throwing the dog out. There are idle weekends to look forward to, loafing about in the garden, watching the grass grow and balmy evenings eating dinner outside with a glass of vino within striking distance. What am I saying? This is not the Canaries and the rain is usually gushing like Niagara Falls, the sun lounger is awash, the slugs have ejected their shells and are scurrying for shelter and everything is wet, wet, wet.

What is most depressing, apart from the weather, if you stay at home is having to listen to people with perma-tans who have just come back from their holiday saying things like: "You really should splash out and go to Florida. It's just fantastic. And the weather…." Being sensitive souls, they'll proceed to offer you a mountainous selection of photos showing themselves in various stages of undress, lounging around, stretched out on a beach or sipping gin from a floating tray in the pool.

Martin seems to have a tan all year round but I suppose that's easy for him, considering that, as a pilot, he can just jet off anywhere for the price of a bus ticket into town. He certainly knows how to look after Number One I thought, looking over at him as he sipped his beer. He doesn't eat red meat, wouldn't touch tap water, has his own gym at home where he does press-ups and God knows what else, and he can be seen jogging on the street every evening like a man possessed after which he drinks a suspicious concoction made from carrot juice. His skin is the colour of Peruvian mahogany, in sympathy with his kitchen, which is one of those real wood affairs with dark cupboards and stained floorboards. I called over one evening and, though it may have been a trick of the light, for a moment I could have sworn he was about to disappear into the woodwork.

Martin had, of course, organised his summer holiday – three weeks in the Bahamas – months ago and he knew my reputation for organising any kind of break left a lot to be desired.

"Speaking of holidays how did the manly camping weekend go?" he asked, catching my eye and smirking. Luke or Adrian had obviously told him about the weekend from hell.

A few weeks before, having had a sneaking suspicion that organising the family holiday was going to be no picnic, I'd thought I'd earn some brownie points with

Lorraine by taking the kids away on a weekend camping to the waters and the wild, just to test the mettle of all involved. Fiona, aided and abetted by her mother, had refused to go. This might have been because I'd eschewed the notion of an organised campsite in favour of the wide-open spaces way out west: oh the glories of setting up camp for the night in an open field, the thrill of sorting the poles, striking out the canvass, finding a shady spot to build a fire and, the piéce de resistance, constructing our very own latrine. It was going to be the Boy Scouts meet the Swiss Family Robinson.

It had been a starry night; the pregnant moon had cast an incandescent glow over the purple hills to the west. A gentle breeze had left a perfume of honeysuckle in its wake as a corncrake wheezed in the distance. The night had been warm and enchanting and a clear sky of dazzling silver lights had promised another splendid day. The view was panoramic, spectacular even at dusk and, sloping towards the seashore, wild flowers had been strung like a necklace bordering quilted fields of clover. The campfire had crackled and inside the tent a lamplight embraced the sleeping forms tucked safely up for the night.

Not exactly...

It had been wet and windy and, just as we had discovered one of the tent poles was missing, the rain came lashing down in bucketfuls. The wind had whipped up from the east and black clouds rolled over the hills. The field was covered in cowpats and there was an anthill nearby. We had managed to cut down a long branch to replace the missing pole but the wind kept bending it. The fire was no brighter than a candle and all we had been able to cook was a tin of beans in a tiny saucepan. This had a devastating effect during the night and the tent flap had to be left open for everyone's sanity despite the cold and the puddles formed by the bubbling cowpats all round. It had been more like the Boy Scouts meet the Addams Family.

As I dwelt on the less than pleasant memories triggered by Martin's question I made a decision. Next time I feel the tug of nature I'm hiring one of those camper vans – not a 1970s vintage with stretch covers and leatherette, either. I fancy an all-singing, all-dancing eight-wheel drive, articulated mother-of-all-campers, fully air conditioned with an en-suite, 10 CD changer, drinks cabinet and ice-maker. I might, if the mood took me, bring along one of those pop-up tents, the kind you throw at the ground and watch in wonder as it springs magically into position. But I would insist on a new house rule: forget all that sentimental cowboy nonsense, there will be no beans of any kind, manner or description, whether fresh, frozen, tinned, packaged, dried, reconstituted or regurgitated. Toast is no bother, sausages I can handle, a bit of bacon thrown on the frying pan wouldn't set my blood pressure sizzling and I would have no objections to a few hash browns for ballast. But Heinz could shove their beans where 'the sun don't shine'.

"I'll tell you something, Martin, whatever about the rain, the sleet, the cowpats, the nettles, the wasps, the flies, the bugs, the cold, the damp and the dew, I don't ever again want to spend another night facing downwind with the tent flap open. There's only so much a body can take."

Gerry nodded with a grin.

"I know exactly what you mean. We actually banned beans up in the Andes for that very reason. Otherwise, we would have had to bring along some kind of fart radar

16

device as an advance warning."

Jim, still concerned about where to bring Cian, was not amused by all this light-hearted talk. "I know if I don't organise something double quick I'll be the worst in the world but, actually, I think holidays can be more trouble than they're worth."

Mick agreed. "You're right. I often wonder whether going abroad in particular would ever be worth the hassle. The lengths some people will go to for a foreign holiday have to be seen to be believed. There's a group of codgers in my local who meet every Friday for a game of cards and a few pints. They normally wouldn't agree the time of day amongst themselves yet they manage to organise what they call a 'didlum', a sort of workingman's saving club. The barman would take a certain amount from each of them every Friday night before closing time and put it all into a huge jar under the counter. They called this their Offshore Account and, not being an overly trusting bunch, would, every so often, during rare moments of sobriety, gather together to conduct an audit of the money. This tends to lend a note of gravitas to an otherwise rowdy establishment as the proceedings are carried out with all the solemnity of a Green Tea Ceremony. Then, on designated dates, the barman would dole out the cash so his customers could pay for their holidays."

An offshore account system is one thing but there are alternatives to all that bothersome trouble of saving for a holiday and then preparing for departure on the appointed day. After my one attempt at organising our holiday, I was already suffering from family holiday fatigue. Feeling desperate I had even tried to convince Lorraine that there were better things to be doing than packing, dragging baggage around and keeping the kids from getting lost while you try to figure out where you are.

"Instead of all that, let's simply lock the front door, pull the curtains shut and lay in provisions to keep all and sundry going for a couple of weeks. We needn't bother to look out the window – it will be raining, anyway. We can keep a few bottles of vino in stock, a few steamy novels by the bed and a jar of fake tan to make like we've been roasting our hides on a far-flung beach. We'll take the phone off the hook in case it rings and sudden reflexes give the game away. Most importantly of all we'll forget to cancel the milk."

After pointing out that the kids wouldn't exactly be thrilled with my holiday alternative she'd told me to dream on, or words to that effect. I had then been advised to make myself scarce so she could concentrate on finding us a proper holiday on the internet.

When I told the lads my alternative holiday idea Martin was the only one who thought it had any merit.

"A fantasy holiday wouldn't a bad idea," agreed Martin, laughing. "It's no more surreal than the holiday I had in Japan last year. You'd practically need a real offshore account to stay in Tokyo. Hotels there cost a fortune but there were definitely some compensations – the Japanese really have a way with words. The attempts they made to write instructions in English were hilarious. Where else would you get a room notice that reads: 'You are invited to take advantage of the chambermaid'? They didn't know, of course, that I certainly wouldn't be taking advantage of her! At the bar downstairs there was even a drinks menu which said they were serving: 'Special cocktails for the ladies with nuts.' I'm still wondering did they mean transvestites only?"

I know what Martin means about signs. English is the

language of choice in hotels and restaurants the world over but most of the time it is nothing like the Queen's English. Even if we got to France we'd have to be on the ball. Lorraine and I had gone to Paris for a romantic weekend the year before and in our hotel lobby we were advised to: 'Please leave your values at the front desk.' I'd been really tempted to obey the strict dress code in one posh Parisian restaurant: 'A sports jacket may be worn to dinner, but no trouser.' Maybe this time around I should suggest we go to Rhodes as apparently there is a tailor shop there that tells customers to: 'Order your summer suit. Because is big rush, we will execute customers in strict rotation.' Rome wins the prize though. According to Martin, in a Roman doctor's surgery they claim to be: 'Specialist in women and other diseases.' I wonder if Lorraine would like to go to Rome...

The thought of what kind of holiday we would end up with was still on my mind as I got up from the table to consult the calendar and get an idea when I might have to take time off in August. The start of the month was still seven weeks away. The present month had a date ringed in red – Father's Day. I had completely forgotten about that one. I began to wonder what delightful little surprises might await me on the day. Would it be a gender-bending bunch of flowers or could it possibly be a nice bottle of whiskey? I was prepared to settle for a homemade apple tart. I only hoped against hope that Fiona didn't come up with the bright idea of fitting me out with the latest line in combats. Like plastic hamburgers, gas barbecues, frozen fish fingers and throwaway party plates, there is nothing lasting or particularly meaningful about Fathers' Day. However, it can be very useful for that extra lie-in on Sunday, toast delivered along with piping hot pot of coffee and a cheery: "Happy Father's Day." And if I didn't at least get breakfast in bed – poached eggs, rashers, the works – with or without the booze, I was prepared to follow little Annie Oakley's advice and get ready to kick some serious ass.

It didn't look like I'd have to, though. I was sounded out about a Father's Day present by Luke of all people, who ambushed me at the calendar.

"What's your favourite CD, Dad? I mean the best one of all, the one you can't stop listening to? Is it Eminem?

Not likely.

"No thanks," I said. "The best present I could get would be to be given free reign of your video games for the day. What do you think?"

My newly found secret passion for video games had all started during a particularly rainy May when all great plans for getting fit with team sports, hill walking, jogging and other outdoor pursuits ran aground. Those activities only lend themselves to real summers, which is why video games are ideal. To hell with the rain, the cold and the wind and the great outdoors I say.

"Most people die of fresh air, anyway," Mick had commented when I'd told him. He sometimes comes over at the weekend to play the games with me. I thought it was a strange thing for him to say considering all the time he spends fishing.

My favourite video game is still *Mortal Kombat*, although I am well aware that this is now considered, like myself, to be a bit of old hat. This clever game, which was the subject of no small controversy when it first appeared, involves two combatants going at each other in a variety of martial arts. In addition to normal abilities such as throwing, kicking and blocking, the different players come equipped with a multitude of interesting skills, including the ability to jolt an opponent with electricity, spit deadly venom, wield a razor-sharp fan, and (my personal favourite) deliver a crushing fist into the genitals of male characters. (I tried using it on one of the two female fighters; it didn't work.) The object of Mortal Kombat is, naturally, to kill your opponent, the more viciously the better. With each blow delivered, blood splatters across the screen, until eventually someone loses. When one player lies dead, the other can reach down and rip out his or her heart, holding it aloft in all its dripping glory while uttering a victory scream.

Luke looked a bit worried at the notion of me playing his video games at all never mind as a present. As he was going off to bed, he said:

"No offence, Dad, but please be careful with the games. You know you're not the best at electronic stuff and you might break it. You probably won't be able to play it for a full day, anyway."

The cheek of him!

"I'm not about to break it, Luke. All I'll be doing is playing it. I know that you kids figure that just because I've been having problems with the DVD player that I cannot get my feeble adult brain around a video game, but I can. Now go off the bed and don't worry about it."

As he went, it occurred to me that he had a point. The DVD had me puzzled. I still have to get my head around the fact that you can't just pop in a movie on DVD, press Play and off it starts. It doesn't quite work like that, as Adrian had been quick to point out a few weeks before.

"Look dad, you can't just press Play and expect it to play."

"Why not?"

Big sigh. "Because that's not how you're supposed to do it."

"OK, enlighten me."

"Look, you put in the disc, close the door… "

"All right, I'm not a complete idiot and I don't have to be treated like an imbecile."

"I know, but you still haven't managed to play a single movie on your own."

Touché.

I had tried every day since then but I still hadn't got the hang of it. Adrian certainly wasn't optimistic about my chances and I wondered if it was just me or whether other dads had the same trouble trying to get their head around stuff that their kids pick up in an hour.

"It's the same with me," said Jim. "Cian tries to show me how to play his PC games but I'm lost. Where do you get this *Mortal Kombat* thing anyway?" he asked, swigging the last of his beer.

"Any games shop will have it – get Cian to show you," I advised, as everyone started to gather their belongings.

If Luke went with my Father's Day present idea my techno-smug kids were in for a surprise, as I remarked to the guys just as they got up to leave.

"What the kids don't know is that I have been brushing up on my skills. *Mortal Kombat* isn't just popular with the over forties. It now has a whole new generation of fans and lots of kids aged fifteen and under play it. I have been secretly practising it with a kid up the road just so I can catch out my own in-house practitioners with a nasty surprise. The minute they start fighting or bickering or try to patronise me on Father's Day with: 'Dad, this is how you get your guy to jump', I will let loose with a vicious karate chop that will send them splattering all over the screen. Than I will wield my joystick with amazing dexterity at my opponent who won't even have time to duck. After that, I will turn, triumphant, my trigger-finger smoking hot, and deliver the final, fatal blow."

"Dream on", said Mick, just as everyone headed for the door. "You have the same fantasy about playing poker. You dream that one of these days you're going to wipe the floor with us. The only trouble is you can't play either game to save your life."

I couldn't organise a holiday to save my life, either. Less than two weeks later during a session in Gerry's house I found myself confessing to the fact that Lorraine had managed, in double quick time, to secure us a huge farmhouse in France for the last two weeks of August.

Naturally, just to prove she was a paid up member of the stronger sex, I knew it would all go without a hitch. In the meantime, Father's Day had come and gone. I was given my breakfast in bed, got to play *Mortal Kombat* and although, I did not quite annihilate all around me, I still acquitted myself very well, thanks to my secret mentor.

In fact, getting good at playing the game had not taken me as long as I expected and it gave me hope for the future. The DVD was still a complete mystery though, but I set myself a goal of learning to master it before the summer holiday. As this was still over a month and a half away, it should just about give me enough time. It would be a comfort to know that if, for some reason, the holiday in France went belly-up and we were forced to spend a couple of wet weeks in Mick's mobile home watching DVDs at least I would know how to operate the damn thing.

Two

Football Fever

We were in Martin's place for the weekly game and he had cooked up some kind of Greek dish that everyone devoured. "Don't ask me to pronounce the name of it. I can't. I got the recipe from my ex."

Jim couldn't resist having a cut.

"I suppose he was a Greek dish, too, was he?"

Martin wasn't the least bit fazed by this. "You have no idea. He was an Adonis."

Gerry decided to change the subject.

"Marriages may come and go, but the game must go on," he announced, raising the bet and obviously confident of taking the pot.

"Who said that?" asked Jim.

"I did," said Gerry, smirking.

"No, I mean who said it first?"

"How the hell would I know? I just heard it in the pub."

Naturally, Martin knew.

"Oh for Christ's sake, guys, did none of you ever see *The Odd Couple*? It was Felix Ungar."

Blank stares all round.

"You know, the movie that became a TV sitcom in the sixties. They still show it now and then on cable. I bet you know it, Dan."

At the mention of my name, I tried to shake myself fully awake.

"What's the matter with you? You look like shit."

In fact, I was recovering from the night before. I could hardly remember the last time I felt so shattered, fatigued, exhausted and downright knackered – it was all the bishop's fault. There are some things that are merely tiring, like fixing a puncture in the dead of night, climbing the wrong side of a mountain with the wind in your face, running a marathon for charity, chasing a bus in the pouring rain or watching the Eurovision from beginning to end. But what can really test the body and assail the spirit is attempting to summon up the energy needed to get a pair of wannabee soccer stars to go to bed after they've been allowed up to watch a Champions League match. All because, as luck would have it, the bishop came to the school and, like the good sport that he is, he declared that night a homework free zone. It wasn't the bishop's fault, of course, that the onset of family fatigue was precipitated by our late return from the farmhouse in France where bone laziness was the order of the day and the only decision to be made every morning was whether to have marmalade or jam on toast at breakfast. He could hardly be blamed for the fact that time out is nature's overdraft and merely a deposit against future withdrawals. No wonder I wasn't looking my normal chirpy self.

Getting away from it all has a way of getting back at you. I think there is nothing worse than getting ready for a family holiday. All that preparation: searching for keys, wrestling with suitcases, losing the plane tickets, finding the plane tickets behind the couch and losing them again, discovering that someone put the passports in the fridge for a laugh, finding a home for Plato, the dog, by pretending that he doesn't piddle on the carpet or chase the postman, and having to pack life's little essentials into

25

a case no bigger than a pizza box. After the 'getting ready to go to the gîte' experience I had even come to believe those surveys that showed holidays high on the list of life's traumas, ranking alongside getting hitched, winning the Lotto, losing a job or going into hospital, as events that trigger the greatest disturbances in people's everyday lives.

We had decided against going by boat because we reckoned someone was bound to be sick. So we settled for a plane, a train and a rented automobile. It had sounded great until we got to the farmhouse and discovered that one of the suitcases had been left either on the train or on the plane and both of them were now 300 miles away. Thank God the suitcase belonged to me and not to Lorraine or the kids. Otherwise, I would have been wishing that I had been back at work. I had ended up borrowing a couple of tee-shirts from Luke and, like most guys, I'd had no problem wearing the same underpants for a fortnight anyway.

If the going away had been tough, the coming back was even tougher. Our first flush of relief on seeing that the house hadn't been burgled or burnt to the ground and that Plato had survived, all too well, the travails of separation had soon been eclipsed by the realisation that all the preparation had to be done in reverse, like rewinding the video. Everything from smelly socks to Luke's tee-shirts, which will never see the light of day again, had to be disgorged and put back in their rightful place. Post-holiday Syndrome can be hell.

On this occasion, I'd decided that there was nothing for it but to attempt to ignore all hints, threats, entreaties and silent daggers, make like I had never been away, and leave the smelly socks to marinate in a bottle of expensive

French wine. I'd tried to explain that there were more important things to be done, like making sure that the beer was at the right temperature, the popcorn was to hand, the couch pitched along the correct viewing axis and the television image adjusted as sharp as the interviewer's tongue. Even though there had been no soccer on, I'd convinced myself that it was essential that I watch the start of the American football season. Lorraine hadn't agreed. My five minutes of rebellion had been the only time I'd sat down all day.

Thank God the following day had been one of rest and recreation. There aren't too many of them around. It had meant that, instead of leaping out of bed and facing the new day with restless wonder, I had been able to burrow beneath the blankets, bury my head under the pillow, pretend to be asleep and make like it was the season to be hibernating.

That, of course, had meant missing the early morning wake-up call from the jackdaws picketing the front garden, skipping the thrill of watching our new neighbours shaving the grass with their state of the art lawnmower and resisting attempts to dash to the shop for the Sunday papers. I'd bribed Adrian to go instead. It had also meant taking a break from my occasional encounters with things theological. This, I know, was a sin and a shame and should never be allowed even among consenting adults, but the man above is the forgiving sort – I'm sure.

The next day had been, horrors of horrors 'Back to School Monday' and things had taken a turn for the worse again. At first I'd thought it was my imagination. Then I'd realised that there was something funny going on. The heir to my overdraft had been stretched prone on the bed, as immobile as a Sphinx, with a countenance

27

of utter serenity. He'd looked like a waxworks model or the Infant de Prague. Calmness and immobility are not Adrian's usual bedfellows. Even at the age of twelve, he is shaping up to be one of life's movers and shakers. He does everything at breakneck speed, tends to make the rest of us look like we are living in slow motion, and remains the only person I know who can catch a fly with one hand. Blessed with the kind of energy that would keep the national grid going, he usually leaps from the scratcher at the crack of dawn, dashes to the loo, races downstairs to leave Plato out and manages to down two bowls of Rice Krispies before the rest of the world knows what day it is or comes to the realisation that he has drunk the last of the milk.

The rest of the day tends to take on a similar pattern – frenetic buttering of bread on toast, constant tugging of my arm and gasps of "we're late, we're late", scrambling for the handle of the car door when we're stuck in traffic en route to school and, in class, greasing through lessons at what the teachers can only describe as warp speed. Lunch is taken on the hoof, homework completed on foot and dinner is dispatched almost before it hits the plate. Then it's playtime when companions are over-run by the pace of events forced upon them, followed by feverish interfacing with the computer until, slowing to a cyclone, it's time to crash out, give the light switch a whip and provide the rest of us with a well-earned rest. Even though I'd had a good idea that it was an Anti-School protest it had been strange and disturbing to behold such a whirling dervish in repose.

Living under the same roof as a real live wire can be problematical as well as exhausting, not least at weekends and on bank holidays when your body clock is languishing in Acapulco and his is somewhere in orbit with no sign of burn-out. Chronologically, Adrian is twelve, but in terms of distance covered and missions accomplished he must be approaching pension age. He has had a head start on most of us. I have no memory of him ever sleeping a full night as an infant. Shortly after taking his first steps, I engineered an encounter with nature for him in the form of a spider:

"See the itsy, bitsy spider, there's a good boy. See? That's right. It's a spidy."

Quick as a flasher, he had the spider in his hand, gave me a quick look and promptly ate it in one gulp. His mother had not been troubled by this news. The quiet, gentle type he ain't.

All of which had made his refusal to be roused a bit unsettling but, as there was no circumstantial evidence of real illness, no fever or sweaty forehead, I'd felt duty bound to get the day's proceedings under way without further delay. Despite a combination of plaintive entreaties, and jocular renditions of "don't be such a lazybones", followed by warnings of dire consequences and issuing of a final notice to quit, he'd refused to budge, save to raise a limp arm and whisper: "I'm dying."

I must admit it had been a fair effort, worthy of an Oscar, but he overdid the hangdog look, went way over the top with the cough and the talcum powder he'd used to make himself look pale had come off on the pillow.

In any case, I had seen and heard it all before, thanks to an older brother whose collection of excuses would make a nice addendum to *The Guinness Book of Records*. His best line had been when he'd pretended he had lost his memory and that was why he couldn't remember his spellings. Another time he had been bitten by a vampire and had the marks to prove it although, remarkably, they washed off with soap and water. My all-time favourite was when he'd said he was hypnotised by aliens who told him he'd best stay in bed or he might be beamed up in the schoolyard. None of his attempts, though, compare with the excuses dreamed up by a work colleague, a master at ducking and diving, forever ringing in sick at work. He once rang his boss in a frightful panic to tell him he couldn't come in because he'd been stung by a jellyfish. The World Cup was on at the time and he never mentioned the fact that he had a small fortune on Germany. He was finally caught out when his exasperated doctor wrote a note describing his patient's illnesses as an 'acute dose of Pluma Lina'. Nobody reckoned on the personnel manager being a classical scholar capable of translating the diagnosis as 'Swinging the Lead'.

As it had turned out, Adrian was also suffering from a variant of Pluma Lina, otherwise known as Anti-School Fever. I'd had to admire the effort it took for him to stay so still and I'd decided to play along for a while, enquiring sweetly as to the exact nature of the ailment.

"I think I've got the Blue Flu, Dad," he'd whispered.

His granny had told him all about the so-called Blue Flue which had become something of an epidemic in her time. It had been the favoured ruse of policemen and women looking for a pay rise. Since they were barred from going on strike they'd gone off sick instead.

"I met a policeman yesterday, outside the shop, and I think I picked it up from him."

I could hardly blame him for chancing his arm considering I was trying to see my way to cadging a few days off work myself to watch American football. The New York Jets were playing and I wanted to see them in

30

action. I had even given serious thought to using the Blue Flu as a means to an end. However, I abandoned that plan because I had been forced to admonish Adrian for trying to hoodwink me and I didn't want to play the hypocrite. I had to admit, though, that I had a sneaking admiration for him when I discovered he had been placing the thermometer under the steam from the electric kettle in order to show a high temperature.

Even the poker buddies were impressed.

"Smart kid. How did you figure it out?" asked Jim.

"Well, I knew that, no matter how sick he might be, he could not possibly have a temperature of 120 degrees unless he was on fire. I thought at first he might have put it in the microwave but I suppose if he had done that the bloody thing would have exploded."

The lads burst into laughter.

"No wonder you look like shit," said Gerry.

Martin used the moment of distraction to pull out a package, neatly wrapped, from underneath the table and hand it to me.

"What's that?"

"It's your birthday present."

This was unusual because none of us usually give each other any kind of present and most of the time we don't have a clue about whose birthday it is. But, on this occasion, it was simply a way of taking the piss out of me. Martin, of course, proceeded to make a big deal out of giving me the present.

"Gentlemen and gentlemen, this is Dan's present and, in my not so humble opinion, it's the only way he's going to learn to play real poker. As you all know, despite his efforts and Mick's endless patience, he plays like a nun."

Then, with a flourish, he told me to upwrap my present.

It was a book entitled *How To Cheat In Poker When You Can't Really Play*.

At first, I was taken aback and even a bit offended that he thought I was such a lousy player.

"Don't worry, Dan," said Gerry, seeing my crestfallen face. "That's how Martin learned himself. I bet he has a well thumbed copy hidden away here somewhere."

In fact, when I brought it home later and examined it, I realised that the whole thing was really a scam and the best part of the book was the title. I figure it should have been called *How To Cheat At Writing A Book About Cheating*. The only thing worthwhile in it was the chapter dealing with luck: How To Recognise When Your Luck Is In.

It's a pity the book didn't have something to say about recognising when your luck is out. As any 21st century father will tell you, there are some rare days when Dadsville is a tranquil and glorious place, a state of grace and perfect happiness where everyone is cheerful, full of joie de vivre and the fat-free milk of human kindness. These are the days to take a gamble. The days when, no matter how hard you try, whatever monumental malfeasance you may attempt to commit or, despite the most awesome neglect of all things that matter, nothing whatsoever can go wrong. Leave the lights on in the car overnight and, hey presto it starts first thing in the morning without so much as a wheeze. Sneak into work in a panic after a late night and, wouldn't you know it, your boss is out with the flu for the first time in twenty years and nobody even notices that you are three hours late. Let the watch you got for Christmas fall in the street and, my goodness, a dear old lady comes panting up the road, gasping: "I think you dropped this but don't worry, it's still working." Forget your beloved's birthday only to discover: hang on a minute; it's not until next week. Forget to tie up the lil' ol' fishing boat on the mooring and, believe it or not, a neighbourly fisherman spots your monumental stupidity and puts everything to rights just before the damn things decides to head for the Azores. You get the picture. This is the day to run a red light, increase the overdraft, buy a Lotto ticket and go bungee jumping with a marshmallow. It's as if a lazy angel, scouring for soft targets, has decided to take up residence in the vicinity of your shoulder having been warned by The Man Above that she is way behind on her quota of good deeds for the week.

But this is not one of those days.

I know it the minute I roll out of bed and a cheerful sun slices through the lattice window, in stark contrast to my own sombre mood. I had woken-up with a massive migraine despite a sensible Saturday night of uncommonly good behaviour. I had an inkling of the gathering storm when, instead of a cup of Sunday morning tea, I am issued with a clothes peg and greeted with a verse of "the loo is blocked again" to the air of a nursery rhyme. I don't have to be told as the pungent aroma of a Moroccan souk fills the house.

I was just about to suggest that, perhaps, it might be a good idea if I donned the Wellingtons and used the thin end of the yard brush to try and free it when I was reminded of my previous attempt to free a blockage.

"You have a very short-term memory about these things," said Lorraine. "The last time you attempted something like this it cost us a fortune. It took two guys to free up all the wire coat hangers you had shoved down the bowl and, in the end we had to buy a new toilet. This time, I'm getting someone who knows what he's doing unless it clears itself."

We wait until lunchtime but the stink just keeps on getting worse. There is nothing for it but to go to Defcon Two and call out the cavalry. Three hours later, he arrives.

"Dad, the stinky-pooh man is here, ha, ha." Giggles and sniggers all round followed by an exaggerated display of noses in the air and melodramatic sighs of "aaagghhh" and "yuck."

The man for the stinky pooh is florid of face with cheeks like ripe pomegranates and appears gregarious, but looks with scorn at the ensemble encircling the television, transfixed watching a Cup Final match. Even Lorraine, normally not the most passionate follower of soccer, is taking an interest in proceedings. She usually prefers the cut and thrust of rugby and can often be found cursing and swearing on the sidelines at a school rugby final or offering post-match analysis and having something to say about the referee's sanity.

"I like the look of that striker," she said, as we all flopped down to watch the game.

I'm beginning to suspect that she doesn't mean his dexterity with the ball. I am convinced she either fancies him or she is trying to pretend that the drain isn't blocked and that the kitchen doesn't stink to high Heaven and that the face peeping round the door isn't really there.

Like most plumbers, he is full of unnecessary chat.

"Don't tell me there's another match on. That's all I hear about these days. I'm sick to death of it. You'd swear the world was the shape of a football."

I hate to enlighten him, particularly as he is here of a Sunday to get me out of the you-know-what but I wish he'd had the good sense to wait until teatime. Despite prevailing feminist sensibilities, this is designated man's

34

work and, volunteers being at a premium, I am forced to show him the offending receptacle while attempting to keep a weather eye on the match. With a shrewd sense of timing, he enrols me as a go-for and general dogsbody. I am not that bothered at first, expecting the game to be a dull affair and figuring that, in terms of excitement, dealing with a blocked loo might have the edge. But it is turning out to be a real cracker and I end up missing most of the first half. Naturally, he decides to have his tea at half time and then regales us with plumbing disaster stories for the first ten minutes of the second half. For a while, he does a solo run and I think it's safe to settle down on the sofa. But it proves to be a false dawn. Near the end of the match, the pomegranates appear through the window that had to be kept open for a bit of fresh air.

"There's a bend in your pipe outside and you won't believe the state of the ball cock. Come and have a look."

Murmuring curses unknown to any thesaurus, I consent to go outside again and be amazed – all the while wondering whether the home team can make a comeback.

"Will you look at that?" he says, pointing to an orange plastic thingy in the ground. "Did you ever see the like?"

I feel obliged to confess I haven't and am just about to contemplate shoving his big, fat face down the loo when a mighty moan goes up to signify the end of proceedings. Even Plato is howling. Two seconds later Luke comes dashing out of the living room with a look of unrestrained glee on his face.

"Too late. It's all over. 'Twas a great game, though."

I figure his mother must have put him up to it. I had missed the dying moments – all because of the phantom of the sewers and his copper ballcock. I didn't even know the score as Luke had made good his escape. I knew I should have stayed in bed but, just for spite, when the plumber finally left, I handed Lorraine his bill. It was even bigger than the man himself.

"Perhaps you should have put down some bleach, followed by a bucket of boiling water," said Jim when I told my story, as he raised his bet during the following week's poker session. "That would loosen all the goo and get things moving."

Naturally, everyone around the table had an opinion, even Mick.

"No, that wouldn't do the trick at all. I tried that once and added some washing up liquid for good measure but the place became full of suds and it took Laura days to mop it all up. Still, the place was spotless afterwards."

It's amazing what will get a bunch of guys animated. Women, no matter what their age or marital status, will talk among themselves about everything from the size of knitting needles to how their own guys measure up in bed but men – even close friends – confine their most animated discussion to sport, DIY and the size of a newsreader's knockers. Unblocking a loo is one of the few things that get them really worked up.

Gerry, being an engineer, had the most gobsmackingly complicated solution.

"What you need to do in these circumstances is to create a vacuum. First of all, cover the whole bowl in Clingfilm and tie it tight around the edges. That will set up a pressure zone. Then, bang down the toilet seat quickly and sit on it. Flush a few times and that should do the business. You might have to repeat it a few times, though, to make sure everything is clear."

Martin thought this was hilarious. "Supposing Dan creates too much pressure and is ejected through the roof? Or maybe he will set up a vortex and get sucked down in the bowl. That would certainly get things moving."

But even he wasn't about to be outdone in the solution stakes.

"Maybe you should have sought some divine intervention," he said, straight-faced. "An awful lot of soccer players, particularly the Brazilians, do that all the time. You often see them kneeling down and blessing themselves before a match. Perhaps you should have done that. Or maybe you could stick a miraculous medal in the toilet. Or hang a scapular of Padre Pio from the toilet roll holder. He's a saint now and that might do the trick if you're really stuck. I've even heard of a few players who go around with pictures of him wrapped around their calves or stuck in their socks. Maybe you should try that."

That seemed more than a little sacrilegious or even blasphemous and I figured I would have no luck for it. In any case, shoving a photo of the man whose claim to fame was his bleeding hands down my socks seemed an act of utter desperation.

What are those soccer players up to anyway? Do they not know that when the chips are down, when the mother of all battles is being waged, when triumph and disaster are tussling for supremacy there is only one person to call upon to get a result? Not the Mother of Good Counsel, not Saint Ignatius of Loyola, not the Little Flower, not Saint Patrick nor even Our Lady and certainly not a rookie saint. I'd been give the tip on good authority from my own sainted Auntie May who lived her life as a celebration of all that is good in Christianity and held her conviction to the day she died.

"If you want the job done," she used to say to me, "you have to go straight to the Sacred Heart. I have nothing against saints. I am sure they are all worthy of the affection in which they are held by many people, but they have their limits. Saints are all right for most everyday things like losing your watch (Saint Anthony), travelling to far away places (Saint Christopher), keeping your purity (Saint Martin) or trying to pass exams (St Jude – for hopeless cases) but if your back is to the wall, The Sacred Heart is your man."

Whatever about asking the Sacred Heart to unblock a loo, perhaps I should take Auntie May's other piece of advice and go to confession. It might even help my poker. However, it is highly unlikely that admitting sins to a stranger in a dark closet would make any difference to most of us. Although if latter-day psychologists, mystics and common or garden Jesuits are to be believed, it would do us all the power of good and, of course, is a hell of a lot cheaper than employing a therapist. Even though it has never been proven to help you score a hat-trick, land a stunner of a goal from a corner kick or win your first poker game, confession is sauce for the soul. Mind you the power of religion has never been particularly evident in poker schools or, now that I come to think of it, plumbing matters.

The funny thing was that Gerry, Jim, Mick and Martin were all fully convinced that only they had the proper solution to my problem and that everyone else's suggestions were rubbish. Not only that, but they each fully expected the rest of us to conform to their way of thinking.

"Dan needs to flood the toilet bowl with a power hose," said Gerry. "That is bound to work."

"Bollix," said Mick. "He'll end up soaking the place

and it will still be blocked."

There appeared to be no end to the debate my plumbing problems had generated. The only good thing that came out of it is that, while they were all talking they didn't notice me pushing my luck. I was having a 'How To Recognise When Your Luck Is In' epiphany. The others were so busy arguing, that even my ham-fisted bluff worked and I ended up taking the pot. Maybe the Sacred Heart had been listening – after all it was my first time winning at poker.

THREE

Father's Daze

Things were getting a bit fraught at the poker session.

It was Jim's turn to play the host but at the last minute it was switched to my place because he was in the process of moving. He was now going to be sharing with two other guys and Mick had promised him the loan of his truck to move the rest of his stuff. The house was in a nice area and at least it was better than the awful flat he had moved into immediately after he got divorced from his wife of ten years, Darina. We all felt a bit sorry for Jim but none of us dared show it, knowing that, of all things, a display of public sympathy would be bound to piss him off. He was far too macho for that. Yet something was clearly bothering him.

"Jesus, Jim, are you going to play or do we have to wait for the climate to change?" asked Mick who clearly didn't seem to notice anything amiss.

"Getting divorced is like being knocked down by a bus," said Jim, to no-one in particular.

Mick, unusually for him, was getting impatient and ignored Jim completely.

"I have to be home early tonight. I am playing a match in the morning. It's a league game."

Even at the age of forty-one, Mick is still in big demand on his local rugby team. He is a tight-head prop which basically means he is there to hold the scrum together although, according to Martin, who went to school with

40

Mick, his real job is to scare the other side.

"All he has to do is just stand there, all 6'2" and 22 stone of him. That's enough to frighten the crap out of half the guys on the other team and, of course, he never lets on that he's really as gentle as a lamb," he said in an effort to steer the subject away from Jim's problems.

Mick started angrily pointing out what playing a tight-head prop really meant but Martin ignored him. He began gathering up all the beer cans scattered around the place. He was putting them into a special bag.

"Kid's orders," Martin said, by way of explaining the recent edict of my pint-sized gruppenführer on the subject of recycling. "Your little one, Fiona, has warned me, under pain of death, not to leave anything lying around. I even have to put cans and bottles in separate paper bags and label them. She'll be some formidable woman when she grows up. She's already into Save The Whales and wants to join Earthwatch when she's older."

Conformity rearing its head again – nowhere is the doctrine of political correctness more marked than in the debate on the environment. It was all very well for Martin to be making fun of gathering up the beer cans. He didn't have to listen to the goody-two-shoes routine all day long. The new religion of recycling is awesome and omnipotent and has even permeated the inner sanctums of primary and nursery schools. Four-year-olds who wouldn't know a guardian angel from a Teletubby have no trouble in remembering the latest 'save the world' mantra and can recite the litany of pure living gospel according to the self righteous. I have been through it all vicariously by way of getting a constant earful on the demise of the Chinese red panda, the wilting rainforest and the state of the whales – all this from a pert little blonde no bigger than

41

an endangered koala bear. She knows all about recycling; she's learned off by heart the latest creed on protecting the environment; she makes like a fishwife whenever someone steps out of line; she's found a whole new use for her AK47. Extolling virtues of saving string, brown paper bags and tins has become second nature to her and we have all learned to conform or suffer a verbal mugging. Woe betide anyone rash enough to leave the light on in the landing or throw away old newspapers and, as for tossing cans in the waste basket – it has become a hanging offence. I had discovered the hard way that if you value a quiet life, domestic harmony and something approaching personal sanity, it is essential to remember that filling a bin with plastic bags can only be done in the dead of night, preferably when the moon is shining somewhere east of the Urals.

The influence of the political correctness brigade tends to get even more obvious if you happen to throw a kid's party. Among the throng bursting in the hall door there is bound to be a fair sprinkling of the environmental lobby's offspring bent on ensuring that only conformist goodies are consumed. Try to cheer up a sullen child with a packet of Smarties and you're likely to be scolded with: "I'm sorry, but I can't have those. They're full of E numbers. Don't you have any homemade popcorn?" There is also sure to be some kid who says he can't eat anything but rice cakes and, as for breaking out the bottles of Coke, you'd better keep a cask or two of pure apple juice handy for the offspring of dentists who won't be long telling you that sugary drinks are bad for their teeth.

Fiona had a birthday party planned for the weekend with the kind of precision her mother usually puts into organising the family holiday. I had grown to cherish the wondrous ways of a malleable eight-year-old when, all of a sudden, Fiona decides she's nine and I'm finding out the difference the hard way. I was beginning to realise what a change a year can make. Only that evening I had returned home from town with a Barbie birthday cake the size of a small car. I was prepared for endless praise and squeals of delight, only to be told by a very cross Fiona to take it right back and not to come home again without an organically produced carrot cake with a Chinese panda drawn on the icing. She clearly wanted to impress her environmentally aware friends.

Organising the programme for a birthday party is, in itself, a matter not to be taken lightly. Even I, despite a natural inclination to be economical with my physical energy, have occasionally found myself having to sort out some entertainment. I have some experience in this regard and have been known to amuse children for considerable periods with a selection of tall tales and true and a natural gift for mimicking all and sundry, particularly those nearest and dearest. Sometimes it gets me into the height of trouble but I can't help myself. Fiona has declined my services.

Maybe all of this environment lark is a girl thing. None of that stuff ever seemed to bother the boys when they were Fiona's age. For them, organising a party usually involved battening down the hatches, putting all the ornaments out of reach, finding a safe haven for the valuables and readying ourselves for three hours of mayhem. Apart from hiring a bouncer, donning the chain mail and electric fencing the perimeter, we'd thought we had it covered. Although prepared for the onslaught we were in no doubt that there were still a few kids who would probably take the greatest of pleasure in eating us

43

out of house and home. But we felt ready for those little tykes who try to drive everyone to the brink of suicide.

When Adrian had his ninth birthday party we had to practically glue the ornaments to the mantelpiece. By contrast, I was sure that all fifteen of Fiona's guests would be models of decorum, grace and manners. You'd probably find more mischief in a convent. I don't know if I'll ever be able to get used to such good behaviour. I am feeling nostalgic for the days of mayhem when the place would come alive with mischief and it would be all I could do to hold on to my sanity. I now thank God for those kids who would shout and roar, wipe noses on someone else's sleeve and who had never been weaned on a diet of guilt-ridden political correctness. I still believe it's important to have at least one or two of those kids at any party, and I am considering inviting some to Fiona's party myself. My favourite out of Adrian's friends had been a red-haired lad who bounded in the door with his space-gun blazing, gave any pigtails in sight a good tug before tucking into the cakes, crisps, jelly beans and every E-ridden sweet in sight. If I hadn't caught him in time he had been about to proceed to dribble a football straight through the flowerbed. I wonder if he has any sisters. His mother had been a revelation, rearing six children on a slim budget with homespun good sense and a constant smile. The secret of her success, she told me, was "to leave at least half an hour between slaps". It didn't seem to have done the kid any harm. I can't remember what he's called now but I remember his nickname; all the kids in the school called him Keano.

Watching Jim glaring morosely at his cards, I wondered what they might call Cian, Jim's son and what would happen at his next birthday party. Cian seems to be a remarkably cheerful kid, despite the fact that his parents no longer live together. It must be tough having your parents separated especially when you're nine years old and don't really understand what's happening.

Jim must have been thinking the same thing.

"I'm sorry guys, but I have to go. I'm just not in the mood."

Mick finally got the message that something more important than his match was bothering Jim. "Are you OK? You don't look too good."

"No, Mick, I'm not. It's Cian."

"What's wrong with him?"

"Nothing. He's fine. It's just that I'll be seeing even less of him than I am now if Darina has her way."

"What do you mean? She hasn't found herself a new guy, has she?"

"You got it in one. A barrister she was doing a case with. And that's not the worst of it. They're now talking about moving and if that happens I might as well say goodbye to being a father."

With that, Jim put down his cards and started to head for the door but Mick stopped him by putting a huge arm around his shoulder.

"Jim, I'm sorry. I shouldn't have said that. It was stupid of me. It never occurred to me that Darina might actually have gone off with someone else."

Then ushering him over to the couch, he looked at me and said: "Come on, sit down and Dan will get you a drink."

Jim complied, sat down and put his hands to his face, staring at the floor. When I brought over a glass of whiskey, he looked up and there were tears in his eyes. "Sorry, guys, I didn't want to spoil the night but the thought of losing Cian... It's bad enough getting divorced."

Martin and Gerry sat on either side of Jim. Martin squeezed his shoulder while Gerry patted him reassuringly on the knee. "Don't let that bother you in the least, Jim. What you're going through is far bigger than any poker game."

I brought the bottle of whiskey and some glasses over to the coffee table by the couch and we all had a slug or two. For a while, nothing was said but I could see that Jim was looking a bit better. He finished his whiskey in one gulp and stood up.

"Thanks for the drink, Dan, but I really have to go."

This time, nobody tried to stop him as he made for the door and I escorted him out. The others were finishing up their drinks when I came back into the room. Mick was shaking his head.

"Jesus, I wouldn't wish that on anyone. It'll kill him if he can't get to spend time with Cian. Even though my own gang can be exhausting at times, I wouldn't swap with him for the world."

Gerry and Martin nodded but, though I had all the sympathy in the world for Jim, I felt he had brought a lot of it on himself. As they left for the night, I thought about what Jim had said to me earlier when I was chatting to him about my own, admittedly, minor child rearing problems. I was telling him about my latest project to get the children to use language in a manner other than the dreaded TV-speak of shows like *The Simpsons*. I had become thoroughly fed up with listening to remarks like "Don't have a cow, man" or "whatever…". It was beginning to make my blood curdle.

When I had mentioned this to Jim earlier in the evening, he had as usual, acted like he had all the answers.

46

"Just ban the TV or dock pocket money for every smart-assed phrase. That'll fix them."

It's a pity someone couldn't fix him and his 'no problem' attitude. The mood he'd been in I hadn't dared mention it at the time, but Jim likes to have his cake and eat it. Despite his current situation and the fact that he tries to spend what time he can with Cian, Jim still expects Darina to do the lion's share. He never stops complaining that he doesn't see enough of Cian but he still has no intention of cutting down on work and never once have I heard him mention anything about Cian's schooling. Even when he and Darina were together, he never once corrected the boy's homework. When I had pointed this out a few weeks before, he'd become immediately defensive.

"I bought him a top of the range computer. He can learn from that."

I couldn't believe what I was hearing. "Computers are all very well, Jim, but all they are is a tool. No computer can independently raise or educate kids. Cian needs his father far more than he needs a bloody computer." He hadn't responded but had started to shake his head to indicate that he didn't want to talk about it.

The more I have thought about it since then, the more convinced I have become that, despite all the hype, computers are little more than a glorified hammer or chisel. In fact, computers are occasionally imbecilic. I have learnt not to rely too much on the high-tech dictionary on mine that insists 'Jack Charlton' should be changed to 'Jack Charlatan' and 'pathos' should be 'paths'. What it threatens to do with words like 'wink' and 'bullocks' doesn't bear thinking about.

Language, not computers, is what makes the world go round. It shapes our culture and describes our relationships

47

with one another. Ever since Neanderthal Man exchanged grunts in the cave, words, written and spoken, have defined our ascent from the planet of the apes. It is part of what we are. Unfortunately, bad language, silly language and downright nonsense are also part of what we are. Tune in any night and you'll see what I mean. Have a listen to schoolyard chatter and you'll find much the same thing – kids as young as five advise each other to: "Eat my shorts" or "Go suck a lemon, dude". You cannot blame children for picking up TV vernacular, anymore than you can expect them to speak correctly unless someone takes the trouble to teach them.

Discovering that my own children were well on their way to graduating with honours from the Bart Simpson Academy of Rotten English drove me to the verge of despair. In anti TV-speak mode I tried various devices to amend the situation. I even took Jim's advice and banned certain programmes (declaration of war), replacing them with suitable videos like *The Railway Children* (boring, boring) and inventing a points system for full sentences in good English (I'm still waiting). I enjoyed some measure of success when I borrowed a friend's collection of stupid newspaper headlines. But even though they laughed themselves silly at, '500 Blind Boys See Pope', 'Death of Well-known Secret Agent' and others in similar vein, my success was short-lived.

I finally discovered a better way to verbal nirvana and it is all thanks to that early master of the sound bite, the wartime British Prime Minister Winston Churchill. Churchill was, of course, a brilliant orator and not beyond indulging in mass manipulation to get his own way. He loved language but despised the pedantry of War Office mandarins who often went to ridiculous extremes in order to avoid grammatical sins when corresponding with their great leader. He once wrote his Cabinet Secretary a stinker, warning: "Up with this I shall not put." He believed that a good grounding in the classics was all that was needed to perfect the art of rhetorical discourse. Once in a while, though, even his great skills let him down. On the eve of war he broadcast to the Empire with a few choice words, advising his listeners: "It will be long; it will be hard but there will be no withdrawal."

Taking Winston's belief in the classics on board rescue came in the shape of that crusty old man of letters, Charles Dickens. If Dickens was writing today he would probably be doing episodes of *Friends*, *Coronation Street* and *Married With Children*. It was, as he might have said himself, with a measure of uncommon delight that I chanced upon a dog-eared edition of *Oliver Twist* and resolved to employ it as a bedtime tale. *Superman* and the like were consigned to the shelf and for a whole month the story of the boy who asked for more was revealed a chapter a night. It wasn't what you'd call an overnight success and for a time I considered putting Mr Dickens back into the dustbin of history, but I persevered.

After a month's solid work vindication finally came on a beautiful autumn day. There was a schoolboy's soccer match on and one of the parents came along driving a top-of-the-range Lexus. I expected the usual exclamations like, "Wow, what a cool set of wheels". Instead *The Simpsons* aficionado was heard to remark: "I believe he is a man of considerable means, Dad."

Well, eat my shorts. It looked like the kid done real good in the language department. That encouraged me to go for broke in the kid-improvement stakes. Big mistake. I forgot my limitations. Luke, the eldest, had been moaning about wanting a guitar for ages. He wanted one for his birthday that was coming up in early November. The only trouble was all the local classes were full and there didn't seem much point in getting the guitar unless he could get a bit of help learning how to play it. I got my solution from Gerry, of all people. I have always admired his sense of dedication and focus on the task at hand, something I have rarely been able to emulate myself. Gerry is an engineer and, in many ways, he is a typical one. He always takes a straight-down-the-middle, no nonsense approach to all problems and attacks them in a scientific way. "There are no insoluble problems; only problematic solutions," he is fond of saying. When I mentioned the business with Luke he had the perfect answer.

"Buy him a book and I'll loan him my old guitar until he gets good enough to have his own. You can learn most things from a book. Go into town and buy *Learning Guitar in 10 Easy Lessons* by WB Crommitch. It comes complete with full instructions on tuning and all that and has all the chords set down. It couldn't be easier. I tried it myself less than two years ago and now I play in a Green Grass band and we have gigs once or twice a month."

"What's a Green Grass band?"

"It's like Blue Grass, but with an Irish flavour."

There was no answer to that, so I took his advice and bought the book. It couldn'd be simpler – or so I thought."

Lesson 1 – A Minor: "OK, Luke, look at this chord, do a little strumming and Bob's your uncle."

I kept this up for a couple of weeks, fully expecting that he would become expert in no time. I thought everything was going swimmingly until one Wednesday when it was my turn to host the poker game and Luke was practising in the room next door while we played. I was used to the noise but to the other guys his playing was a revelation, particularly Martin.

"I'm sorry Dan, but you can't be serious."

"What do you mean?"

"Luke. The Guitar. The racket. Jesus, man I can't hear myself think. It's like listening to a pair of cats humping. It's impossible to play."

"Well, it was all Gerry's idea."

"I know, but didn't you know that he once was convinced he could learn to swim from a book? That was an even crazier notion and he nearly got himself killed. He read the whole thing and swore he was able to swim but he never bothered putting it into practice. Tell him the rest, Gerry."

"The trouble was I should have practised what I'd read and at least tried out a few lengths but I couldn't be bothered and, anyway, I never liked the water. Then, one day on holiday in Lanzarote I got thrown into the pool and that was how I discovered the hard way that you can't learn everything from a book."

"Anybody under the age of twelve could have told you that," Mick commented.

The only real difference between adults and children is that, while grown-ups think they know everything, kids really do. When I was about four years old, I had an unshakeable conviction, which no amount of reasoning or religious indoctrination could shift, that the world and all its works had been created, not by God or some other omnipotent being, but by a gravedigger of my acquaintance called Dinny. To this day, I don't know who or what put the idea into my head, but I can still remember at the time doing a sort of stand-up comic routine at the behest of my father who would parade me in front of his pals in the pub and ask: "Tell us, now, who made the world?" Dutifully, I would reply: "Dinny made the world." Fuelled by enough drink to launch a flood tribunal, this always brought about howls of raucous laughter and loud guffaws, followed by a round of manly thigh-slapping and remarks like "isn't he gas?". For my efforts, I was invariably awarded a bag of boiled sweets and a glass of orange.

Everyone in the neighbourhood had known Dinny. He hadn't been just a gravedigger, though that was his principal vocation. He was also a raconteur, a philosopher, a mischief-maker and a chancer of the highest order. Though digging graves was his job of work, technology was his passion and, while he never lived long enough to see the age of the microchip or satellite television, he could see it coming long before works like internet or DVD became so much part of our everyday vocabulary.

"One of these days, we'll have telephones strapped to our wrists like watches, manual work will be a thing of the past and we'll be able to travel from here to China in the blink of an eye," he would tell me, while working on what he called "me little invinsins".

His 'invinsins' had generally been mechanical contraptions powered by an electric motor and designed to take the back-breaking labour out of digging graves in the stony soil of the cemetery. The problem was that anything he made never worked properly, but he had carried on regardless until one day the local council threatened him with the sack. There had been complaints from a party of grieving mourners who had arrived at the cemetery shouldering a monumental coffin to discover, to their horror, that Dinny had forgotten to dig the grave.

I don't know what Dinny would have made of our

current obsession with computer technology, but I think it would have thrilled him no end. I can just picture him surfing the net with a laptop resting on his dirty dungarees, having placed his rusty shovel, as it so often was, in repose at the side of a handy gravestone. Even he might have baulked, though, at producing an " invinsin" that would put us all out of Luke's misery.

"Are you going to get him to stop or what?" asked Gerry.

I got up to try and put a halt to Luke's racket. Mick called over his shoulder as I left the room. "Maybe you can get an interactive CD-Rom that will teach him how to play."

He didn't know how right he was, I thought as I returned to the table after persuading Luke to give us all a break. "You're know you're not far out, Mick. In case you hadn't noticed, there has been something of an explosion recently in the number of websites devoted to toddlers, brought about by the launch of a software program for children under two. The makers claim that it is a developmental tool like books or educational toys. The CD-Rom was put together with the help of – wouldn't you know it – a team of psychologists and it is designed for use by babies sitting on an adult's lap."

Gerry was intrigued. "How does it work?" he asked, the engineer in him anxious to learn about any new technological device.

"The child can select activities by pressing pictures on a colourful mobile above an image of a teddy's cot, while drooling in the arms of its parents, bringing a whole new meaning to the notion of laptop computers. You'd think that it would be enough that the likes of Bill Gates has the adult world in hock, but now those genies of the techno world are trying to ram CD-ROMs down the throats of infants too young to handle a spoon."

What the makers have not reckoned on, though, is a child's capacity for mischief. Shortly after I acquired a new laptop, I'd had the misfortune to allow Mick's youngest, a toddler, have a go at stomping the keyboards to keep her quiet, thinking that, whatever she might get up to, at least she could do little harm. Bad decision. Before long, the computer screen had been showing signs of delirium tremens, the keyboard was awash with the remnants of a glass of orange and the CD-Rom drive had been trying to make sense of a large and indigestible digestive biscuit. Just to finish things off, on closer inspection at home, I'd discovered that the control mouse was on the missing list. I hadn't said anything, as I wasn't even sure if it had made it to Mick's house in the first place.

I reminded Mick of this scene of chaos, just as he was leaving and we had packed up for the night. "Remember when your little one put the kibbosh on my laptop, Mick? She'll probably grow up to be the new Bill Gates."

Bizarrely enough, the missing mouse did reappear a few days after the game and in circumstances that created something of a seismic shift on the home front. A near neighbour, known to everyone as Auntie Nora, came calling and was sitting with her usual cup of black tea when the dog came streaking in, barking loudly and trying to dislodge something resembling a comet attached to his tail.

Auntie Nora, fragile at best, jumped up in fright, exclaiming, "Oh my God, what is that?" and spilling the tea all over her gingham dress.

"Don't worry, its only Plato with the mouse, but I

think his tail is on fire," she was told, helpfully.

With a cry of "Jesus, Mary and Saint Joseph", Auntie Nora suddenly became as agile as a fox and jumped up on the footstool, all the while screeching in a high falsetto like a demented banshee.

In response, Plato barked all the louder before someone took pity on him and doused his tail with a glass of orange. Both the culprit and her pet then dashed out of the house in panic. That was the last I saw of the mouse and I can only surmise that, in a fit of pique, the dog buried it deep in the bowels of the garden along with my mobile phone that he had dispatched the week before.

Whenever I endure a close encounter with some technological wizardry gone haywire I always think of that old gravedigger who was so bewitched by scientific advancement. The more I consider the march of technology, and the capacity of mere mortals, not to mention dogs to screw it up, the more convinced I am that I was right all those years ago and Dinny, God bless him, did make the world.

I am less sure, though when I encounter the dark side of humanity or when I have a run-in with a new generation of kids far more streetwise than I am. Things are very different now to Dinny's time. The world is fast becoming populated by wolves, sharks and quick-buck merchants whose social conscience rarely stretches further than their ample cheque books. I can even detect a metamorphosis among the very young. I find it hard to recall the last time Adrian expressed any interest in becoming a fireman or of helping to put the world to rights. There was a time when all he dreamt of was donning a bright red suit with a shiny helmet to save everyone from harm's way.

Luke, as older brothers do, had put paid to any such

childish notions, remarking: "Fighting fires is hard work. It can be very dangerous and, anyway, firemen get paid buttons."

For one awful moment I thought that Adrian was about to be advised to become an accountant when he grew up but common sense prevailed. Kids are still kids and, after a long debate, it was decided that becoming a pilot was the business. I figured they must have been talking to Martin. Sure enough, that was it.

"He flies to New York and Chicago, all over the place, and next year he'll be going to LA."

"Cool."

"He's even talking about getting a house in San Francisco."

My heart leapt – but only for an instance. What clinched the deal was not any exciting tales of Matin's derring-do or soaring above the clouds or great adventures flying around the world. No the clincher, guaranteed to make any job every 21st century kid's dream, was: "They make buckets of moola."

I think that this kind of career pragmatism and steely determination must come from their granny. She was – and still is – trés formidable. The local shopkeeper has good reason to ensure that her newspaper is always there on time and in good order even if it means disappointing some other customer. As for the butcher, he is never able to go more than two rounds. I once overheard him tell his apprentice: "Jaysus, boy, what are you doing? You can't give that one a fillet like that. If she doesn't get exactly what she wants she'll be beating down my door on Sunday and I'll never hear the end of it. Give that old scrap to old Mr Mooney. He's a lovely man and never complains."

Making your presence felt invariably works a treat for my mother, even if the price to be paid is a little embarrassment all round. I still balk at the memory of standing amongst a crowd of customers in an electrical shop at the age of ten, feeling sorry for a pimply-faced lad who had been commanded to: "Take that scrap-heap of a television set in from the car and tell your boss hiding in the back that we want our money back."

When the boss had finally decided to emerge from his hidey-hole he had made the fatal mistake of attempting to argue the toss. He'd declared that, whatever was wrong with the set, it wasn't his fault and maybe she might like to get it touch with the manufacturer. He was soon told that he had better come up with the readies unless he wanted to meet his own manufacturer. No prizes for guessing who won that little skirmish.

Despite or, perhaps, because of these early experiences, I never learned to play hardball, never learned to raise so much as a whisper when confronted by shoddy purchases or indifferent service. It just isn't in my nature to complain, to make even a frisson of a fuss or to demand first-class treatment. I prefer to let things lie rather than risk a potentially bruising encounter. But now all that is about to change. I have decided that this is no way for a grown man to behave. This decision has nothing to do with being influenced by my streetwise offspring. This metamorphosis is thanks to a certain blue-rinsed old dame who always pushes past me in the supermarket, mumbling about how some people have no manners. The last time it happened I found myself almost prostrate with regret, apologising for being ahead of her, not to mention for being there at all. It was only when I scrambled outside that I realised what a sorry excuse I was. I vowed that at

57

our next encounter I would smile sweetly and say: "Take a hike, you old bag, and go to the back of the queue where you should have been in the first place."

Letting things lie cannot continue. I will have to grow a bit of backbone. In fact, I have a few people in mind who could do with a little bit of retaliation from me. The butcher has it coming to him. The next time he throws me a steak that looks like it came out of an Egyptian tomb I'll spit in his eye and tell him to feed it to his Rottweiller. I won't take any nonsense from the guy in the paper shop, either. If he hasn't held my newspaper I'll just insist on taking his own one. Any audacious parking tickets will be met with a declaration of war and the phone company will get an earful if they insist on sending me any more reminders. The bank manager had better watch out, too. No more gentle mea culpas for the state of my overdraft. After all, banks are only glorified moneylenders and how else would they make their obscene profits if it weren't for the likes of me? I will demand even more money, expect it to be delivered in small notes, and insist he counts it out himself.

The environment can go to hell as well. Those champions of the whales will have a more robust me to contend with. The whales themselves can go skinny-dipping with Pamela Anderson for all I care and the rainforest will have to fend for itself. As for global warming, the whole place can burn up and I know exactly where I'd like to shove the ozone hole. My streetwise kids had also better wise-up to the fact that their dad is no longer the wimp he once was. My language project was just the start. From now on they will all have to deal with a new ass-kicking 21st century man.

FOUR

Family Values

Planning to become a new, more assertive version of myself was the easy part: putting the plan into practice was much harder, particularly in the face of overwhelming odds and ferocious opposition from buddies, kids and even pets.

We were in Mick's house for the weekly session and I had to admire how all of his five kids were wonderfully behaved while we were in the sitting room and Laura was baking one of her wonderful pies in the kitchen. This was a slow food house where parents and kids sat down every day to meat and vegetables cooked on a massive range. Mick took pride in all this, even while he did little to bring it about. He also managed to get the kids to do what he wanted without making a big deal about it. He was assertive without even trying. I have never once heard him raise his voice to his kids but they always seemed to do what he asked and it wasn't as if they were sickeningly well behaved either. He didn't seem to notice my wide-eyed appreciation of all this old fashioned domesticity as he dealt the cards and slurped his can of beer.

"The children are a credit to you, Mick," I said, full of admiration.

"That's Laura's doing," he said. "She was determined that we wouldn't become like one of those American families who never say a word to one another and rarely eat together. She knows what she's talking about, having grown up there."

Laura's belief in the importance of families eating together struck a chord somewhere. It reminded me of the week before when I was scurrying about in search of a missing video and I'd come across a bundle of old greeting cards tied with string and apparently saved for posterity. On top of the bunch was a cheery greeting from Four Star Pizza and it reminded me that those kindly folk are usually the first to send us a card every Christmas. In fact, we always get two, one from each branch of Four Star in town. Not that we are old friends or anything but, like all good business people, they see no harm in using a bit of PR to hang on to their best customers, particularly the ones they know by name. All the delivery guys know our house. Not one of them has to be told directions. The card normally would not have cost me a thought but, for some reason or other, it occurred to me that this was really a very strange state of affairs. We never, for instance, get so much as a nod from the grocer up the road. He would be unlikely to know who I was even if I took to dancing in the nude outside his establishment. That can only be because we do not frequent those establishments often enough to be regarded as regular or even familiar customers.

All of a sudden, as I looked around Mick's tranquil home and smelt good home-cooking, I began to feel parentally inadequate and terribly guilty about our fast food lifestyle. I had always regarded the thoughts of the back-to-family-values brigade as the bleatings of a few cranks. I had dismissed the latest campaigns in Britain and America designed to bring back the family dinner as ridiculous and po-faced, but maybe I was wrong. I had just read that morning that Kellogs, of all people, had commissioned a survey that showed most families eat on the hoof and don't bother to sit down together at mealtime. If what the analysts were saying was true, it probably made me a member of a disorderly if not quite a dysfunctional household. It was time to put the thinking cap on.

Was the demise of family dinnertime the end of civilisation as we know it? Yes, according to the latest breed of child rearing gurus in Britain who believe that the average family is on the brink of extinction because they no longer like to pig out together. For some reason, not altogether explained, the very act of breaking bread together provides the super-glue that bonds families, prevents divorce, keeps kids off drink, drugs, heavy metal and bad company and is generally A Good Thing. On the other hand, according to them, sending out for a video and Chinese takeaway or ringing up for a large pepperoni pizza is not A Good Thing at all. In fact, it is A Very Bad Thing and Shouldn't Be Allowed.

Just in case we didn't get the point, these gurus had managed to dredge up an old PR style black and white photo of the traditional family (mother, father, boy, girl), sitting around the dinner table gazing in awe as daddy dearest dissected a leg of lamb, as if he was the hunter-gatherer returned from a day chasing a herd of wildebeests. Side-by-side with this, there was a still photo from a modern TV programme showing everyone slouched on the couch and staring blankly at the telly. The message was clear: families in the 21st century are sullen-faced couch potatoes, unlike the wholesome gatherings of yesteryear. They clearly intended it to be a lament for some kind of lost world where fresh-faced youngsters raced off to school in the mornings full of good cheer and porridge. In the evenings they could hardly contain their

61

excitement as they tucked into prime roast beef and broccoli cheerfully prepared by mother while father smoked plug tobacco and read the evening paper as he parked his ample rear in his favourite armchair and waited for his cup of cocoa to be delivered.

Although I am concerned about our fast food lifestyle, I am still not convinced about the worthiness of such images. I have always figured that family meals were overrated and the notion that the kids couldn't wait for the sizzling Sunday roast was sentimental nonsense. I have never known anyone under the age of twenty to get excited over a leg of lamb. As for broccoli, green beans and asparagus, they can only be enjoyed by nerds, nuns and people with bowel disorders. I had to admit, though, that the tranquillity of Mick's place was something to be savoured and it set me thinking on the way home after the game that perhaps we should give it a try.

The following morning at breakfast I let my own gang know how I felt.

"Look, kids, it's not like I expect you change into angels or anything, but a little bit of consideration, a teeny bit of politeness would not go astray."

They took not the slightest bit of notice. It was as if I was The Invisible Man. I clearly hadn't made my presence felt and needed to be the more assertive me. There was only one thing for it so, I got up on the chair and roared:

"Listen up, everyone. Tonight we're all going to sit down and have a meal together – even if it's just a pizza. No ifs or buts, and I don't care if you're not hungry."

There wasn't exactly a huge response, so I couldn't say for sure if I had got the message across but that night we did the family dinner thing and made like *The Waltons*. We kept it up for a week and, to my utter amazement, it seemed to have brought about a sea-changer in their behaviour. Suddenly, they went from constant warring to co-operating and actually being polite to one another.

After a few days, I wondered if they had come down with something. Fiona, the tearaway, became a paragon of virtue and even seemed to be having a benign influence on her older brothers. Over the years I had become accustomed to steeling myself outside the front door in the evening, getting ready for the traditional hurricane rush to the door and the usual greetings of moans, groans, and complaints of who did what. It took a while for me to get used to living with the fact that a transformation of glacial proportions had taken place. From either being roared at or totally ignored, I found myself being ushered indoors, my jacket dislodged by a pair of eager hands, an icy gin and tonic pressed into my hand, before being gently guided to the couch amidst enquiries of: "How was your day, Dad?"

This was just too bizarre, so it was with a tiny bit of relief that I realised that, in fact, they hadn't really been taking any notice of me all along. They were up to something. The kids had been playing me for a patsy and this was merely a tactic to get something from me. I suspected it had something to do with wanting another dog, but I didn't really care. Before I called their bluff, I decided to milk the situation for all it was worth. I had already sworn that I would never have another pet in the house after both Plato and Sylvester the goldfish died in the same month.

The new assertive me was determined that this would remain the case, no matter how much the kids protested. I still missed Plato, though, although I would never admit it. He had been the cutest looking dog you ever saw but not the smartest. He'd never really 'got' the idea of being house-trained and his antics with the dead and buried laptop mouse were typical enough behaviour. As Jim had remarked shortly after we got him: "He's pass Maths. A bit of a dope really."

Plato was barely two years old when he got himself run over on the road. He was always racing after cars and it wasn't the driver's fault. It wasn't as if he hadn't had narrow escapes before but, depending which of his funeral mourners you talk to, he was either accidentally and tragically killed by a gentle soul doing twenty-five miles and hour or brutally murdered by a maniac in a Fiesta. The truth is he was killed by his own stupidity and anyone who tells you a King Charles is an intelligent dog is either dumber than the animal or trying to sell you one.

Sylvester had been next to bite the dust. It wasn't that he was particularly cuddly or anything and, anyway, you can't exactly bounce a goldfish on your knee. It's just that all dumb mammals have, in common with petulant soccer players and other people's babies, a peculiar way of creeping into your affections. It's as if their very cuteness is nature's way of making up for their vulnerability. Instead of shark-like aggression or the kind of prickly defences favoured by hedgehogs, Mother Nature sometimes indulges in a little Freudian psychology, enticing huge rugby players to go all gooey at the sight of her dumbest and most defenceless creatures.

Why else, for example, do we tolerate David Beckham's nonsense on and off the field? If he didn't look so good – with or without the ever-changing hair – he would have long ago been dismissed as just another over-rated and overpaid soccer player. Roy Keane, was never given that kind of latitude. But, then, he was never exactly adorable, unlike, for example, George Best. No-one cared about George's wild excesses with the world's most beautiful women or his lifelong love affair with booze so long as he remained Gorgeous George but as soon as he began to lose his attraction both on and off the field he also began to lose the affection of his legion of fans. As any member of the plain people of the world will tell you – a pretty face goes a long way.

It was a bit like that with Sylvester. He was like an underwater Best: sleek and lithe with a passion for dribbling between the miniature rocks at the bottom of his tank. This made his passing all the more dramatic. To witness the demise of one of Nature's tiniest life forms is nothing short of a near-death experience. My own final encounter with Sylvester was just too traumatic – discovering his upturned corpse floating in melancholy pose at the bottom of the sink; lifting the lifeless form with trepidation and the aid of a spatula, swaddling it in kitchen paper and finding a Hamlet cigar box of appropriate size for a coffin.

I'd launched an immediate investigation while, at the same time, keeping an open mind as to the manner and circumstances of death. It wasn't that our Syl could not be energetic at times or was in any way a stranger to the finer points of underwater acrobatics. He had, in fact, been an Olympian when it came to synchronised swimming and his most endearing quality was a stunning ability to execute a 360 degree turn in cold water that would make *Flipper* look paraplegic. But even I could hardly fathom how such a tiny deep-sea diver could suddenly choose to rocket skywards and embrace cold steel without some outside corporeal assistance.

My initial suspicions had been aroused by the

coquettish sniggers of his minder who could hardly contain herself at the crime scene and who had on at least one previous occasion confessed to a certain partiality to goldfish cuisine. In the end, though, I'd been unable to lay the blame for the slaughter on anyone's lap and was forced to record a Scottish verdict.

We'd buried him with due ceremony, beside Plato, at the bottom of the garden, to the left of the magnolia. It had been a beautiful winter's day and even the cat from next-door had come with bowed whiskers to pay his last respects. We'd played ABBA's greatest hits album – Sylvester's favourite – to mark the solemnity of the occasion. Yet I felt aggrieved that we had hardly done him justice. For Plato, the kids had insisted we'd at least had a bottle of whiskey and a saucer of untipped cigarettes in the hall to offer mourners. That had been a real Irish wake. We had considered cremation, of course, on both counts, but I had felt that such forms of dispatch did not quite accord with Christian doctrine. I know my Penny Cathecism.

After all that grief I'd decided that our homestead would have to remain a pet free zone for a long time. There was little in the way of wild life in the house for weeks, apart from an occasional ladybird that might have found stowage on a daffodil extracted from the garden. That was until a weak moment found me the proud owner of another King Charles spaniel no bigger than a toothpick and far lighter than the wad of notes required to seal the transaction.

The kids worked together for weeks to wear down my defences. Their tactics had not developed – they were still using a mixture of gin and tonics and TLC – but all three children had kept up a constant barrage everyday.

Sometimes they worked separately, sometimes together but always the demand was the same: "Can we, can we?" It's amazing how kids know instinctively which buttons to press to get what they want. They also know who to target. It had been building for weeks.

"Dad can we have a new dog, can we, can we? Please, please, please. Can we?"

"Why do you want another dog?"

Luke, the smartass, of course had the perfect answer to that: "It'll make us more of an old fashioned kind of family," he said, proving that he did listen to me now and again. Fiona – aged nine going on nineteen – had the best response. "I really miss Plato, Dad. The O'Briens have a dog, and the McCarthys got a Dalmation. It's gorgeous but it doesn't have its spots yet. The new people up the road have two dogs."

"All right, all right I know you miss Plato. But just because half the neighbourhood has a dog that doesn't mean we have to get one. Anyway, dogs are big trouble and, as you know, they have a habit of getting knocked down. There's another thing. You promised to care for the last one and you never did. You're supposed to feed it, wash it and clean up after it, not let your fool of a Dad do all the hard work."

"We will, we will. We promise. Please."

"Ask your mother" didn't cut any ice, either.

Lorraine was not amused by this tactic.

"Oh no, you don't. Don't you try this 'ask Mum' lark again. That's a real cop-out. I don't mind getting another dog but I'm not having this one in the house. He will have to sleep in the garage. I'm not going to be seen as the big, bad killjoy on this one. It's up to you. If you want to let the kids have a dog that's OK by me. Just don't come home with a bloody Alsatian or Rottweiller which I wouldn't put past you."

I can't remember exactly when I gave in but I will always have a clear memory of placing a ball of fur in a cardboard box for the journey home, mindful of the awesome responsibility that accompanied him and with the passionate advice of his previous owner still ringing in our ears. Plato had been three months old by the time we got him but this guy was a tiny puppy.

"Don't feed him too much or more than once a day. Don't forget to clip his nails and, whatever, you do, don't allow him to make total idiots of you."

We duly ignored it all but learned to be mindful of our little darling's foibles. His name is Spenser, with an S in the middle and I reckon that makes him a Protestant dog. He must be one because his tastes aren't exactly Catholic. Unlike Plato, Spenser doesn't fancy dog food, is a stranger to bones, prefers Farley's Rusks, likes milk and water mixed at a temperature of 98 degrees, crys like a new-born infant, and has discovered an ingenious method of emptying his bladder through the cracks in the kitchen floorboard. Raising triplets would be easier.

I always thought that brains and brawn were no match for native cunning and prided myself on having at least a little savvy, but there is no way to explain why it is I alone who managed to end up, yet again, with the job of pooper-scooper and general dogs-body. Despite my attempts at being Mr Assertive of the 21st century, it looked like I was destined to remain forever a canine slave and I ended up, once again, as the dog minder.

One night I found myself in the position of doggy therapist, attempting to mollify this whimpering ball of wool that gazed up with the soulful eyes of Sammy Davis

Jnr. If I could, I think I'd have breast-fed him if only to halt the infernal noise. A yapping dog is worse than a dripping tap, a constant drain on fraught nerves. Putting a dishcloth under it doesn't help either, although transferring the cloth to the jugular might do the trick. Obviously, my parenting skills – such as they were – needed to be called into play. The solution, as always, was simplicity itself. An overture of *Nessun Dorman*, sotto voce, and a soulful rendition of *Faith Of Our Fathers* followed by *How Much Is That Doggy In The Window* did the trick. I fell asleep on the couch in the company of a gently snoring puppy. It wasn't long before I got used to sharing the couch with a second pedigree chum.

I got so attached to Spenser that the following week, in a moment of madness, I brought him along with me to the poker game. Mick was playing host again because Gerry couldn't. DIY Gerry has been up to his neck in painting and papering at home for weeks now. We can't wait to go around and slag off the results. The advantage of playing in Mick's house, of course, is that there is the usual bonus of a slice or two of Laura's blueberry pie so it suited everyone.

I knew that arriving with a puppy wasn't going to do my reputation as a hard man any good but I reckoned the poker guys had probably always regarded the new '21st century ass-kicking' me as a bit of a joke anyway. I quietly put Spenser on my lap and for the first few rounds he didn't let even a squeak out of him. Everything was okay for a while but then Martin gave a huge yelp and jumped nearly three feet off the ground, scattering the cards and nearly knocking over the table.

"Holy shit, get that disgusting animal out of here," he roared.

69

Spenser had pissed on his leg, ruining his new shoes and the yellow residue of dribbled pee had formed a puddle by Martin's chair. The rest of the guys weren't too impressed either.

"Laura's not going to be happy about this," Mick muttered. For once he actually got up and started searching for some cleaning stuff. I thought it might be a good time for me to leave. Head bowed, I made a hasty exit for the door with Spenser under my arm. The worst of it all, though, was that I had missed out on Laura's pie.

My, by now half-hearted, attempts to rule the roost were finally annihilated by another wild creature not long after that. Coping with domestic animals is one thing but trying to tackle wild creatures is another matter entirely, particularly if they arrive unannounced.

I woke up on Saturday morning in a state of high anxiety to find a stranger in my bed. Not in the bed exactly, but certainly on it, all curled up and sound asleep without so much as a by-your-leave. I was quite put out, particularly as our uninvited guest offered neither apology nor explanation on being awakened by a well-aimed clout with the aid of an indignant roar. Instead he proceeded to give a throaty squawk before darting from the safety of the bedspread towards the open window, flinging himself, Kamikaze-like, at the glass in search of a quick exit.

For a moment I thought I was hallucinating or reliving a particularly scary scene from Bram Stoker's Dracula which had been the late night movie on TV the night before. I cursed myself for having been stupid enough to stay up for every blood-sucking moment of it. It's all very well to watch horror movies in the company of others where you can pretend to laugh it off, letting on that it's all great fun. But if you happen to be watching alone in the dead of night you might find yourself leaving the light on in the hallway on the way to bed.

But this was no vampire – it was either a bird or a bat, or at least an airborne creature of the wild that had no business making free with the frugal comforts of suburbia. There was nothing for it but to wrest myself from self-imposed stupor, make like Clint Eastwood and go on the attack. That was easier said than done. It's one thing to kick a dog out of the house or wrestle with a cat. It's quite another to attempt to rid yourself of a flying phantom when all you have to hand is yesterday's newspaper and your adversary is equipped with the kind of manoeuvrability and firepower that would make the Mafia weep.

The mother of all battles it was not. I tried lunging; I tried coaxing; I tried cooing. I even flung a shoe and nearly broke the window, but all the while it darted overhead, leaving its calling card all over the bedroom.

As in all moments of panic, crisis, national emergencies and public beheadings, a crowd appeared. They were clearly mesmerised by the ensuring scramble and my attempt to bring order to a discordant universe. Naturally, there was no shortage of advice.

"Dad, you're doing it all wrong. You'll never catch it like that. You'll have to get a towel or something to throw over its head."

Luke was lucky I didn't throw something at his head. For once, Lorraine, tried to restrain herself from advising me how to accomplish the deed but she was none too shy about letting me know what she wanted. Even though she refused to take any hand, act or part in evicting our intruder. In fact, she vowed she would not go in the room again until she was assured categorically that the problem had been sorted out.

"Just get rid of it. Get that awful thing out of here before I throw up. It gives me the creeps just thinking about it flying around the place."

We had for years divided household chores into Blue Jobs (him) and Pink Jobs (her). Blue jobs included things like taking out the rubbish, fixing the garage door, cutting the grass, fixing the garage door again. Pink jobs involved washing clothes (as in shoving them into the washing machine and pressing a button) and dead-heading the roses. It may not be exactly politically correct but it works most of the time. Clearly, this had been designated a Blue Job. I wasn't convinced, though.

"I think this is probably a Pink Job. It doesn't require brute force and ignorance so it can't be a Blue Job."

"I swear to God that if you don't get it out it'll be a Black and Blue Job."

"But, how?"

"How the hell would I know? I don't care if you drown it, shoot it or beat it to death. I don't mind even if you have a little chat with it and coax it out the window. You can nuke the bloody thing for all I care. JUST GET RID OF IT. NOW!"

Then, just as I perched one leg on the end of the bed and tried to gain a foothold on the wardrobe for a final offensive, the mobile phone in my pocket rang. It was Mick enquiring about the venue for Wednesday's poker game.

"I'm sorry, Mick. I can't talk. I'm a bit preoccupied. I'm trying to get hold of a bird at the moment."

"Oh, you sly fox. Playing away from home, are we?"

"No, you fool. It's not that at all. This is a real bird, with wings, and it's in our bedroom and I can't seem to get rid of it."

He laughed so loudly that I dropped the phone, right on Fiona's foot. She was, at the time, in the middle of a tirade about the cruelty of her horrible parents.

"You're both cruel and mean. You'll kill the poor little thing. It's one of God's creatures, you know."

There was no time for further debate. A wet dishcloth was employed by Luke from somewhere along my left flank but it only served to spread the bird's little messages to a wider audience. While it found a handy perch on the curtain rail, commonsense flew out of the window and the words of wisdom grew ever more shrill.

"If it's a sparrow you'll have to give it Rice Krispies, they love that."

The assistance became ever more farcical. Adrian even brought in a mousetrap. It might have been my little whispered prayer of desperation or perhaps the dive bomber grew bored but, eventually, fate intervened in the form of a gust of wind that ruffled a few feathers and, with an 'up yours' loop-the-loop, the airborne trespasser glided past, out through the open window, soaring in a north-easterly direction as dawn broke. The place was blitzed by our intruder's evacuations, requiring a major mop-up operation. He had even managed to deface the cover of Robert Fisk's book *Pity The Nation* which I had somehow never got around to reading.

A quick perusal of *The Birds of Britain and Ireland* revealed that it was probably a sparrow or a finch. Then again, it could have been a thrush, I really couldn't tell the difference. I was quite sure, though, that it could not have been a robin – at least not like the kind you see on Christmas cards. My most memorable previous encounter with birds of the feathered kind occurred when I was about eight and my mother and I had arrived home from town to a strangely silent house and a strong odour of leaking gas. Exclaiming, "oh, my God, the budgie", she rushed past my father who was sound asleep in the armchair, to check the resident of a silver cage in the corner of the room, a yellow and green bird which she had been tutoring to sing *Moon River*. It's a pity she wasn't around when that wild thing flew in the bedroom window. She would have had it eating out of her hand and whistling Dixie in no time.

I, on the other hand, have never quite got the hang of dealing with birds in the wild unless they happen to be served up with a nice gravy. Neither had I been able to catch the creature that had taken domicile under the floorboards in the kitchen. At the time, I would gladly have diverted any spare cash in my possession in the direction of someone – anyone – who could have rid me of the unwanted guest who could be heard in the dead of night. Was it a rat? Was it a mouse? All I knew was that it liked to be heard and not seen and had taken to scurrying to and fro beneath the floorboards and making a rustling noise that sounded like someone reading a newspaper in the toilet. It had been devious, clever and wily, had a PhD in diversionary tactics and shunned all attempts at capture. I tried everything from humane traps (useless) to the more usual guillotine variety (even more useless) and had the bruised fingers to prove it. I'd heard that, despite what you might see on old *Tom and Jerry* cartoons, mice actually prefer peanut butter to cheese, so I'd put six traps in place with a tidy dollop on each.

Next morning the peanut butter had been gone but the traps remained unsprung. I tried sausage, then rinds of bacon, a lump of smelly stilton, even a suggestion of paté – all to no avail save to ensure plenty of protein in the creature's diet. I could only assume that, as a result, I was producing a fatter, stronger mouse. There had been some nights when I'd dreamt I could even hear it snigger.

In desperation, I had even tried surfing the net, in the forlorn hope that some internet nut out there in cyberspace might be able to offer a solution, but I'd found the association between the PC mouse and my living, breathing nemesis strangely disconcerting and I had to give it up as a bad job.

My last hope lay in the Vatican. I knew their experts were well-versed in the art of driving out devils. Surely, I'd thought, they'll be able to tell me how to drive out a mouse. I had seen in the newspaper that they'd just published a new guide for exorcists, *De Exorcismis et Supplicationibus Quibusdam*. It's the Catholic Church's latest manual for driving out the devil, the first to be issued since 1614. It is ninety pages long, bound in leather and, naturally, is written entirely in Latin. It clearly affirmed the Church's teaching that Satan was alive and well. "The Devil," wrote Cardinal Jorge Arturo Medina Estevez, the Chilean prelate who supervised its preparation, "goes around like a roaring lion." My devil went around like a roaring mouse but the Vatican hadn't been interested.

I never got the better of it. In the end, it was Luke who managed to rid us of our unwelcome guest. After spending a few hours in the garage, he had emerged triumphant, shouting, "I've got it" just like Archimedes. He had been grasping what looked like a miniature coffin and looking very pleased with himself.

"What's it worth to you?"

"What do you mean what's it worth to me? Just see if the damn thing works," I'd responded in desperation. "If you get rid of it I'll give you the money for yourself and your buddies to go to the cinema."

"No dice. I can go to the cinema any time. How about you do something big for me?"

"This sounds like extortion."

"It's more of a business transaction. I can guarantee you I'll get rid of that mouse and all I want is for you to pay for six golf lessons. Consider it an early Christmas present."

"Why you little bollix. I'm already getting you a new set of irons for Christmas and God knows what else you're going to get from your mother."

In the end though, I'd had little choice and I must admit his device worked a treat. Luke placed the 'coffin' upside down in the kitchen. It was raised up on one side with two matchsticks and had a string at one end. Within minutes the mouse had ventured inside, allowing Luke to pull the string and capture it alive. I'd been amazed.

"The real trouble, Dad, was that you were trying the wrong kind of food. This is a twenty-first century mouse, not a *Tom and Jerry* kind of mouse. He has more sophisticated tastes. He wouldn't touch the cheese but he went straight for the piece of leftover pepperoni from last night's pizza."

I hadn't figured on our unwelcome guest being a Mafia mouse and, as I broke Spenser's rusks into bite-sized pieces for him, it dawned on me that my attempts at morphing into a butt-kicking superman were clearly not about to bear fruit. There and then I decided to throw in the towel and go back to being the mild mannered wimp I had always been.

FIVE

Brave New World

I always feel sorry for Jim during certain times of year like Christmas or holidays or on his son Cian's birthday. It's tough enough trying to be a good dad when you have the support of a spouse and a reasonably stable and normal lifestyle. It must be murder when you only have restricted access to your child during what should be the family fun time of the holiday season.

The Christmas holiday season is a testing time for fatherhood. It's the time of year when dads, young and old, either come into their own and manage to make up for past and future transgressions or they are shown up for their lack of parenting skills. Gerry and Martin don't have children so it's just one long party for them but Christmas can be hard work for anyone with kids.

Mick has five – three girls and two boys ranging in ages from three to fifteen – but he is hitched to the queen of homemakers so Christmas is a rosy-coloured affair for him. He has it unbelievably easy and rarely lifts a finger except to fix the lights on the tree and put a few logs in the fire. "Laura prefers it that way", he says. "She doesn't like me getting in the way. Says I'm too awkward."

We have to have a traditional affair as well, whether we feel like it or not and it is usually great fun. For Jim, though, since his split with Darina, it has turned into an endurarnce test.

"I hate and detest Christmas most of all," he said just

77

after we had piled into Mick's place for our weekly session. "I can't wait for it to be over. It's a nightmare. If I could, I'd go off somewhere for a week and forget all about it. But I can't of course, for Cian's sake."

It was my turn to start the dealing and Jim was seated on my left, so I dealt him first. He looked terrible.

"Are you feeling okay, Jim? You don't look great, if you don't mind me saying so."

"No, Dan, I'm not okay and it has nothing to do with looking good or otherwise. Darina told me yesterday that she will be taking Cian to her parent's place for Christmas and, as you know, that's almost 200 miles from here and Christmas is less than four weeks away. That means all I'll have with him is the usual Saturday McDonald's time between now and then. Life's a bitch."

"So is Darina, by the sounds of it," Martin muttered.

Jim gave a long sigh. "No, she isn't. It's just that, as far as Cian is concerned, she gets everything her own way and I know enough about the legal system to know that most guys in my situation haven't a snowball's chance in hell when it comes to access to your children, let alone custody."

Jim isn't wearing well. He looks and sounds old even though he is actually a young divorcee, at just thirty-four. He got married when he was twenty-four and he and Darina had just left college. They had built up a good solicitor's practice together and made plenty of money. The real, everyday problem, though, is that they still work together in the same office.

"Why can't you take him down to that place you bought by the sea for a few days? I know it's winter but he could still go fishing off the rocks or something," suggested Mick.

"You could always take him to the sun for a week," said Gerry. "There are some great bargains at the moment and it would do you both good."

Gerry was right. Jim certainly looked like he could do with a break.

"Darina won't have it. She says that taking him away like that is too disruptive for him. Anyway, there are no school holidays between now and Christmas so all I'm left with are Saturdays."

None of us were much in the mood for poker after that so we decided to take a break. We cracked open a few cans and sat around talking for a while. The rain was pelting down outside and there was a definite nip in the air. Autumn had definitely given up the ghost, kicked its gently falling leaves into the gutter and done a runner. It's the same every year. The onset of winter always means bye-bye open windows, open shirts, Calvin Kline underwear and low-cut tops. It's time to say hello central heating, woolly jumpers, sensible shoes, roll-neck sweaters, y-fronts and thermal vests. It's a bit like a wayward nun being forced back to the convent after spending her parole in a bordello. It also means you'd better watch out. Jim had just reminded us all that unless we were planning on emigrating to the far side of Pluto, it's time to start making that list.

As I started moaning about buying Christmas presents, Gerry, organised as ever, pulled out a little black leather diary. The diary not only had the names of all the people he had to buy presents for but also what he intended getting them.

"I do the same for birthdays," he explained, as our collective mouths gaped open. "Sometimes I buy someone both presents at the same time. Even if, say, their birthday is in July, I get the Christmas present with it. I can even wrap it because I always keep wrapping paper handy."

Mick couldn't be consoled. "Jesus, Gerry, that beats everything. That's weird, even coming from you. I have five kids and I don't go to that kind of trouble."

In fact, knowing Mick, he probably went to no trouble at all. It was more likely that his wife Laura did all the hard work. It was a miracle that he ever got around to buying her a present.

Not for him the days spent scouring the shops, the panic over some toy or other and the last, mad rush to shops for someone you forgot. Buying for some people is easy – grannies and granddads are fine: just a few golf balls here and a cardigan there. A book or two will do for aunts and uncles and, as for partners, there's nothing like the glisten of gold to earn a few brownie points. The real trouble comes in smaller packages. Kids want it all. Gone are the days when a pair of guns and holsters or a doll that wets itself would set their little hearts pounding.

Not being one of life's long distance planners, I usually end up in a mad flurry on Christmas week with a list the length of my Aunt Matilda's nose, tearing around the shops trying to scramble together presents for people I should have thought about a month before. This year I had promised myself that I would start making that list early. Otherwise I knew I might find another kind of list waiting for me. Not so long ago, I came across a sample Christmas list on my computer. I have kept it to treasure. It is called Document One so I can only assume that it was something of a work in progress. It was written by a ten-year-old, now twelve, who even then could usually outsmart people three times his age. With a winning smile, he had informed me, when questioned, that he wouldn't

80

dream of asking for anything prohibitively expensive if his parents had to pay for it but, seeing as it would all be from Santa, he'd reckoned that money was no object. The list had been a classic:

Dear Santa For Christmas I would please like the following.
1. Gameboy Advanced SP
2. Tony Hawks Pro Skater3 for Dreamcast
3. Final Fight for Gameboy Advanced
4. Jet Set Radio for Dreamcast
5. A BIG SURPRISE

At the time, I'd thought about setting up an e-mail all the way from Lapland. It was to go something like: "All I can say to that lot is Ho...fxxxxing...ho." Luckily for all concerned, I'd thought better of it.

Everything on that list, from the Gameboy to the Dreamcast radio – had been a Japanese or American product and that's still the name of the game nowadays, from Gameboy to Pokémon. Pokémon cartoons can still sometimes get the kids up in the morning and keep them awake at night, dreaming about the adventures of Ash and his sidekick Pikachu. The army of new toys gets bigger every year.

"I was never that organised Gerry, even when the kids were younger. Do you remember the first toy invasion force – the Teenage Mutant Ninja Turtles? There were four of them and they lived in a sewer with a Japanese rat as their mentor where they indulged in male bonding and practised all manner of hand-to-hand combat with broom handles. I'll always remember them because that Christmas, 1990, psychologists started warning parents that the stress of hunting for them in the shops could result in marriage breakdown and schoolteachers blamed them for increased violence in school playgrounds. I still ended up getting the full set."

"I remember them," said Jim. "Darina had a nephew who used to go crazy for them. He was about eight at the time and he made his parents buy all the turtles. Then – and this is the really mad thing – he insisted that they buy him four real turtles in tribute to his toy heroes. Of course, the inevitable happened. After a while the toy turtles were thrown out and they were left with the real ones. They had grown from the size of a coin to dinner plate size. The kid is in college now but his parents are still stuck with the real turtles."

Martin thought the whole thing hilarious. "Those turtles will be around when that kid is a grandfather. They might even be still devouring wildfowl chicks and bird's eggs well into the next millennium. People seem to forget that turtles live longer than Tom Jones."

It was all very well for him to scoff. Although he often got me some of the new kids' stuff in the States, he's never actually had to go scouring the shops for toys like the Mighty Morphin Power Rangers or a Tamagotchi – an electronic pet that lived for up to thirty-five days if fed, cleaned, disciplined and exercised through the pressing of buttons. If care slipped, a tiny angel descended and took the pet away and you could hear the cries of bereaved children from Belfast to Bangkok. Bandai, their Japanese manufacturer, sold ten million of them in six months but by Christmas 1997, Tamagotchi had been put six feet under by the Gameboy explosion. Beany Babies, polystyrene cuddly toys that have since become collector's items, were another craze. My favourite had been when

Adrian asked for the Snickers Ball, a contraption you were meant to strap to your thigh and jiggle about. I never managed to find out exactly what it was supposed to do but I still suspect to this day that it was not meant to be a child's toy at all and had more to do with family planning.

As per usual the thought of all that manufactured childhood was getting me down. I reassured myself with the thought that there are always certain things you can do to regain a little simplicity on the home front. I must confess that the Teenage Turtles that went missing from Luke's toy chest had actually been abducted in the dead of night, secured in a plastic sack and dumped in the bin. As for the Tamagotchi, it didn't die of old age or neglect but was cleanly dispatched by way of the considerable gullet of a neighbour's child known, far and wide, as The Destroyer. He is like a miniature Arnie Schwarzenegger, all brawn, no brains, with the personality of a hammerhead shark and the amazing ability to munch through anything – either manmade or organically grown. I swear that kid could cut the grass with his teeth. I am also guilty of telling porkies when I swore blind that the Power Rangers were no longer on TV and, hand on heart, I cannot deny a sense of relief when another kid ran off with Fiona's hand-bag carrying Teletubby, Tinky Winky. In case you have to resort to such tactics and the little horrors get suspicious, keep some old favourites handy, like a pair of six-shooters, just to show them how it used to be. They will cost next to nothing in the Discount Shop and your kids will probably think they are really cool.

We decided to deal out another hand but I was finding it hard to get my mind back on poker. Despite all my good resolutions for this year I knew when it came to the crunch that it wouldn't be easy to take pleasure in the notion of wading through the shops in search of the latest 'must have' toy. Going shopping was even harder when I knew I could just as easily be enjoying liquid lunches with friends while soaking up the Christmas spirit in the pub. In fact, I have managed to get away with not shopping on occasion, thanks to Martin who is a prodigious shopper and who loves to spend other people's money. He had managed to get most of Adrian's list that time in New York, even the big surprise. If he ever gives up the airline business, I don't know what I'll do. I suppose I'll just have I'll do it myself.

Even though Christmas shopping for kids can be exhausting, I know, in a way, I will miss it when mine grow up and I don't have to do it any more. When they get older they will, naturally, want to do their own shopping. Luke is already buying some of his own stuff. It means part of the spirit of Christmas will have left for good, but I will still look forward to everything else about Christmas in a childish kind of way. I always do. I adore the way over the top campness of it all: the beta waves of flashing coloured lights and the relief when you finally manage to get them to work; the milky way of tasteful tinsel; the shiny, gaudy baubles; the crackers and their bad jokes; the oversized turkey; the endless squeals of the kids who seem to be running on empty. Not to mention the wall-to-wall display of cards that shows you still have a few friends left; the endless array of unsuitable presents – the ties that nobody wears, the aftershave that smells like sweat, the jumpers three sizes too big, and the books that will never be read until the day you find yourself stuck in hospital. Best of all, though, is the tree. I'm not talking about those big plastic things that cost a fortune in the department stores or the ones that look like Tinfoil but the real Fir or Norway Spruce variety. A Christmas tree is the ancient symbol of pagan lifeblood that ennobles the living room and starts shedding its needles the minute it's brought indoors.

Only once did I ever come close to not having a tree at Christmas and that was when I was about five years old. The tradition then was to put the tree up on Christmas Eve when my father would cart it home under his arm and plunge it with full ceremony into a bucket of wet sand like he had just conquered Everest. On that particular night before Christmas he'd arrived home full of far too much good cheer and bad whiskey. He had obviously taken the scenic route from town and had been indulging at every pub, safe house and crossroads. When he'd eventually stumbled in the door we were waiting, with wide-eyed anticipation, for the pungent aroma of pine needles. But there'd been no sign of the tree. Words had been exchanged, accompanied by weeping and wailing that went something like: "That's all you were asked to do. Now go back out and don't come back without a tree." Just like a Christmas miracle, the tree had been there in all its splendour the following morning.

"Santa brought it," my father had explained. "He promised me he'd drop it in on the way here with the presents."

It was only years later that I discovered that the same night a strange, hooded figure was spotted with an axe, feverishly chopping down a stately tree under a full moon at the local cemetery. Like all good neighbours, the inhabitants never let on.

We buried my father on a fine summer's day in that same graveyard and, despite the sadness and solemnity of the occasion, I couldn't help but smile as I fancied that I spotted a bit of a gap in the hedging of tall spruce surrounding the normally wind-swept cemetery. I still marvel at how he'd managed to cut down a full-grown tree and cart it home under the cover of darkness while so much the worse for wear. I reckon it must have been sheer terror at the thought of what would have happened if he'd failed to deliver. The real miracle of it all is that he didn't chop his leg off in the process. I often wonder if I would ever have the nerve to do what he did in similar circumstances.

Of course, the downside to Christmas ever since is that he has not been around to share the day with us and engage in a fine old slagging match. He would have delighted in learning from his grandchildren all about my failed attempts to be Dad of the Decade.

There are, of course, other downsides to Christmas as Jim was discovering. The season of goodwill can test the limits of human endurance in many ways. The trouble for Martin and Gerry is that they find they are expected to visit relations they can't stand on Christmas Day. It drives Martin particularly mad.

"I have this aunt who lives on her own and I am regarded as the worst in the world if I don't go to see her at Christmas. The problem she is forty miles away and it means I can't even have a drink until late on Christmas night. It's a real pain."

"It's the same with me," said Gerry, as he looked at his hand. "I know you think I have it easy with no kids and only one sister but Fionnuala has a huge gang and we are always expected to do the rounds. It means I end up driving around all day."

My problem is the opposite. I never have to move out

of the house for Christmas but I do occasionally have to endure a crusty old retired British Army colonel who every now and then gives notice of his intention to grace us with his presence. He does so in a manner that suggests we should all feel eternally grateful for the fact that he has, yet again, decided to sponge off us. My abiding memory of him will always be that he makes Scrooge look like Father Christmas and he can peel an orange in his pocket while wearing mittens. He is a staunch Tory, likes to reminisce about the great days of Empire and lives in a run-down house in faded grandeur where he dreams of past glories and future grants. He despises socialism in all its forms and once told me when I was a teenager dossing about in London: "I wouldn't mind your working class attitude if you'd get a job." He has definite views on everything, from taxes (a Communist plot) to refugees (denizens of the dominions) to drug addicts (hang the lot of them) to Irish whiskey (gut-rot. Give me a half-decent Scotch any day). He mourned the death of Enoch Powell although he considered him to be too much of a liberal for his liking. He always brings out the worst in me. Just for the hell of it, I like to leave a copy of *The Socialist Worker* lying around when he arrives and make sure there isn't a drop of Scotch in view. I usually stick a bottle of Paddy under his nose just for the pleasure of watching his eyes water.

He has often professed a fondness for dogs so, one Christmas, I'd hoped he might give us a bit of a break and take our wild and windy pet out for a canter. The only trouble was Plato had gone on the missing list at the time. I'd found myself fantasising about what it would be like to have my own virtual pet, a little creature comfort without the grim reality. Something of a docile companion, programmed to sit, roll over and yelp on command, without all that bother of having to feed him or help put the vet's kids through boarding school. Considering that Plato had gone AWOL after a well-executed drop-kick when I'd discovered that he had eaten half of granny's Christmas cake, I'd thought I might have years of vet bills to come. I'd issued a health warning to visitors (with one exception). As I'd fully expected most declined the offer of sharing the leftovers. But one greedy monster proceeded to wolf down what the dog hadn't got with exaltations like: "Simply delicious. How on earth did she manage to get it so moist?" I'd had a pretty good idea but I hadn't had the heart to tell him.

In any case, Plato had finally turned up and I'd outmanoeuvred Colonel Blimp by suggesting he either go walkies or stay and watch the movie *Michael Collins* on video. Observing his outraged expression I'd decided that watching *Michael Collins* on Christmas Day was going to become my newest Christmas tradition.

The trouble was that the very thought of having Colonel Blimp for another Christmas was making me wilt and, like the tree, I could feel my needles beginning to shed. The lads all knew about my annual curse.

"I know what you should do," said Gerry, as he turned his cards face down on the table, paying nothing into the pot to indicate he was folding. "Tell him you, Lorraine and the kids have decided to spend Christmas with him for the next couple of years because you found his company so compelling. I bet that'll frighten the life out of him."

That didn't seem a bad idea but it was really a coward's way out. Plus being a wimp was no fun – I was still hanging on to some idea of the new assertive me.

"You forget, Gerry, you're not playing with a wimp

any more. The new, improved me don't take no shit from no-one, no more. I'm going to tell the old fart that he's no longer welcome – plain and simple."

Then, as if to justify this monumental decision, Eureka, I played a winning hand. A flush of excitement spread across my cheeks as I pulled in my second poker pot with a pair of sevens in Five Card Draw. The rest of the guys could hardly believe it – for the second time in not too many weeks they'd been taken to the cleaners by a beginner. I'd quickly suggested that we call it a night after that.

My winning streak galvanised me to take another kind of gamble the following day. I decided it was time to brave the shops and be ahead of the posse. All the talk of Christmas lists at the game had made me determined not to end up in a mad flurry on Christmas Eve. I had resolved that I would get everything under wraps early when the shops would be quiet and I'd have the pick of the crop. The funny thing was, everyone else seemed to have the same idea.

It began easily enough: list all made out in alphabetical order (computers do have their uses), a gentle meander down the aisle where they keep soaps, candles and those nice smelly things all neatly wrapped up in baskets, then on through the knick-knack department where any amount of presents could be picked up for aunts, grannies and ladies of a certain age. A quick whip round the books secured another fine haul without too much bother and, although things were certainly looking busier, it was, at least, civilised. This was shopping as it should be: comfortable, convenient and without fuss. In a flush of enthusiasm, I made a dash for the toy department – big mistake.

No wonder the rest of the shop was quiet. Half the population was there, engaged in a mad scrum to get hold of whatever was already on the kids' must-have list for Christmas. There was roaring and shouting, tears and lamentations, grabbing and pulling and a crush of bodies you wouldn't find at a rugby match. It was like mud wrestling without the mud: fun to watch but a hell of a way to spend an evening.

Early Christmas shopping was all about trolley rage with a difference. Forget road rage – it's only for wimps. Never mind tut-tutting over soccer hooligans on and off the pitch or moaning about those drunken lager louts you see falling about the place in town after a match on Saturday. If it's blood and guts you're after, if murder and mayhem happen to be your notion of sport or if you hunger for the kind of no-holds-barred fight where the Queensbury rules don't apply, there's a ringside seat to be had to the meanest, dirtiest mother of all battles near you. All you have to do is grab the purse or wallet, break the bank or raid the hole-in-the-wall and enter a pre-Christmas toy department.

A bit daunted, I put out a hand for the Barbie Biker which I was sure would be Fiona's toy of choice. My reasoning was that even Miss Environment would surely want some toys on Christmas Day.

"EXCUSE ME."

The voice was ten times bigger than its occupant, a tiny, pinched, withered old dame of the kind Daniel O'Donnell never tires singing about. All I managed to mumble by way of reply was a meek "sorry?" but she was having none of it. Just as I was about to politely step aside, this silver-haired mother of somebody or other nudged her way forward with both elbows in battle station formation, like a rooster trying to take off.

She tended to speak in capital letters and, landing a nasty sidewinder, declared: "THAT IS MINE, THANK YOU."

Just in case I didn't get the message, she repeated the exercise, again and again, for all the stuff on my list, all of which were in short supply. You could tell she was a veteran at this kind of thing. Every advance was accompanied by a verbal ejaculation like: "DO YOU MIND?" and "HAVE YOU NO MANNERS?" Through gritted false teeth, she kept up this barrage, all the while lunging in my direction with rapid bursts from her trolley, which she employed with practised ease.

The only thing for it appeared to be to remain above all that nonsense, but the high moral ground is a lonely place and, anyway, I was damned if I was going to let her get her gnarled old paws on the last of the Ken and Barbie Combo sets.

There then ensued what I can only describe as the Battle of the Barbies. She pulled one way, I the other. She yanked; I dragged. She cursed; I swore. She shouted; I roared. It didn't do either of us much good because, by this time, Barbie had begun to take on the appearance of Michael Jackson and Ken looked as if he had just undergone a none too successful sex change. No prizes for guessing who won the day. By the time I got home, I was cowed, bowed, and bruised all over and I never managed to get my hands on the Combo set.

The whole encounter taught me a valuable lesson, though. I swore that the next time I met her I would either give her a wide berth or else don a suit of armour and get ready to do battle. As a former boy scout, I knew how to be prepared. Next time I went Christmas shopping

I would wear a pair of woolly knee-length stockings and a brace of stout walking boots to ward off all attacks from walking sticks, high heels and shopping trolley wheels.

Most importantly of all, it taught me that I should find out what exactly to go into battle for before I left the house. As it turned out, I need not have bothered fighting over Barbie and Ken. When I got home that evening I was flabbergasted to find Fiona putting a whole battalion of Barbies in a box. Horrified, I asked her what she was doing.

"It's OK, dad. Don't worry. I haven't gone crazy or anything. As you know, I don't play with dolls any more because I've grown out of them. I'm bringing my old Barbies to school tomorrow to sell them and raise money for Chi Chi. He's a very rare red panda who lives in a zoo in China and they have no money to feed him properly."

At least shopping early had been worth it in one way. It was just as well I hadn't waited until Christmas Eve to find that out or I'd have been in even bigger trouble than my father.

SIX

Growing Old Disgracefully

There is nothing like a bout of binge eating and drinking, particularly during the Christmas season. I'd had a blast but the only problem was the results of all that excess weren't so much fun – especially for those afflicted by middle age. For weeks after the holiday season, I tried to cut down on both the buns and the booze but I didn't put too much effort into it and, as a result, it didn't seem to be having much effect. The trouble with reaching middle age is that, unless you are one of the greyhound breed there is a tendency to grow out as well, to expand further than your normal horizons and way beyond the confines of the body beautiful. I know there is nothing particularly unusual in this and that anyone in the region of forty-years-old is bound to put on a bit of extra padding now and then. What had me concerned though was the fact that my poker pals seemed to be holding up better than I was and this was brought home to me one Wednesday not long after we had started a session in Martin's place. I made the mistake of complaining that I seemed to be showing signs of grey hair and a bit of general wear and tear after the Christmas festivities and I wondered if any of the others had the same problem.

"See that?" said Martin, grabbing a fistful of jet, black hair and giving it a tug. "All my own, every strand and not a grey hair in sight, or, at least, not so you'd notice."

I was trying to listen to Martin and, at the same time, take heed of the poker advice I was getting from Mick. I needed all the help I could get because I had made a complete cock-up of the opening round.

"Look, Dan, pay attention. This is very basic stuff. Betting goes in sequence. The player to the left of the dealer usually makes the first bet. Now your mistake was that you opened the betting even though you didn't want to. Actually, you didn't have to. You could have passed it onto Gerry who was on your left and if he didn't want to, he could have passed it on as well, and so on. Got that?"

I wasn't sure, but I just nodded dumbly. Anyway, what Martin was saying sounded a bit more interesting. He was in full flight, appropriately enough for a pilot, and, in any case we felt obliged to listen considering we were in his place and it was his beer we were drinking.

"Guys, listen up. We're all either approaching forty or past it. . . ."

"No we're not, at least not all of us." It was Jim, reminding us that, at thirty-four, he is still the baby of the group. "Of course, unlike a slip of a young fella like myself, some of you guys will never see forty again so you have to take a bit more care of yourselves. Remember, exercise is not a disease and some of you are getting a bit paunchy. Look at you, Dan. Since you gave up the cigarettes you must have put on two stone. You'll have to hit the gym or take up jogging or something. You're in worse shape than any of us. Martin and Gerry are holding up well and, even though he's built like a brick shithouse, at least Mick keeps himself physically fit by playing rugby, but you're heading for trouble."

I felt Jim was holding all the aces in more ways than

94

one and that this might just be a clever way of trying to put me off my game. Not that he needed to resort to such tactics: Jim is one of the best players around.

"It's all very well for you, Jim. Now that you're single again you can afford to take the time to look after yourself. Gerry has loads of time to himself as well because he doesn't have kids. As for Mick, Laura makes sure he doesn't have to lift a finger."

As far as Martin was concerned, this sounded like one big moan. "Give us a break, Dan. It's not like you have it so tough. Lorraine is great and so are your kids. Look, it's what I was about to say before Jim jumped in. The real problem is that we are all going through the Forties Fear Factor. It happens to a lot of guys in middle age. It's a scary time."

It didn't seem to bother him.

"You're just as bad as Jim, Martin, you don't have to cook for yourself when you're working. The airline puts you up in the best hotels and I am sure they all have gyms. You're not married, you don't have kids; you never have to do the school run or spend all your time driving a bunch of twelve-year-olds to matches."

In fact, I was about to add that all he really had to worry about was how to spend his pay cheque and where his next one-night stand was coming from, but I thought better of it. He was right about one thing though – the forties are scary for men. When a man turns the wrong side of age forty he can do one of three things: ready himself for the long and gentle journey into the twilight world of cardigans, slippers and potted geraniums; sprout an earring (or a ponytail if the follicles are up to it) and take to wearing loud shirts; or become a born-again slob – unworldly, unshaven and occasionally, unsightly.

95

Cardigans have never suited me and as I don't happen to be an aging disc jockey, an artist or a minor poet, joining the ponytail set would make me look ridiculous, so for the time being I've settled on the third option and have been dedicating myself to becoming a middle-aged slob. This decision had also been reached thanks to an Armani suit, a phantom bottom pincher and a wayward pet.

I have never been what you might call a flashy dresser, have never gone in much for overstated style and have always viewed the dictates of fashion with a sense of wondrous detachment. I'm not talking about cleanliness here which is obviously another matter entirely. There's nothing quite so refreshing as a good dollop of plain soap to baste those places where shower gels don't reach and there's no harm either in applying a dash of designer aftershave to a newly scrubbed face. Perhaps this attitude comes from growing up in mortal dread of falling under a bus and being found wanting in the hygiene department. No, I'm just talking about designer clothes.

I like my shoes either black or brown – not both – and prefer the sartorial elegance of a blazer and grey trousers to the madness of expensive designer suits or the horror of those checks and stripes that you sometimes see being paraded around golf courses by a lost generation of failed sportsmen with dodgy taste in clothes. As I looked round the table, I noted that each of us had a very different idea of style. Mick, for all his bulk, always looked the neatest and rarely sported anything other than the country squire look – tweed jacket and corduroy trousers. I suspect, though, he simply wore whatever Laura bought him. Whatever Jim wore always looked expensive – usually a check shirt and blazer. Gerry favoured polo-necks and Martin always looked as if he had just stepped out of a designer clothes shop. My notion of a fashion wardrobe is brief: one suit for weddings and funerals, a sports coat for taking a stroll in the woods and a sweater and jeans for when you're pretending to cut the grass. I could not imagine spending a day's wages on a designer vest when it could be better invested in the pub and I still can't understand why any sane person would volunteer to wear anything with the label on the outside.

Despite this highly developed anti-fashion phobia, strangely enough, my journey into the middle-aged nether world of slobbery all started when I had an uncharacteristic flirtation with fancy clothes while on business in Italy. Everywhere I'd looked there'd been guys flashing designer labels and it had seemed a shame not to take advantage of the fact that using plastic to pay for everything felt painless. One Armani suit and half a dozen shirts and ties later and I'd felt ready for anything. The only trouble had been that what had looked positively understated in a sun-drenched climate seemed totally daft when viewed against leaden skies at home. Nevertheless, the new clobber would have to be given an airing and, as luck would have it, the opportunity soon arose in the form of a fancy 'do' populated by the bright and the beautiful and what passes for high society in our neck of the woods. It had been when I grabbed my third drink from the waiter that I felt an all-out, no-hands-barred, over-the-top, full-blown pinch in my Armani region.

The culprit, a Madonna lookalike, had proceeded to give the thumbs up sign to her sisters in crime who'd fallen about the place in howls of laughter, slapping each other on the back like a bunch of lager louts at a stag party. Bemused and bewildered, I'd affected an air of haughty indifference but couldn't quite get over feeling discommoded by such an unwarranted intrusion. The hussies, meanwhile, had set their sights elsewhere and, while their husbands were discussing the price of crude oil, I'd overheard them giggling about what they would like to do to a baby-faced guy in the corner if only they could lay their hands on him. Lucky for him, he hadn't been wearing an Armani suit.

I had taken an instant dislike to the suit and thrown it on the couch in disgust when I got home. Not a good idea. The following day I'd discovered that it had been turned into a bordello by my frisky dog who had invited a stray partner over for a little hanky panky. They'd been at it again later that morning. Puppy love sounds better than it looks and before you could say 'designer label', they'd proceeded to do what comes naturally right in front of me, without any regard for haute couture.

The suit has been in a bottomless drawer ever since and the slob within has reigned supreme. No more suits or fancy shirts. Even my long-held passion for carbolic soap has faded. Now it's a three-day beard for poker nights and the economical use of water for the rest of the week. After all, this is how people used to live before electricity and running water and it has a certain Bohemian charm, if you can manage to stay downwind. I swore that the next time I found myself at a fancy soirée I would arrive wearing an egg-stained shirt, ragged cardigan and Jesus sandals and dare anyone to lay a painted fingernail on my rugged corduroys.

Whatever about our different lifestyles, we were all agreed that it was still a great shock to the system, though, when you begun to realise that middle age had arrived without so much as a by-your-leave. Mick stifled a yawn, as he played his last hand and stretched.

"You must be right, Dan. It's only ten o'clock and already I feel like it's past my bedtime. Middle age is a bitch. It's like a cross between a double-glazing salesman and a zealous Jehovah Witness. You're never ready for it, no matter when it arrives."

I was exhausted as well, which was probably why no amount of instruction from Mick throughout the night had done anything to improve my playing. It didn't look like I'd be winning at poker again for quite some time.

Middle age was clearly catching up. I should have been better prepared, should have seen the warning signs, should have noticed those extra few wrinkles and lines around the face, the increasing aluminium sideburns, that ingrown toenail, the little ache where no ache existed before, the paunch.

For a while, after choosing the middle-aged 'slob' option, I'd resigned myself to all of it even the growing paunch but late one drunken Friday night I'd found myself in a chip shop. There had been a long queue of customers. Some had been dodgy looking characters but mostly they'd been business types who had sidled over from the pub across the road at closing time. They had all been men and it was as if they'd been cloned – each one in turn was making a brave attempt to walk a straight line while clutching the metal barrier that corralled the queue. Then, one by one, and, with as much dignity as possible, they'd given a loud belch and mumbled something like: "Giz a shicken supper with lozza peas." The whole queue had been reflected in the stainless steel counter and when I'd spied myself mirrored among that bunch it shocked me. I'd seen a middle-aged man staring back. It'd been a major Forties Fear Factor moment. I'd fled before it was even my turn swearing that I would never return and that I'd immediately start fighting the onset of middle age. I had been having too many late nights, anyway, and even the poker lads had begun to remark that I was looking knackered.

"You'll have to cop yourself on," said Gerry, as we were nearing the end of what had turned out to be a marathon poker session. I had stupidly complained about my aching back. Gerry knew I had to be up early the next day and that this was my fourth night out on the trot.

"You run around morning, noon and night like you were eighteen-years-old. You're not. You're married, with kids and a responsible job and you act like you were living in a bedsit and going to college. You think you can keep up with the guys in the office in the drinking department, but you can't."

"Actually, you're wrong, Gerry. I can drink the lot of them under the table."

That, though is no great boast. I would be much better off if I had a smaller capacity. It would mean I wouldn't fall asleep at awkward times. You'd think that dozing off at half time in the middle of a Premiership final, snoring in the chair during a bout of the new *Simpsons* board game or being comatos after trying to teach Spenser how to walk in the park would have been hints enough, but, no, I put it all down to underwork or overindulgence. It's easy to fool yourself, to act like Mr Invincible, imagining you are as fit as a fiddle even though you're shaped like a cello, thinking all your friends are showing their age but not you, or taking mean spirited pleasure from the fact that an old school pal two years younger is as bald as a baby's bottom. It's only when something startling occurs, something monumental and unequivocal, that the inevitable dawns and you know that if, for instance, you were hit crossing the road, the newspaper would describe how a ' ...middle-aged man was knocked down by a double-decker bus near his home yesterday. . . .'

My drinking bravado was just a front for Gerry. After the chip shop revelation I'd had a second startling occurrence that had been almost as bad as getting knocked down by a bus. It had involved been savaged by a skinny kid in an arm wrestling contest. He wasn't even twelve at that stage and he'd had something of an advantage, using two small arms instead of one big one, but, for all that, it was a fair fight and the worst of it is that he hadn't even noticed me turning the colour of a cardinal's robes while I'd tried in vain to stem the onslaught. Adrian, bless his heart, had thought I was indulging in a little paternal power play, doing what I'd often done before – allowing him to win. What he hadn't suspect – and I'll never tell – is that Papa hadn't had the strength of a pussycat and would have happily broken a little finger to win the day.

That whole episode was on my mind as we rose to get our coats and Martin began throwing the empties in his special beer can bin. I bet Jim will never face that with Cian and I certainly can't imagine any of Mick's brood getting the better of him, even if the whole five of them tackled him together. Maybe I should think about taking up weight training.

Driving home I started to think about Adrian's new competitive spirit. Bouts of combat are unusual in our neck of the woods. The will to win, to succeed against the odds, whatever the cost, to jump higher, run faster, to taste victory, has never had much currency. A more humane spirit generally abounds, where everybody goes about their business without the compulsion to go one-on-one or do battle to the death. But lately uncompromising competitiveness has invaded our homestead. Lorraine has already found out that sometimes it can be used to advantage, like finding out who can bring in the shopping in less that five minutes, who can haul up the bins while holding their breath or who can drag in the washing from the line before it rains.

The underlying theme of these manly pursuits is not so much the desire to win as the fear of failure. This seems to a peculiarly male affliction. Sensibly, women of all ages no longer seem to hold such fears. A woman used to be regarded a failure if she couldn't do the hoovering at warp speed, have her brood shiny as a beacon and have the house scrubbed like an operating ward. She also had, on pain of ridicule, to be the hostess with the mostest, ensuring that her sponge cakes rose three feet off the ground. Most women nowadays couldn't give a toss about such nonsensical competitive one-upmanship but men are still in the Dark Ages. Witness the explosion of gyms and keep-fit classes catering to men alone, most of the inmates being overstressed, overweight and, of course, middle-aged. Thankfully there are always a few notable exceptions. I have to admire that diehard old trooper down the local who refuses to buy into anything approaching a keep-fit regime and whose notion of competing is raising his drinking arm faster than the man beside him.

For most of us, though, middle age is not a competition; it's a disease, and an incurable one at that. Even Martin, fit and all though he is, has started to get a bit pudgy and has taken to going to the gym more often. He even has a portable flab buster that he brings along with him whenever he's on a long-haul trip so he can work out in his hotel room. The fact is that you know a major bodily transition has taken place when you wake up, look in the mirror and have that morning-after feeling even though there wasn't a night before. What's worse is then being beaten to a pulp in a trial of physical strength by an eleven-year-old. I can only pray that the next time around Adrian will show a bit more respect for his elders, do the compassionate thing and let his middle-aged Dad win.

In the meantime, I am going to totally ignore most of Gerry's advice about slowing down and giving into the middle-aged disease. I will cut back on some of the late nights and their chip shop finales but that's it. What does he know anyway? He's only thirty-seven but I know livelier eighty-year-olds. Apart from poker, his idea of a really crazy night out is going to a meeting of his gramophone society. It's amazing to think that he was once a serious adventurer who lived among the natives with a mountain tribe in Tibet.

There are even some good things about the middle-aged disease –one sure thing it brings is an inability to ignore a pretty face, particularly when it is smiling sweetly at you and hoping you wouldn't mind answering a few questions, if it wouldn't be too much trouble. Of course not, no trouble at all. And, of course, I was enthralled to hear that the week before, while half the world was in slumber, the population of Planet Earth rose by one to bring it over the six billion mark. I had nothing whatsoever to do with this state of affairs and I can only plead that my insider knowledge of the momentous event was derived from a new-found passion for questionnaires. This was brought about as a result of being inveigled by an overly attractive visitor to fill out a questionnaire for the purpose of analysing the modern European family. Some of these things are thicker than a telephone directory and demand patience, perseverance and no little imagination and, once begun, there's no giving up. Whoever sends out these questionnaire bearers certainly knows what they're doing. I'll bet that less than 1% of them are unemployed lumberjacks in string vests. Like the Avon Lady, the Clipboard Lady will not take no for an answer, unless, of course, you are asked whether you happen to be: (a) a serial killer, (b) an escaped convict or (c) a congenital liar in which case it would be wise to say No to all three, despite constant assurances that your answers are 'treated in the strictest confidence'.

But the real problem with these questionnaires is not that they take longer to fill out than a tax return but that they demand equal economy with the truth. For example: Do you watch more than one hour of television per day?

Answer: No – Lie. It's a stupid question anyway, a bit like asking a fourteen-year-old boy if he has ever had impure thoughts.

Do you take more than half an hour of exercise daily?

Answer: Yes – damn lie. Do they really expect people to admit to being couch potatoes?

Do you do the household shopping regularly?

Yes – statistic. This one, of course, is meant for men only and is designed to prove that Neanderthal Man is alive and well. I suspect the hand of that hoary old feminist, Germaine Greer, in this.

I'll bet that, statistically speaking, nine out of ten people who fill out questionnaires lie through their teeth, anyway – especially if they are middle-aged.

In any case, as Martin keeps saying, I must seize the day and accept whatever is flung in my path. So, I've decided to seize it in my own way and enjoy my new sloblike lifestyle. It won't be easy because I am not the best at coping with change. I generally prefer the comfort of the familiar and dislike any notion of new things. But I've made the decision. Instead of competing with the onset of middle age I'll just avoid chip shop mirrors and Adrian's arms from now on. Besides, there are plenty of other life changes that I have to cope with. Take sardines for instance. It doesn't seem that long ago that opening a can of sardines demanded the kind of attention necessary for a triple by-pass and it wasn't everyone, hurlers and golfers apart, who could turn a flick of the wrist into dinner for one. There was that key you had to turn, tease, twist and swear at until it finally broke free of its moorings to reveal a mass grave of tiny creatures that only a bachelor reared on his mother's stew could stomach. All's changed, changed utterly. The key has now been replaced by a ring pull system of the kind you will find on a Coke can. It's supposed to make life easier but, in fact, successful manipulation demands the dexterity of a contortionist and muscles like Adrian's.

There are other life changes that take even more getting used to, like sharing life with a computer that looks like something out of a sci-fi film. To the initiated, this might seem like the pathetic groan of a technological Neanderthal but, despite his lack of creature comforts, at least the only glowing orb Homo Erectus had to come home to was a fire in the middle of the cave. He might have had to club a bear for tea but I wonder how he would have coped if everytime he came in the door he had to consult an oracle that warned "you've got mail", or had to worry about whether some deranged member of a lonely nerds chat-line would be sending him a message?

Not all life changes are for the better, either. Growing

105

prosperity has also brought about many new social customs. It's no longer considered the done thing to drop by on a whim – you must be invited. There was a time when if you felt like calling on neighbour, friend or family all you had to do was go round to the back door and shout: "Is the kettle on?" No more – particularly among the denizens of the so-called café society who would regard an unexpected visit as some kind of assault. Even some funerals are now by invitation only. Gone are the days when you could turn up to a rural dispatching, safe in the knowledge that friend and stranger alike would be welcome and there'd be no worries about where to stay the night.

There are, of course, some things I hate being invited to and will do anything to avoid: those delicate cocktail parties with champagne that tastes like liver salts; the horsey set outings where everyone slobbers over disgusting green dips; ghastly charity dos that specialise in five-course meals by way of helping the destitute, and not forgetting the annual office dinner dance, refuge to spinsters and dirty old men hoping to drop the hand. Far superior to such events are the little unexpected happenings that seem to arise organically from a consensus of like minded people out for a bit of fun. It's hard to beat those after work binges on Friday or the rush of blood you get when you decide to drop everything and dash off to the seaside for a weekend. The best fun is by its nature unplanned and sometimes it falls into your lap like manna from heaven.

One of the best invites I ever got was when Lorraine and I went to Greece one year and we found ourselves standing outside a tiny Orthodox church on a pimple of an island. As we passed by, a shaft of bright sunshine illuminated the gloomy interior to reveal an attractive young woman scrubbing the stone flagged floor. Garlands of native greenery and bunches of bright Mimosa lay scattered around the oak benches and the little chapel exuded an air of expectancy.

"It looks like someone is getting married," I'd said, more for want of something to say than anything.

"That's right," she'd replied. "Me."

It had turned out she was an Australian on the grand tour, had fallen for a local Adonis and planned to make a decent man of him before the day was out. It had been taken as read that we would hang around for the celebration and everyone in the village, native and visitor, had a ball.

That magical moment seems like a long time ago now. It took place while we were still in college, before marriage, before we got the house, the kids, the pets and the hedge. It seemed the most natural thing at the time to accept an invitation like that, to 'seize the day'. Nowadays I'm not sure if I would be so quick to attend the wedding of a complete stranger. That's another thing that middle age tends to do – it makes you a bit paranoid. Believe me, if you happen to be growing old, balding, on the brink of advanced middle age, get ready to develop the heart of a mouse.

If we met a bride-to-be scrubbing a church floor nowadays, I think I would probably turn to Lorraine and say: "What a nutter! She must have escaped from some lunatic asylum. Let's get out of here quick before she pulls a knife on us. We're too young to die."

SEVEN

The Wrong Stuff

The Americans make a big deal about being born with what they call The Right Stuff, a term used by the US Marine Corps to suggest a sense of daring, adventure and a fearless disregard for your own safety. I think I must have been born with The Wrong Stuff and it seems to get worse the older I get. That time all those years ago when Lorraine and I were in Greece we hopped on dodgy boats and planes without a thought. Nowadays, flying in particular fills me with dread. Even the thought of flying has me reaching for the bottle of brandy I keep hidden under the sink. It must be something to do with reflexes but every time a plane flies over my house I duck, run for cover, cower in the corner and reach for a nice bottle of Crozes Hermitage. I don't gaze up in wonder and envy at those flying off to some sun-soaked holiday resort. I don't for a moment wish I was on board. Instead, I count the seconds as it passes and thank my lucky stars that I was born with The Wrong Stuff.

When you are young – and by that I mean full of joy, with restless energy, horny as hell – there are certain things you take in your stride, like rock climbing, deep sea diving and snowboarding. It's as if you have a cloaking device or a protective shield to ward off all sorts of nasties. No matter what you do, or fail to do, you still manage to escape unscathed. Planes are just a means to an end, a way of getting from A to B and back again, and it never causes you a thought that there might even be the slightest bit of danger involved. But as you get older all it takes is one close call to make you realise that things like rock climbing and flying aren't the same as hopping on a bus.

I blame my own fear of flying on a near death experience during a later trip to Greece when we managed to skip off on our own for a week while Granny looked after the kids. The plane was little bigger than a mini-bus and it didn't take long to realise that we were in the hands of a serial killer piloting his vomit comet from Athens to one of the islands off the Greek coast. Even while we were on the ground, moving towards the runway, the plane slewed to the left before taking off with a hop, skip and a bump. In the air it was worse: one minute droning on, the next dropping a hundred feet in a bungee jump before climbing again and suddenly veering from side to side like a demented roller coaster. The pilot must have been on Ouzo. It would not have been so bad but, just as I was about to conquer my terror (with a little help from a brace of large brandies), I spied across the aisle a frail, elderly lady, her head bowed in what looked like the crash position. She was fingering a set of rosary beads the size of golf balls and was muttering copious incantations in a disturbing monotone. I decided to get up but my legs took exception to the notion – nothing to do with the brandy. I made a vain attempt to open the seat belt but I had it tied so tightly that an escape artist would not have been able to shift it. I tried to shout, holler, rail against the dying of the light or at least make some attempt to announce to all who would care to listen that this was the final curtain. All I could manage was a feeble whimper.

"Jesus, Mary and Joseph, this can't be happening.

Flying is supposed to be fun or, at least, businesslike but this bloody thing is going to go down and we're all going to die. I can feel it in my waters. This wasn't the kind of Mile High Club I had in mind."

What really got to me was the thought that one of the last things I was going to see in my life was the overstuffed backside of an American woman snoring in the aisle opposite.

"This is the end of the line, babe, and we haven't even made a will."

My beloved, a fearless champion of in-flight decorum, turned puce with rage and looked as if she would gladly have thrown me out the window if that were anyway possible.

"Would you ever get a grip? You're making a right show of yourself. You're probably too drunk to see that she's a nun, for God sake and she would be saying her prayers even if she were on a bus to the convent. I don't know why you had to drink all that brandy like it was going out of fashion. And why do you always have to go on the brandy every time we fly anyway? I think you use it as an excuse to get well and truly pissed."

Maybe so, but all I could think of was that we were all nearer my God and, by the sounds of her mantra, the nun had to be reciting the Sorrowful Mysteries. When we finally landed without incident, the captain strode through the aisles, his belly almost bridging the gap between the seats, and bellowed: "I hope you all had a very nice flight."

I wanted to murder him. I wanted to smash his face against the cockpit and make him suffer. I wanted to gouge out his eyes, rain curses on him and his family and watch him beg for mercy. Instead, I staggered meekly off the plane, mumbling a polite: "Thank you."

Fear of flying I went on to discover is a bit like suffering from piles: a painful condition if you are on the receiving end but hilarious if you aren't. Worse still, you will be assured categorically, and without question, that travelling 30,000 feet off the ground in a tin box is the most natural thing in the world.

I plucked up the courage to tell the lads the vomit comet story one evening during our poker session. I was hosting and had won a couple of rounds out of sheer luck. Gerry had set the mood by telling us about his years of adventure. We were enthralled by tales of the time he went climbing high in the Andes and how he had gotten in tow with a bunch of Born Again Buddhists, particularly since such an exciting lifestyle was now at such variance with Gerry the DIY king.

"The most embarrassing moment of my life happened one night when I was with the Buddhists. I was sitting naked, in the lotus position on a mound of snow and chanting my mantra when a familiar face strode right up to me. It was my old geography teacher. 'I'm glad to see not all my lessons were wasted on you,' he said. I nearly died. He was always a sarcastic bugger."

Mick didn't have any embarrassing tales to tell – probably because he is incapable of being embarrassed about anything. Jim was saying nothing for the moment and Martin was too busy lecturing me on the joys of air travel.

"It's still by far the safest way to travel, Dan, you can't deny that. Sure there are accidents but, statistically you are much safer in a plane than in any other form of transport. I fly for a living and, in fact, I feel safer 30,000 feet up than I do driving or even crossing the road. Wait till Adrian becomes a pilot, he'll be doing loop-the-loops, probably with a busty stewardess on his knee. He'll want you to be his first passenger, so you'd better get your act together."

That didn't exactly fill me with confidence. It's all very well for him to start spouting statistics at me about flying being the safest way to travel. If The Man Above had intended us to fly, he would have given us alcohol patches.

"In any case, Dan, you were lucky you weren't arrested on that plane," said Martin, as he dealt me what looked like a very poor hand indeed. "The airlines have become very strict about that sort of thing, you know. How long have you been afraid of flying? That can be cured nowadays. We have a programme at the airline and they say it has a 99% success rate. You should give it a try. At least it might help you to stop making a fool of yourself in the air. Did you know that fear of flying even affects some pilots? They say it can come on in middle age. You could just be having a mid-life crisis."

That was the thing. I used to be able to fly anywhere without a thought. Now I would take a slow boat to China to avoid it. Of course, I used also have no problem driving at 90 miles an hour on a country road at night with the lights off, just for the hell of it. I suppose fear of flying isn't the only thing that gets worse as you get older.

"That's a load of bull," said Mick with uncharacteristic vehemence. He had thrown in his hand very early and it was down to the wire between Martin, Gerry and myself. Mick's quitting the round had taken me by surprise. I had figured he had to have a winning hand because he was animated and full of chat. I clearly had a lot to learn

112

about poker. He leaned back in his chair and gave us all a steely look.

"You don't have to be middle-aged to be afraid of something or to have an embarrassing moment. Screaming your head off at 30,000 feet isn't the only way to make a complete idiot of yourself either. It can be done at ground level. Remember Bill Clinton. Who would have thought that an American president could make such a complete toss of himself?"

Mick was right. Before he managed to rehabilitate himself, Clinton mortified not only himself and his family but also the nation he governed. For a while, he was the comical President, saved only by the very quality that got him into trouble in the first place, his irresistible charm. Embarrassment is not an impeachable offence. If that were the case, Ronald Reagan would have been hanged, drawn and quartered on the steps of Capitol Hill years ago. Even Nixon, the tricky master of Machiavellian double-speak, was not without his awkward moments. When he went to China for the first time in 1973, he was heard to exclaim: "What a great wall."

Most of us can recall in vivid detail our embarrassing moments or times when we made complete and utter fools of ourselves. But the great thing about being an ordinary mortal rather than President, or any other kind of inmate of an institution where everything is done for you, is that the everyday tasks of life soon intervene. If you didn't have to get up early to make sure the kids were ready for school and all the sandwiches were made, you might find the time to dwell on the fool you made of yourself at the office party. That would be enough to plunge any man – pauper or President – into em-barrassment rehab.

In terms of embarrassing moments it is possible to have a midlife crisis even if you are far from being middle-aged. Sometimes your wife can have one for you. That's what happened to David Beckham when the world found out that he enjoyed wearing his wife's underwear. It's one thing to gossip about who wears the trousers at home, it's quite another for the whole world to be told who likes to wear the knickers. Beckham must have felt more than the cheeks of his face go red when he heard his wife, the truly scary Posh Spice, announce on TV that her husband had taken a shine to slipping on her thongs, those minimalist items of underwear no bigger than his bootlaces.

He wasn't the first to be made a fool of in public, and he won't be the last. In fact, most people need nobody else's help in doing so. Tony Blair's wife, Cherie, once found herself on the wrong side of the law as she headed for her first day as a judge and suffered the embarrassment of being fined for not having a ticket for her train journey. At least she only made herself look foolish and not stupid. Ronald Reagan's sidekick, Dan Quayle, once did both when he apologised to an audience in Latin America for not being able to speak Latin. "I'm real sorry but I don't speak any Latin," he said by way of a mea culpa.

Even movie stars, who should know better, have moments when they wish the spotlight wasn't on them. That great old ham actor, WC Fields, once attended an international soccer match in the company of a fellow thespian, an Irishman whose friendship with him was sealed forever through the bottom of a whiskey bottle. He had been allocated prime position to view the proceedings and, much to his delight, the crowd expelled a huge and joyful roar as he was escorted to his seat. Naturally, being famous for being notorious, WC immediately assumed the cheering was for him and imparted a Hollywood wave to the packed gallery. Imagine his consternation when a voice bellowed from behind: "Sit down, you stupid old tosser, we can't see the match." However, like the old trouper he was, he took it all with a nonchalant shrug.

Most people know what it's like to suffer the fallout from a moment of singular stupidity and would like to forget them but there is always someone around to remind you. Mick winked at me and then looked across the table at Jim.

"Don't you remember, Jim, that conference you went to in Chicago? You surpassed yourself at that."

We all looked at Jim.

"OK, OK, so I was feeling out of my depth because the conference was attended by the great and the good of the legal world. Instead of lying low and keeping my mouth shut, I drank far too much and my colleagues still laugh at the memory of me grabbing the microphone and singing every verse of *Patricia The Stripper* before being escorted out the back door."

Even children are not immune to embarrassment, if Martin's experience was anything to go by. "That's nothing. When I was about seven, I became the victim of a neighbour's delinquent daughter who was a right little bitch. She used me for target practice with bottles of nail varnish she had got as a birthday present. She couldn't decide which colour to wear so she painted each of my fingernails a different shade and left me for two hours sitting on a hedge with my arms outstretched, waiting for the paint to dry. The embarrassment factor was huge, particularly in church as I was an altar boy and I got a severe roasting from the parish priest for keeping my

115

fists clenched. He thought I was being blasphemous.""

"I can beat that one," said Gerry, clearly feeling that his Buddhist story was being outdone in the embarrassing moments contest. "My Uncle Joe has four teenage daughters. Just before Christmas he came home from a night on the tiles and was snoring so loudly in the armchair that the girls couldn't sleep. They decided to get their own back by painting his toes and fingernails a vivid purple and giving him a new backcombed hairstyle. The trouble was that an hour later he was carted off to hospital with chest pains. Luckily, it was nothing serious but he nearly had a real heart attack when he woke up in the ward, surrounded by giggling nurses and looking like a transvestite on a bad hair day. Their bedside manner consisted of wolf whistles and requests for a song. He was out of there faster than you could say: 'Pass the thongs, darling.'"

After my mildly embarrassing tale of flying phobia, I had decided to keep my mouth shut, quite an unusual occurrence for me. The problem was Gerry decided to talk for me. Just in case anyone might have not heard it before, he proceeded to remind us all of my seminal moment of monumental embarrassment.

"Who can forget the time you went to the chemist and asked for a large packet of Viagra for a headache?"

A painful memory if ever there was one.

Had I mooned in the shop window, done cartwheels on the counter or declared myself to be a visitor from a far off galaxy, I could hardly have created such a jaw-dropping response. Heads has turned as one, and mouths flew open wide enough to catch seagulls. The two teenage girls in the corner had halted their nail varnishing in mid-swipe and even the muscle-bound health freak stopped admiring himself in the mirror.

"The only place you'll get any of that stuff is by getting a job in Pfizer's," said the smart-ass at the cosmetics counter.

My glazed look must have convinced her that she was dealing with a complete dodo.

"You know, Viagra, the Pfizer riser."

Recognition had finally dawned. "Viagra, Oh, sorry, I meant whatchamaycallit, that thing for migraine, it starts with a Vitriol ... Voltoral or something like that."

It was clear that she had regarded the explanation as about as credible as the *X-Files* and I was not going to be allowed make a dignified exit.

"I hear Viagra is a great cure for migraine," she'd bellowed, by way of her version of "have a nice day".

Mick gave a loud guffaw. "That's brilliant Dan – a clear case of suffering from Foot and Mouth. Mind you it should really be called Foot-In-Mouth Disease because every time you open your mouth, you put your foot in it! But fair is fair Gerry, it's your turn now and don't think you'll get away with it just because of that geography teacher thing or the bit about your uncle."

Gerry turned red. "Fine. The very worst moment of my life so far happened less than six weeks ago. I was in the hairdressers and this new girl was there. She was a real stunner. She asked me what I wanted done and I said: 'A cut, wash and blowjob.' I was monumentally embarrassed but the funny thing was that she wasn't. She just gave a little laugh and said: 'that'll be extra.'"

That gave the rest of us more than a little laugh and I reckon that it doesn't get much more Foot-in-Mouth than that. The putting your foot in it affliction, though, can affect anyone and political animals are often the worst.

Ronald Reagan once had the misfortune to have his solution to the superpower struggle recorded on tape. His exhortation, "Let's nuke Moscow", not only scared the hell out of the Russians it even had his own side gasping and wondering if their President was playing with anything approaching a full deck. Even Hillary Clinton lost her usual gift of the gab when she was tackled about her brother, Hugh Rodham, after it was revealed he got $400,000 from a drug trafficker for his efforts to secure a pardon from the outgoing President. All she could manage was: "He's my brother. I love my brother." George W. Bushisms are of course legion. Jim emailed me this priceless collection only the other day:

"They misunderestimated me."

"I know the human being and fish can coexist peacefully."

"Families is where our nation finds hope, where wings take dream."

"It's clearly a budget. It's got a lot of numbers in it."

Faux pas, Freudian slips, call them what you will, when your mouth is crossing the finishing line and your grey cells are still at the starting blocks it can lead to all sorts of trouble. Sideline banter produces some of the best, particularly when the heat is on: "Jesus, would you rise it McMahon – if 'twas a skirt you'd lift it!" Not to mention those all time classics from soccer commentators. One radio commentator in a quandary once asked the nation, "Is the ref going to finally blow his whistle?" and then quickly answered: "No, he's going to blow his nose!" Another classic is one of Mick's all time favourites: "Teddy McCarthy to John McCarthy, no relation. John McCarthy back to Teddy McCarthy, still no relation." My hero, though, has got to be Henry Ford who was top of the

Super League of Foot-In-Mouthers. On seeing a sundial for the first time, the man who regarded history as 'bunk,' declared: "What will they think of next?"

Embarrassing moments can happen to anyone. Who can forget that broadcasting moment on *School Around the Corner* when the host had the misfortune to ask a country school kid to tell him about 'a funny incident'. The incident in question concerned the boy's father having to put down a horse that had fallen into a pit on his farm. The funny incident wasn't so funny until the presenter asked: "And did your daddy shoot him in the hole?"

"No sir," replied the boy. "He shot him in the head."

Other sources of embarrassment include confessing some fixation to your friends. My Trojan efforts to extract their red-faced moments had borne some fruit and I thought I might finish off by telling them my big secret. The session was breaking up anyway and everyone was almost ready to leave.

"I have a confession to make," I said.

All eyes were fixed on me but I paused for dramatic effect.

Eventually Jim couldn't take it any more. "All right. Is it scandalous, subversive or shocking? Will it set loose tongues wagging or net curtains twitching? Will it get you a ringside seat on Oprah?"

I was almost sorry to disappoint them.

"It's not that I harbour any dark and deadly secrets or anything, lads. I haven't taken to wearing fishnet tights or anything like that. It's just that lately I've taken a shine to Daniel O'Donnell."

The others were visibly shocked but Martin was impressed. "You mean you fancy him?"

Now it was my turn to be shocked. "Of course not but

119

it's just that he has cured my insomnia. I've bought loads of his CDs. Although the computer doesn't seem to happy about playing them."

It's at times when sleep becomes a stranger, when you're tossing and turning in the bed, worrying about all the things you have to do the next day, when you've just spent three hours listening to the news from inner Mongolia on the BBC World Service that you come to appreciate the anaesthetic properties of that crooning, lilting, swooning voice. Half the nation's grannies can't be wrong.

There's nothing like a turn of Daniel singing *The Magic Is Here* to put all your cares to bed. It's like being rocked to sleep in a hammock. The trouble was that all the while he was having a similar effect on my computer, even sending it into a coma. It was a new model, too, with more ROMS and RAMS than you could shake a mouse at. It still refused to play any other CD properly. I couldn't figure out what was wrong, mostly because the language used in the world of computers is a foreign country to me, and I imagine, to most people whose mother tongue is English. I defy anyone to sit through an hour of computer-speak without reaching for the sick bucket. Switch on your computer and you will be thrilled to read that 'Your mouse has been initialized'. Marvel at the notion that it includes a 'Fixed desk Quantum Fireball'. Take comfort from the fact that there is 'No active format for break'. But, beware, you could be told that 'Shell can't run a Batlite', there is 'Not enough width left for inst' or, horror of horrors, 'Unit life ends'. No wonder it was driven demented by wee Daniel.

Jim got up and yawned and stretched. "You know, that guy Bill Gates. I bet he was a fan of Captain James

T Kirk and his crew aboard the *Starship Enterprise*. So many home computers are riddled with the kind of language first generation Trekkies love. Wouldn't it be lovely if Bill had his very own Chief Engineer Scottie? I can just picture Scottie gasping for breath, his face scarlet with exertion. After being told 'Windows has detected a fatal error' Scottie would appear: "But Captain Bill, the lithium crystals will never take the pressure. We're doing our best in engineering, but ye cannae expect miracles."

Jim's impression of Scottie had us all laughing but there was a serious side to his comic analogy, the realisation that technology can be beyond your grasp and displaying your ignorance in that regard can be most embarrassing of all. I've tried everything to get myself acquainted with the mysteries of PC land – pressing a button here, tapping a key there, talking nicely to it, barking at it, all to no avail. I'd thought when I bought the new laptop it would be a doddle but even Adrian, the computer expert, was thoroughly stumped by my techno-phobia. After many attempts to just teach me the basics he'd declared: "Let's face it dad, you really don't know what you're doing." I think his exasperation reached breaking point when I failed to get his *Kombat Zone* game up and running. But it was only when I'd confessed that I did not have a clue what he meant by 'rebooting' that he'd finally walked out in disgust. I suppose he was ashamed to think his dad was such a technological Neanderthal. How was I to know that 'rebooting' had nothing to do with tying shoelaces?

If there was a patron saint of computers I might even take to saying a little prayer. I suppose the nearest is George Boole, the father of modern mathematics. It is said, though, that Sir Arthur Conan Doyle based the character of Sherlock Holmes' arch rival, Professor

Moriarty, on the Irish mathematician, in which case he is hardly saintly enough to invoke even if you are being told 'Host cannot connect to proxy server.' I could try Saint Jude, the patron saint of hopeless causes, but she'd probably be off-line and I don't have time to wait for the Vatican to announce the result of its search for a patron saint of the web. Perhaps the problem is that my new computer is overworked, suffering from a case of terminal illness at the hands of amateurs and is in need of a good night's rest. I think the best thing to do is unplug the whole thing, but, before that, I'm going to put *The Very Best of Daniel O'Donnell* into the CD-ROM thingie. If Danny's rendition of *The Twelfth of Never* doesn't do the trick I might even try obeying my favourite command: 'Put disk in drive and close door or shut all windows.'

Martin got up and gave a little shiver. "OK, guys, I can't take any more of this. I'm out of here. The thought of being put to sleep by Daniel O'Donnell is enough to give me nightmares."

The rest followed suit. Mick and Gerry said nothing but Jim was trying to suppress a raucous laugh. "Thanks, Dan. The lads in the office will get a great kick out of that one."

Doh! Was there no end to my embarrassment? Now every lawyer in town would know my fetish. Well, at least I had made Jim laugh. After everything he had been through with the divorce, he needed it.

EIGHT

Celebrity Squares

"Do any of you guys know someone by the name of *Harry Potter?*"

For a minute, we all thought Mick was trying it on as a way of putting the rest of us off our game. It wasn't beyond him to pull a stunt like that, particularly if he had a losing hand and no prospect of a win in sight. It didn't matter to me as I had already thrown in my hand and was out of the game anyway, but Gerry and Martin were neck-and-neck and Jim was just about hanging in there. Mick had tried to bluff, betting big to let on that he had a really good hand. But, for once, his ruse didn't pay off. Martin caught him out.

"You're bluffing, you big fat bollix. I can tell. You don't realise that every time you play a bluff like that you put your hand inside your shirt collar and start rubbing your shoulders. It's a dead giveaway and I feel so stupid that it's only now that I've copped it."

Mick ignored him and repeated the question: "All I'm asking is who the hell is *Harry Potter?*"

We were still sceptical about his apparent innocence but, on the other hand, Mick did sometimes seem to live in a parallel universe, untrammelled by thoughts of popular culture or what excites kids, despite the fact that he has five children himself. Even though most people in the latter stages of middle age have heard of the world's most famous wizard, that didn't seem to bother Mick.

"I think this is your territory, Dan," said Jim. "All your kids still seem to be *Harry Potter* mad. Perhaps you should enlighten him."

I didn't really see the point in enlightening Mick but I felt obliged to say something.

"He's like yourself Mick, a bit of a character."

Martin snorted. "For Christ sake, Dan, just for once, be serious." He then went on to give Mick a quick rundown on the *Harry Potter* explosion.

"He's been around for a good while now, Mick. He's a character in a series of books for children and the author of the books, a woman called J K Rowling, has made hundreds of millions out of it. She is the biggest publishing phenomenon of the past twenty years. Every kid from Boston to Bangkok is reading some Harry Potter book or other."

I still couldn't believe that Mick had never heard of it, considering he had five kids. Perhaps Laura didn't approve. I felt obliged to go to bat for my own children's favourite read.

"When Luke got his hands on the first book, he couldn't put it down and would pine until the next one came along. I was delighted because it meant he hadn't his head stuck in the television. It was the same with Adrian and Fiona. They started devouring the books Luke had already read and now they are all good readers. Some schoolteachers don't like it because they feel kids should be reading Dickens or Hemingway or some other heavyweight but I think they are being unrealistic. They forget that when they were young they used to sneak under the covers with a torch to scour through Enid Blyton or The Hardy Boys."

Mick could relate to that. "I remember I used to often

fall asleep reading comics. I must ask Laura. Maybe she has heard of *Harry Potter* and we should get some of those books for the kids. It's certainly better than kids not reading at all, spending their free time spellbound by TV or playing with those hideous toys dreamed up by international conglomerates. Neither of us want to raise kids like that."

Martin was mesmerised by the fortune to be made from writing children's books. "It's incredible. What a way to make a living. It certainly beats flying. J K Rowling was once broke you know. Now she earns millions a year and she could live royally on the interest alone from all the money she makes."

That's the beauty of being in the money. Even while you're sleeping you can make it work for you, instead of the other way around. The only trouble is you have to get your hands on some of it in the first place and, unless you happen to be to the manor born or have a kindly maiden aunt who has died and left you considerably more than you deserve, you will have to do a bit of hard graft yourself.

Don't be fooled into thinking that all it takes is hard work and dedication. Those two virtues may be very worthwhile but they will only get you so far. There are millions of people the world over who drag themselves out of bed at the crack of dawn, work hard in the factory, shop or office and have little to show for it but a clapped-out second hand car and a mortgage they cannot afford. Even after forty years work with a company, many cannot afford to retire.

Minding your money is not always the answer to a future of lazy living either. Jim's former brother-in-law, is a case in point. Jim never tires of telling us about his misfortune, particularly when he is in a foul mood or having a bad run at poker. I looked over at Jim and could see the signs. He was not a happy camper. He hadn't raised a bet for at least an hour. All he seemed to be doing was seeing whatever was bet and calling, not prepared to take a risk but not folding either.

"I feel like Darina's older brother, Nigel. I've done everything right, played my cards right and I'm still losing money. It was the same with him. He was always very careful. In fact, he literally saved up his Confirmation money and spent all his time slavishly building up a tidy nest egg. He's very clever and has worked in the computer industry where the pickings are good. He worked all the hours God gave him and then some. He was far too mean to go anywhere or take a holiday. His clothes were mostly hand-me-downs or something he might pick up in a charity shop or jumble sale for a pittance. Nigel decided early on that he couldn't afford to have girlfriends and he had few male friends either because he was in the habit of sponging off everyone he knew. He never drank and the only obvious vice he had was cigarettes. He smoked like a trooper but the cigarettes were never his own. He was utterly shameless.

Week after week and year after year Nigel scrimped and saved, waiting for just the right investment opportunity to come along. It eventually did, in the shape of a fast talker who majored in bullshit and soon persuaded him that this was the chance of a lifetime. Within a month the guy had cleaned him out and skipped the country. Nigel was taken to the cleaners by a clever con artist who played on his voracious greed and mean spirit. He didn't attract much sympathy from me, I can tell you but I do know what it's like to lose money," Jim concluded, finally

126

throwing in his hand.

I nodded, knowingly. "I suppose he learned the hard way that money isn't everything. I would hate to think that my kids might be short of money, though. Luke wants to be a doctor or a lawyer, like his mum. He's no fool. Adrian wants to fly, like Martin, so that will have him well fixed up too. It's early days yet, though, and, for all I know, they could both decide to other things that might not be half so lucrative. Fiona is too young yet to really know what she wants but she's as bright as a button and I think she'll do well after saving the world first of course."

It was getting late and we had been playing for hours but the pot wasn't up to much. Gerry finally took the lot, but it didn't amount to anything. We decided to call it a night.

Gerry hauled in his takings and yawned. "Time to head for the hills. I won't get very far with his lot, though. It won't even pay for the crisps and the beer at the next session. Remember, you're in my place next week."

There are, of course, other ways of making money. Despite what parents tell their children, a university education and a shirt and tie job are no guarantee of future comfort. Forget all your mother ever told you about doing your homework, studying hard, going to college, getting a degree and finding a steady job where she can buy you a leather briefcase for your first day at work. The real high rollers these days wear overalls and carry saws and hammers and screwdrivers and wouldn't be seen dead with a briefcase, except maybe to carry their day's takings in. If you happen to find yourself a skilled bricklayer, promise him your daughter's hand in marriage at once and she'll be set up for life. Beware, on pain of eternal penury, the hiring of a plumber unless you happen to be in the building trade, in which case you can well afford it, anyway. I will have to take out another mortgage to pay to get the toilet fixed if it gets blocked again. I'd be better off having a bargain triple bypass instead. I'd say I'd need one if I have to see an electrician's bill any time soon. Electricians are making more than architects. Get one to change a light switch and he's bound to feign shock and horror and tell you that your house is a danger to civilisation as we know it and has to be rewired at once, at great expense.

It's the same with carpenters. The dapper young man who arrived to do a bit of measuring for my new front door nearly had me reaching for my DIY magazines when he gave us his estimate of what it would cost.

"I think I could do that myself," I suggested when I showed his estimate to Lorraine.

She was having none of it.

"As I'm always saying you have a very short memory. Do I have to remind you of the garage door debacle? Not to mention your attempts to sandpaper the hall floor, which left huge gouges in the wood. Or how about the attic window that we can neither open nor close?"

Point taken but I have to admit I was a little jealous of Supercarpenter when he arrived on Saturday morning. He was driving an *S type Jaguar* and it looked like it had all the trimmings. He then threw an expensive looking raincoat over the banister and carefully placed a laptop on the floor.

"What's the laptop for?" I asked. "Is it part of some hi-tech way of making doors?"

Not at a bit of it.

"No, it helps me keep in touch with the broker."

"You mean your insurance broker?"

He smiled indulgently, as if he was dealing with an imbecile, which, in a way, he was. "No, my stockbroker."

No bloody wonder it was his stockbroker. I had to pay twice the going rate to get him to come on a Saturday.

There was no answer but to grin and bear it but Lorraine couldn't stand me moping about. "Go for a walk or do something. It'll be all over and done with when you come back."

I decided to take a stroll through the backwoods to contemplate the bounty of nature, the beauty of spring and the wonders of the universe in general. It's the kind of day you'd give your eye-teeth for – if you had any left. Bright and crisp, with a gentle breeze whispering through the trees just cool enough to hint of the winter just past and to pat the cheeks into a frenzy of rosy ripeness. Then who did I happen to meet but Samson and Delilah. I hadn't seen them for ages. They both appeared to be in great form, skipping along the pathway without a care in the world, the two of them the picture of rude health and sound constitution.

I was – as we used say in school – 'on the lang', except in those days we at least had the energy to spend our misspent hours smoking on street corners. On this occasion, I was busy doing what I should not have been doing which was precisely nothing, and I was taking my time about it, too. I know I should have been home making myself useful. The garage – if that's not too strong a word for it – was a temple to sorry neglect and, as always, demanded immediate and rigorous attention. I just couldn't be bothered. The garden (and that is certainly too strong a word for it) I left as Nature intended – around the time of the Neolithic Period.

129

Gerry, the former rake, would not be amused. He had become something of a greenfingers since he hooked up with Fionnuala and, according to him, I should spend every Saturday on my knees, not in supplication but busily dead-heading the roses, squishing the slugs, making the hedge ship-shape and – horror of horrors – scarifying the lawn. I used to think that meant shouting 'boo' to make the grass stop growing but I am assured it involves buying some mechanical contraption even harder to start than a lawnmower that will actually help grass grow even faster. What a dreadful notion. I did have a pang of conscience though, as I sneaked out quietly, passing the variegated ivy that, even I can see, is beyond redemption. The drooping willow seems to have toppled over like a drunk under its own weight and it is plain to see that the climbing roses – my great white hope – are beginning to turn back, having failed to reach base camp. The grass, at least, is green again thanks to all the rain, but the Dahlias are definitely pouting.

Naturally, I gave none of them the slightest thought on my trek through the woods, happy in the knowledge that I was somehow cheating the weather out of a leftover summer's day. As I rounded a mighty oak, Samson spotted me and immediately bounded over, licked my hand, jumped up and down, dribbled on my new walking boots and let out a tremendous fart by way of 'howya doin'. I should mention that both Samson and his twin sister, Delilah, are members of the canine fraternity. They are magnificent Dalmatians, graceful and gregarious, loud and uproarious with a keen sense of theatrics – a bit like their owner, really, one of Martin's old flames.

He is what passes for a Media Personality and has never been one of life's wallflowers. The forest shook with his greeting.

"Dahling. How are you? You look wonderful. Have you been working out?"

As I spied the apparition before me, conscious of the attentions of fellow walkers nearby, the thought crossed my mind that this was the revenge of the Dahlias. The corpulent frame of Mr Personality, stood sandwiched between his pair of hounds, shrouded in a black-and-white three-piece outfit as loud as his voice. The jacket was like an optical illusion, in the shape of a chessboard and designed to empathise with the natural polka-dot coats of the Dalmatians. He looked like a hot air balloon that had crash-landed.

To make matters worse, Mr Personality began to relate, in a voice as loud as a disco, how he had recently discovered the joys of naturism and how we should all be converted to nudity as a way of life and the path to eternal salvation. The crowd around thickened and, sensing an audience, the showman in him could not resist describing the wonders of nude bathing, nude jogging, nude wrestling, nude bowling, nude cycling (ouch) and even nude shopping. Apparently, he had been on holiday in some town in the south of France where birthday suits were in vogue and you could wheel your trolley through the local supermarket in the all-together. I suppose you'd have to be careful where you put the melons. Mr Personality ended his command performance with a flourish and a bow and exhortation to the masses: "Nudes of the world, unite." Then, by way of 'cheerio' he grabbed me by the arm and, with Samson and Delilah at our flanks, rushed me over to the oak tree which he encircled with his arms. He was waving frantically at me to join in, roaring: "Group hug, group hug."

131

I made up my mind there and then, hugging that tree, to give the clippers a sharpen and put the Dahlias out of my misery. They wouldn't even see me coming. I usually prefer the thrill of chance to the boredom of certainty but, with the onset of middle years, I have been devoting my energies of late to the cultivation of what I hope will be a monument to posterity. The rest of the garden, I'm sure, is happier left to its own devices but I have to have my little piece of history. It's big, it's grand, it's green, it's organic and, better still, it's growing at the bottom of the garden. I decided to christen it the Millennium Hedge because I reckon that in one hundred years time no-one will even suspect that it was actually planted in 2003. I'm not one to boast and I know that, on occasions, gardeners can be ruthless, cunning, self pitying and conceited, but the hedge will be hard to beat. I will devote my ever-waking moment to it – especially as the woods are clearly out of bounds from now on.

My hedge-growing efforts were mostly due to a former neighbour from hell, a postmistress whom I shall call Bridie. This is not her real name and I will never divulge it for fear she might come after me with an ash branch. Some gardeners spend their time creating a haven of beauty designed more to be envied than admired. Bridie was a bit like that. Despite the fact that she showed every outward sign of being a stranger to soap and water, saw nothing wrong in slobbering over a parcel in her post office, licking the stamp with her evil tongue before handing it back to a customer, when it came to her garden, she was an unmerciful style snob. I'd had the misfortune the year before to ask her expert opinion of my efforts to turn what was a building site into a little oasis of nature. She'd looked surprised at my new-found enthusiasm for work in the garden.

"I always thought you were more of an armchair gardener. I don't ever remember you doing anything much more than cut the grass and, even at that, it was none too often. I suppose it must be the onset of middle age."

She had then given my efforts a cursory glance and quickly dismissed my herbaceous border with one wave of a grubby hand.

"It's all wrong. Too much colour. It looks like a circus."

My climbing roses, those darling buds that I'd sweated buckets over, she rejected as: "Silly little hybrids." She'd thought my mounds of heather looked like cow dung and declared my pansies to be horrible, unfit to share the same general acreage as her masterful peonies. She'd saved her most spiteful comments for the young hedge, describing my pride and joy as: "Cheap but none too cheerful."

She hadn't taken too kindly either to the new fountain which I had installed when she hadn't been looking.

"You cannot be serious. What do you think you are trying to recreate, The Hanging Gardens of Babylon? That fountain is the most vulgar thing I have ever seen. It belongs in a drug dealer's mansion. Get rid of it at once and take those sickly looking pansies with it."

I was sure she had not been referring to the two strapping lads I had hired to help me who were at that very moment in the middle of installing a pair of coloured lights at the base of the fountain. They were the height of rugged manliness and looked as if they had never had a day sick in their lives.

Funny thing is, Bridie reminded me of Elizabeth Taylor. Not her face, of course, which would be best appreciated during a solar eclipse, but Liz Taylor, star that she is, also understands style snobbery. Her relationship with Richard Burton was punctuated by her screaming tantrums, his drinking bouts and gifts of diamonds the size of a moon rock. She was wearing one of them – the Krupp diamond, not the biggest Burton ever gave her but at thirty-three carats, almost as big as her ego – when she attended a charity bash in London and bumped into Princess Margaret. Her Royal Highness took one look at it and told Liz that it was the most vulgar thing she had ever seen.

"Like to try it on?" asked Liz.

The Princess slipped it on and flexed her finger.

"Doesn't look so vulgar now, does it?" said Liz sweetly.

I was glad I'd remembered that great put-down the day I'd showed Bridie the little heart-shaped pond I had just had put in at the edge of the patio. She'd dismissed it in her usual regal fashion.

"How kitsch and vulgar," she'd exclaimed, looking as if she might faint at the very sight of it.

I'd gone straight for the jugular. "The odd thing is, Bridie, it doesn't look half as vulgar as the exact same one on your side of the fence."

Once Bridie had moved away I'd gone back to my usual bad habits but my hedge lived on.

As I dodged my way back home through the woods, keeping one ear open for anymore "Dahlings" I was thinking that like Liz Taylor, there are some people – among them kings, queens, living saints and Mr Personality – who are born to greatness. Others have it thrust upon them; still more arrive at that blissful state by happy accident, murderous manipulation or a bit of the other. Most people, though, never even get to dream dreams of inventing that new computer, whizzing off to the moon, having their names up in lights on Broadway or gliding along the red carpet in an overpriced dress or tuxedo for the Academy Awards ceremony. That's a bit of a shame because within each of us there's probably a bit of an Einstein or Edison trying to get out. At least that's what Hollywood, with its cutesy clichés, likes to tell us. And the people who do the telling are those who decant themselves into extravagant ball gowns and dress suits for Hollywood's annual salute to itself. The Oscars are always a bit over the top – even by American standards.

Great Oscar moments are guaranteed. There is always bound to be some starlet sobbing with delight and spluttering on top of her little statuette. Then there are always the no-shows. When Woody Allen was considered a name to be reckoned with, he never bothered attending, preferring to play the clarinet in *Michael's Bar* in New York. Nowadays, nobody misses him and a whole generation has barely heard of him. The Oscars wouldn't be complete, either, without somebody making an impassioned plea on behalf of the Navajo Indians or decrying the destruction of the Amazon rainforest. There's nothing to match the pleasure, though, of some of he more obscure directors of foreign language productions or watching some drunken unknown director from east of the Urals thank his mother in three languages.

In between, there is always the parade of the Bold and the Beautiful; the kind of folk who take themselves seriously and consider that acting is a natural condition, a real job for grown-ups. We may not all have the wherewithal to be Einstein or Edison but which of us hasn't at one time or another, fantasised about making like Sean Connery or Meryl Streep even if only in the safe haven of our bathtubs? We all indulge in a little play-acting every day of our lives. Remember that insurance salesman who persuaded you that you were worth more dead than alive; or the butcher who swore that his stringy bit of steak was the finest ever to be extracted from the backside of a heifer; or the car you sold, insisting that it purred like a kitten and you were only getting rid of it because your Significant Other never liked the colour; Oscar winners all.

I once worked as a waiter in a hotel by the sea where the receptionist was a friend to all (at least, all the men) and it usually took an acting ability in the manner of Laurence Olivier for us all to remain on the right side of decorum. The place was inhabited by a strange bunch of misfits. The head waiter was a head banger with an endearing habit of cycling around the dining room on quiet nights, ringing a bell and shouting: "Who asked for their steak well done?" The chef, I am convinced to this day, was a serial killer in a previous life – the things he did to lobster don't bear thinking about.

That early role-playing experience came in handy later on when I got a real acting job – although it was only as an extra. I'd managed to get myself a small part in a film being made about the first great train robbery. It had been filmed at the local railway station and I'd got to play the part of a country gent but, for me, it was a silent movie, as I'd had no speaking role. The costume was great, though – Victorian waistcoat and breeches. I'd even had a top hat and a silver walking cane and all I had to do was get off the train and walk along the platform. The main actor was Sean Connery and he'd been a real charmer in between shooting scenes. In the end, though, the whole experience was mind-numbingly boring and only the thought of a hot meal every hour or so had kept any of the extras sane.

I was reminded of my moment of fame the following Wednesday night as Mick, Martin and I drove over to Gerry's house for the poker game. We had started a car pooling arrangement and it was my turn to do the driving. Jim was working late so he was making his own way over. Mick asked Martin what the most popular movies were on his flights.

"No contest there, Mick, James Bond wins every time. It's always the same. The airlines love the Bond movies because it keeps the passengers mollified for at least two hours. It also means they don't have to worry too much about whether the film is suitable for kids or not. There's never any serious nookie in a Bond movie and there's always plenty of action, so most passengers are happy enough. The cabin crew love them, too, because passengers don't bother them half as much when 007 is doing his thing."

That led onto a debate about the best 007 ever. Martin thought Pierce Brosnan was the best. Mick didn't agree.

"Sean Connery was better than all the rest put together. Compared to him, the rest were wimps. He always looked like he might strangle you and enjoy it."

"When I was a rookie newspaper reporter I was sent to get an interview with Connery. Like all the other reporters looking to talk to him, I wasn't allowed near the set, so I hit on a brainwave. I signed on as an extra and managed to get the interview with Connery." As I told the lads, he turned out to be great fun after I introduced him to the delights of Murphy's Irish stout in the pub across from the railway station.

"Fair dues to you," said Martin. "That was pretty smart for an apprentice hack. I must admit to feeling just a teensy bit envious. Have you ever tried to get another part? You could sign on for another movie some day and maybe even get a speaking part this time. That's one way of making money without breaking a sweat. Even the bit-part actors make big bucks. It's enough to make your eyes water."

I didn't know if he was serious or not but I decided to play along.

"I think Wilde had it about right when he said that most people are modest because they have every reason to be but I don't intend to practise what he preached. There's nothing for it but to inform all those international talent spotters that, should a blockbuster be going a begging, a certain artiste of proven acting ability could be persuaded to put aside his ploughshare and make himself available in Tinseltown. I would, of course, observe the proper protocol of resisting all exhortations to wear the mantle until overwhelmed by duty. I might even be prepared to promise never to be too busy to collect my Oscar and I would never, ever get drunk and start singing *Patricia The Stripper*, like Jim did when he went to that law conference – unless, of course, I was as pissed as he was that night.

Martin was mildly amused but Mick was having none of it.

"Dream on, boy. You have about as much chance of that happening as you do of Lorraine letting you indulge in your DIY fantasies. She remembers past disasters only too well."

The whole idea of making a quick buck seemed to really animate Martin. He was still rattling on about it even as I parked the car outside Gerry's house. According to him, the easiest way of making money legally, apart from writing a *Harry Potter* style children's book or acting, is to become a professional gambler.

"Look at all those professional poker players in the States. They have big tournaments with huge money involved. Did you know that they even have riverboat poker games where players are wined and dined? Lots of them just go from one game to another and they make a fortune. I'd love to have a go at it."

Mick gave a loud guffaw. "You'd lose your shirt. Supposing some guy hit you with a straight that you had no answer to, what would you do then?"

Making an exaggerated display of ringing Gerry's doorbell, Martin went all camp just to annoy Mick, knowing that it would drive him crazy.

"You've got it all wrong, honey. Don't you know that a queen beats a straight any day?"

NINE

DIY Disasters

Making money is one thing; hanging onto it is another. One way, of course, is to behave like Darina's brother, Nigel, and put a little by regularly for a rainy day. But it didn't do him any good in the end when he was conned out of everything. According to Jim, the only thing he managed to hang onto was his virginity. In any case, there are far too many rainy days for saving. I always find the notion of hoarding mind-numbingly boring but I do still love the thought of saving money by making and fixing things myself. I look back on my DIY years with mixed emotions but Lorraine, eyeing some of the evidence still around us, looks back on them with unrelieved horror. She calls them my Restoration Tragedy years.

It must be something built into the male psyche that makes the very thought of getting out the electric drill a matter of wild excitement. From the day he gets his first carpentry set, the male of the species is conditioned to think he can change the world with the aid of a hammer and a few nails. After all, women have been doing just that for generations with little more than a vacuum cleaner and a dishcloth. I was no exception and neither was Gerry who showed evidence of having made the full transformation from adventurer and daredevil to DIY Man.

It had been a while since we had played poker in Gerry's house and when we arrived on Wednesday night it was obvious that he had been doing the handyman bit around the house.

Fionnuala answered the door and her first words as we went into the living room were: "Mind the Waterford chandelier. It's a bit low. I have to get Gerry to fix it."

Mick obviously hadn't been listening because the very next second all of his six foot two inch frame smacked right into the enormous light fitting and, for a moment, the sparking edifice looked like it might come crashing to the ground.

"Jesus wept! What's that? Sorry Fionnuala, I'm afraid I didn't see it till 'twas too late." Mick lifted up his giant hands and managed to steady the glass chandelier before any damage was done. "Anyway, Fionnuala, it looks like you've been keeping a certain person busy."

He turned to Gerry who was sitting on the couch with his mouth open and a look of horror on his face. "Well, Gerry," he said, as he continued to mollify the twinkling pieces of glass, "you've come a long way. I bet you never came across too many chandeliers when you used to go backpacking all over the world."

All Gerry could manage was a faint smile. He was clearly dumb with relief that Fionnuala's pride and joy hadn't been broken.

The chandelier wasn't the only triumph, either, of the DIY man's art. The suspended oak floor sparkled like diamonds and there was a hall-stand which, according to Gerry, he had "thrown together" over the previous weekend. The rest of the house was equally wonderful.

"Oh my God," screamed Martin as we were escorted into the 'study'. "Look, guys, a specially built card table. It even has that green felt stuff on it."

"That's not felt. That's baize," said Fionnuala in the kind of tone that suggested we had all better keep any

141

smart remarks we might have to ourselves.

Jim couldn't resist a dig in my direction, though. "You must have given Gerry a few tips, Dan. He obviously couldn't manage all this without your expert advice."

The bastard knew only too well my own lamentable attempts at home improvements. You don't have to be a thug or a soccer hooligan to cause mayhem. I used to manage it quite nicely through a breathtaking combination of brute force and ignorance, the latter due to a lamentable gap in my early education.

In school I learned to conjugate Latin verbs, was forced to digest the rivers of Europe in three languages, discovered how Alexander the Great built an empire through terror and recreation and even ruminated on the social deprivations that galvanised those bothersome French into revolution. But I was never taught how to paint a windowsill (use diagonal strokes) put up a shelf so it stays remotely straight (rest it on top of a level table and work up) or even how to wire a plug (ask your mother). Yet I'd once had the temerity to join the brotherhood of Do-It-Yourselfers, imagining marbleised paintwork in the hall, eat-your-heart-out parquet flooring in the living room and wall-to-wall plaster cornicing in the bathroom. I'd had all the tools a handyman could wish for: the drill, the electric jigsaw, four foot level, belt sander, copper pipe cutters, soldering iron, even a plug-in glue gun.

I'd tried them all out on our first house, a plain but serviceable semi-detached that has since been restored to its former mediocrity. The first onslaught occurred in the vicinity of the bathroom which had been no bigger than a bar of soap and had one of those coloured plastic tubs that squeak and shift position like a diva on a waterbed, only not half as much fun. It had been a narrow

142

room and I'd figured what a pity it was that the bath wasn't half a foot shorter so that it could be put along the short wall under the window rather than taking up all that room. Brainwave: plug in electric jigsaw and amputate the top of the bath.

As brainwaves go, it had been in the Neanderthal class. To make matters even worse than worse, after an hour of hauling and huffing, I'd made the mistake of proclaiming the deed to be yet another triumph of human endeavour. Lorraine had been less than impressed.

"What about the taps?"

The enquiry had seemed strangely out of kilter with my feelings of pride and elation.

"What taps?"

"The (expletive deleted) taps that were on the (expletive deleted) bath before you decided to castrate it with that (expletive deleted) electric (expletive deleted) jigsaw or whatever you call the (expletive deleted) thing in your hand."

The taps were gone, cut off in their prime along with the six inches of bathtub. The conversation that followed had been less Mills and Boon, more Stephen King. Imagine *Night of the Living Dead* with knobs on. Undaunted, I'd attempted a pincer movement along the hallway, putting down a cork floor that had had more craters than the dark side of the moon and installing a power-shower the wrong way round so that it sucked water out instead of delivering it.

The solution had been simplicity itself:

'For Sale: sturdy family home in need of some repair. Enormous potential. Reasonable reserve.'

For all his bull about the need to make a full inspection of the premises and 'not expecting too much', the

143

auctioneer had never even noticed the absence of protuberances from the vicinity of the bath and we had been far too shy to mention it.

I had to admit that I was just a little envious of Gerry's skill.

"Take a good look, Dan. This is real DIY," said Jim, having given up on trying to draw me out with sarcasm. "You obviously never got past DIY kindergarten."

I tried to ignore him but I couldn't help myself.

"You're one to talk," I said. "I never saw much DIY around your old place. Darina put up more shelves than you ever did."

Martin caressed the soft baize of Gerry's handmade card table while Mick dealt the first hand of the night. "Stop bitching you two and feel the force. This is the first time we have played on a real card table. I'm going to rub it all night and hope it will bring me luck."

But Jim just wouldn't let it go. "Gerry, on the other hand, has put all those days of fending for himself in the jungle and on mountains to good use. He can do anything with his hands. Even when you moved house, Dan, you didn't learn."

He was right, though. The 'new' house was, in fact, an old house and in far worse shape than the one we had left. When we moved in it proved impossible for me to suppress the DIY gene for very long. No sooner had I got a week off work than I found myself scrambling about for the tools I had promised never to use again but hadn't had the heart to get rid of. After a few months the house had looked like it was falling apart around us. The rain gutter at the side of the house had collapsed in a tangled heap in the garden and it'd had all the rustic appearance of a roadside sculpture. I had somehow managed to break, yet again, the door of the washing machine. The kitchen sink was blocked with what looked like chewing-gum, the dog had deposited something unmentionable in the television room and had proceeded to drag his fragile behind along the ridges of the new wool carpet therein. I heard later it was a sign of worms.

At the time I'd ventured to suggest, in what I'd intended to be a measured jocular fashion, wouldn't it be a scream and a howl, if the Hoover decided to lay down its hose and come out in sympathy with the rest of the household appliances. The thought, as they say, was father to the deed and, no sooner had my little mantra been uttered, than it'd duly obliged, evincing a throaty gasp in its death throes before finally thumbing a haughty elongated nose at the dog-style carpet pile.

Before starting to do something about this sorry state of affairs, I'd decided to consult my horoscope. This was an emergency and extreme measures were called for. Sure enough, Mystic Ali had had things sussed. 'Things will not always go according to plan. Matters may have a tendency to get out of hand. It is time to take control, seize the moment and make some hard decisions.'

In retrospect, of course, I should have waited. When life is getting hairy there are a number of thing you can do to rectify matters:

1. Leave the house, forget that it looks like a tip and order a nice meal in an expensive restaurant, washed down with a cheeky Chianti.
2. Call in the experts who will scoff at your best efforts before relieving the swelling in your wallet for twenty minutes work, and making it look easy into the bargain.
3. Pretend you know what you're doing, find a

145

hammer and a wrench in the garage and make a complete botch of everything before finally calling in the experts.

4. Run away from home in the dead of night and join a travelling circus, working your way towards becoming Head Lion Tamer.

Unfortunately for me, my guardian angel had been on sick leave and I'd chosen the third option. I hadn't thought it was possible to make matters worse but I'd somehow managed to snatch defeat from the jaws of victory. When Lorraine had suggested we ring the plumber, I'd taken it as the final insult. She clearly believed I was unable to tackle even the most minor of handyman jobs.

"We don't need to call a plumber. Any fool can unblock a sink. All it takes is a handy plunger, a spanner and a little know-how."

The tools had been readily available but the know-how must have taken a hike. I'd whipped out the spanner like a six-shooter and proceeded to attack the pipes under the sink with gusto, managing to unscrew all those twirly bits of plastic piping and laying them neatly on top of the counter. Guess what? The sink, being full of soapy water, had deluged onto the kitchen floor, creating the kind of puddle that even the dog couldn't manage. Undaunted, I'd dragged the dishwasher from its berth whereupon it had become unbalanced, emptying its contents of dirty dishes onto the sodden floor. The dog had come to investigate, lapped up the soapy water and had then skidded into the gap between the washing machine and the drier from whence he'd had to be rescued with the aid of a wet sweeping brush. This had been just before he barfed on the floor. The Hoover had slipped its moorings and swung to starboard in the direction of the dishwasher. It had looked like a scene from the *Titanic* and I'd felt like I was going under for the third time.

My attempts at looking on the bright side had not been appreciated. I'd been advised that if I wished to hang on to whatever dignity I had left – not to mention my whatsits – I should cease forthwith. For once, I'd taken my wife's advice. Still, it could have been worse. At the end of it all, the house was still standing, the kitchen floor had had a good wash and Superman had arrived eventually with his box of tricks to make everything shipshape again. He had been nothing if not a gentleman. No smart remarks, no mutterings of discontent with the malefactor who mucked things up, save for a good-humoured observation that if it weren't for people like me, plumbers would be out of a job, ha, ha. He had still been laughing as he'd raced off in his BMW.

Jim is wrong because I have since learned the error of my ways, thanks to DIYA (Do-It-Yourself Anonymous). This is a self-help group of former addicts who meet regularly in The Corner House pub to discuss past exploits and mock the efforts of those who, like Gerry, cannot seem to break the habit of fixing, mending and making things around the house. It took a long time and many late nights holding up the bar before I got over my fixation with DIY but perseverance paid off in the end. Nowadays my garage serves as a sort of old folks home for a dusty collection of whatsits and thingies that I know will never come in useful but I haven't the heart to throw out. Among those demons lie an electric jigsaw and a huge collection of multi-coloured rawl plugs. These items, along with electric saws, tile cutters, battery-driven screwdrivers, even the ubiquitous pliers, are the marks of male enslavement, the products of a worldwide conspiracy to entrap men folk into thinking they can make the world safe for democracy with a double-sided, two-speed Hitachi drill with orbital sander and spare chuck. Which is why for years afterwards anyone who dared ask me to lift so much as a screwdriver was told to DIY.

After all those Corner House therapy sessions I am now happy to greet the man in the boiler suit like a long lost brother and watch the proceedings from the comfort of my store-bought armchair. I am also wise enough not to butt in or start telling him how to do his job. After all, I wouldn't take too kindly to him telling me how to sit on my backside. I have since taken up a missionary position, so to speak, with regard to warning friends and foe alike of the dangers of excessive enthusiasm for amateur carpentry and the like. I must confess to smirking knowingly at the misfortune of others, like the one time Mick decided to give DIY a go and drilled through the wall of his home right into the neighbour's front room. The neighbour, a 6'4" policeman, wasn't long telling him where to shove his drill. Luckily for Mick, he was able to match the cop in bulk and brawn, if not in skill.

It still gobsmacks me, though, to see a really handy handyman at work and I find even the exclusive language they employ to be quite poetic in its cadences: "I can see the trouble now. You have a problem with your LCB" or "a three-quarter inch motorised valve should do the trick, but it'll cost you". I can only gasp at the majesty of it all and pray that their younger brothers are all heart surgeons if ever I happen to be in the need of a quick bypass which, judging from what those guys charge, is not beyond the bounds of possibility.

We'd devised a system of collective amnesia with respect to the Day of the Deluge but I suspect that it will be some time yet before I hear my wife declare: "Remember that hilarious day when you tried to unblock to sink and made a mess of everything? What a scream that was."

The game was drawing to a close when Fionnuala peeped her head around the study door: "I'm off to bed. Don't forget to take out the rubbish, Gerry."

I had long ago given up any hope of winning money and I was effectively out of the game, so I volunteered to do the job instead of Gerry. After all, I figured that taking out the dustbins was still the preserve of every member of the male gender, whether or not he knew how to wield a hammer-action drill or an electric saw. The game was finishing up, anyway and Martin was the one holding the pot. Whether it was the power of suggestion or just a bout of good luck, his trick with rubbing the baize seemed to have paid off.

"I'll take it out. Where's your wheelie bin?"

She looked at me as if I had been living on another planet.

"Don't you know? The council won't handle them anymore. We now have to take the bags out of the bins because the rubbish men complain that they are too heavy for them to lift. See you guys, good night."

From what Fionnuala seemed to be saying the council's policy bordered on the paranormal, something my dictionary calls '... observations or occurrences beyond the normal scope of scientific or rational explanation, and therefore not possible to explain in terms of current understanding.'

I have to take the book's word for it. After all, it runs to almost 2,000 pages, is a concrete block of a doorstopper and can provide indispensable ammo for diehard *Scrabble* players who like to play hardball. It explains everything from aardvark (a nocturnal African burrowing mammal with a thick set body, large snout and donkey-like ears) to zygote (the cell that is formed as a result of the fertilisation of a female gamete by a male gamete) and it even has a few curse words thrown in.

Now, you might imagine that the paranormal is a dark and misty world peopled by sad creatures who dabble in high-flying notions of UFOs, little green men and alien abductions; mind-benders in the manner of science writer Erik Van Daniken or spoon-benders like Uri Geller. You'd be wrong. The council was as paranormal as anything you'd find in the X-Files.

Gerry could see I was gobsmacked. "They won't take the stuff out of the bin any more, you know. Maybe they haven't got around to laying down the law in your neck of the woods yet but they will. Then you'll have to do what we do and haul all those big plastic sacks out and leave them by the wall. Otherwise, the rubbish won't be collected."

I nodded gravely but, although I knew Gerry was not given to flights of fancy, I still found it hard to believe. If it really was the policy of the council there were no words adequate to describe it – except maybe for a few choice words in the dictionary that might be near the mark. But, considering the size and temper of some of the binmen I'd say most people would decide, like myself, to keep the choice words to themselves. I certainly didn't want to do myself an injury.

"But that's mad," I said. "That means you could pull a muscle or something."

"Tell me about it – putting out the dustbins is one of the most dangerous things you can do," said Gerry. "A

150

lot of guys injure their backs putting out the rubbish. In fact, most people who suffer any kind of injury are injured in their own home."

Just in case, I wasn't convinced, he brought out a book called *Safe As Houses?* that seemed to prove what he was saying.

"See what I mean? It's true. Compared to walking in the Andes, home can be a dangerous place. Most accidents happen there. When I was hill climbing or camping in the jungle the worst thing that ever happened was the odd insect bite but here at home, while doing my DIY bit, I've nearly come a cropper on a couple of occasions with hammers falling on toes, that sort of thing."

I suppose he knew what he was talking about. Most people would probably agree that there are certain things a body should strive to avoid in order to ensure survival to pensionable age. Most sensible folk would consider hang-gliding for the birds or the incurably suicidal, parachuting out of planes at 10,000 feet an example of utter carelessness and bungee jumping for the seriously deranged. They might if they are, like me, and inclined to be particularly paranoid, even be opposed to allowing a nine-year-old go 500 yards down to the shop for sweets because she might: fall on a broken beer bottle left on the pavement by a drunk; get money out of the cash machine and decide to run away from home; find the shop closed, look for another and get lost; be knocked down by a runaway joyrider in a stolen car.

Most middle-aged scaredy-cats would tut-tut at the notion of rock climbing, hill walking or snorkelling, preferring the more genteel delights of pottering about in the garden or setting down to a cosy cuppa. But, according to Gerry, danger lurks in the most familiar and unexpected places. He was warming to his theme.

"Fancy a cup of tea? If you do, forget all about social niceties and don't dream of trying to keep the pot warm – you'll only do yourself an injury. Every year hundreds of daredevils have to dash to the hospital after a run-in with a tea cosy. Accidents have a way of finding places to happen and most of them are at home. You are far safer climbing the north face of the Eiger, wrestling with a crocodile or chatting with a cheetah than soaking in the bath, using cotton wool or making that hot cup of tea. And you don't have to play soccer to break a bone in your foot either. In fact, studies show that it can happen in bed while you're asleep. Better to invest in a big rubber band and take up bungee jumping. It's much safer."

Martin was enjoying this somewhat surreal conversation almost as much as pocketing his winnings. "What about when you're having a bath? Surely that can't be dangerous?"

Gerry had that one sussed. "You're dead wrong. Having a bath is one of the most dangerous things you could do. You wouldn't believe the number of bathers who come a cropper in the tub, either by slipping going in and out or sliding on the soap."

Jim was glancing through Gerry's book. "Quite a few even managed to get toes jammed in the tap and had to be seen by both a doctor and a plumber," he said. "No prizes for guessing who charged the most."

Even Mick couldn't resist a comment. "Forget the bath. Take to the waters and the wild instead. Try your hand at deep sea diving or, safer still, try a spot of shark fishing. At least you'll have a fighting chance."

Gerry is right about one thing: it is possible to do serious injury at home. My own minor catastrophe had happened very easily. I'd been eavesdropping on a neighbour who was giving her tabby cat a good telling off.

"Now Tabatha, how often do I have to tell not to go wandering in next door? Stay here with mummy. There is a fearsome dog in there that never stops barking and wants to chase you. You could get hurt, my little petsy wetsy... "

As the owner of the fearsome creature, I'd begun to take umbrage and was just about to unleash a few barks of my own when the mug of coffee I'd been holding became detached from my lower lip and descended at the rate of knots. It smashed onto my finger, which had been tapping nonchalantly near the edge of the windowsill. The pain had been excruciating and I was convinced it was broken so I'd taken myself off to the regional hospital. I'd ended up spending four hours in the accident and emergency before being told that although it was fractured, there was nothing they could do about it and it would heal itself.

While there I'd encountered dozens of hapless accident-prone people, all of whom had seemed to have done themselves an injury at home. One little girl had even managed to do damage with a tiny cotton bud. I'd overheard her mother telling the doctor that her daughter's face had begun to swell up for no apparent reason. The doctor hadn't a clue what was wrong with her and it took a wily nurse to discover that the child had stuck a cotton bud up her nose just for the fun of it. She had to be operated on to have it removed.

It just goes to show what can happen, if you're not careful. Thousands of people are admitted to accident and emergency after getting into a fix with seemingly

153

innocuous substances. Even the simplest chores have the potential to be lethal. Thousands of people do themselves serious injury every year trying to start petrol lawnmowers, especially when the grass is wet. Even more get themselves in a tangle with electric machines and you wouldn't believe the number that end up on a stretcher from trying to extract plants from flowerpots. The hospitals are full of over zealous gardeners. Ask the doctors in your local hospital and they won't be long telling you that the first sign of good weather sees the A and E wards jammed with people who thought that cutting the grass in their bare feet was a neat idea.

As we got up to take our leave, Gerry had one last bit of advice.

"If you want an accident free life, better to live a little dangerously – it's much safer. The next time you find yourself side-stepping a herd of wildebeest in Khartoum, abseiling over the Grand Canyon, or hitching along the Ho Chi Min trail, thank your lucky stars you are not doing anything really dangerous like chasing a mouse under the table, opening a can of beans, attempting to change a light bulb or, God forbid, eavesdropping on the neighbours like Dan. You'd want to stay away from the DIY as well, unless, of course, you know what you're doing."

TEN

The Mother of all Househusbands

My experiment with being a househusband was not an overnight success although the transition from lazy devil to house angel did occur almost overnight. It must have been playing on my mind for a while because one day I woke up, stretched, greeted the dawn and decided that it was high time to mend my ways.

Not drastically, of course, that would have been too much to contemplate on an empty stomach. But I decided that, if I was going to have any hope of making a go at homemaking, it was high time I got in touch with my feminine side. For that, I had to become a trifle more demure of disposition, less raucous at office parties, a little kinder, a little gentler, more caring, attuned to the needs of others – that sort of thing. I would also resign myself to fewer 'nights before' to avoid the comeuppance of 'the morning-afters'. The poker school was the first casualty.

"Sorry guys, I know I'm supposed to host next week but you'll have to find a new home. I won't be playing poker for a while. In fact, I might never play again. I'm taking a bit of time off work to stay home and help look after things domestically for a bit. It will be a new experience for all of us. I have other things to do that have absolutely nothing in common with aces, jacks or straights."

"I don't have much to do with straights, either," said Martin, never one to miss an opportunity for a double entendre.

My buddies were very put out, complaining that I was either totally sad or totally mad.

With his tongue firmly in his cheek, Mick got straight to the point: "Look, Dan, you're not exactly a fast learner. You still don't know what beats a run in poker and I keep showing you all the moves. It will take you ages to get a handle on this househusband business. You'll be old and grey before you're any good at it."

Jim just thought the whole idea insane. "What are you trying to prove, anyway, that you can boil an egg? So what!"

I didn't even bother to answer him. If he was trying to get a rise out of me, I wouldn't give him the satisfaction and if he was serious there was no point in arguing with him.

Gerry agreed with the others and, as we packed up for the night, made one last attempt to make me change my mind.

"Let's face it, Dan, you're barely housetrained and now you want to start baking cookies? You've gone off your head. Get a grip."

I ignored it all and, taking my cue from the 'Homemaker of the Year' competition, I donned the apron, wielded the sweeping brush and found out where the vacuum cleaner had been hiding all along. I was so busy for a whole month after that last poker game that I hardly spoke to any of the guys. Even Martin, usually domesticated to the point of fussiness, thought my metamorphosis strange.

"You're behaving more camp than I am," he said when he called over one afternoon.

I was up to my armpits in flour and wearing an apron with pastoral scenes on it that looked like it came from a *Bisto* ad.

"Did you ever think of doing drag? You wouldn't be half bad, if your hair was a bit longer, although you'd have to shave your legs. You make Graham Norton look like Arnie Schwarzenegger."

Just the vote of confidence I needed. After that, it would, no doubt, be downhill all the way.

Adrian, Son No. 2, is a bit bemused by my role as househusband; yet he also finds it intriguing.

"It's weird seeing you cooking and cleaning, but it's kind of fun at the same time."

I felt a similar strange mixture of trepidation and excitement. I never thought it was going to be a doddle but, in fact, there are some aspects of general housekeeping, like cooking and cleaning, that aren't quite as difficult as I thought they might be. I had even got to grips with the laundry and the occasional need to repaint the kids' bedrooms but certain requirements of the homemaker supreme award continue to elude me.

The trouble with homemaking is that you are expected to be able to master the most complex tools every day. Even egg timers are electronic nowadays and manipulating the latest scientific gadget is a complete nightmare. In the past, the nearest I ever got to engaging in anything remotely scientific was in school when I burnt my arm on the flame of a Bunsen Burner and had to be taken to hospital. I'd managed to exaggerate the pain to such an extent that it was recommended I be given three days off school. But according to Adrian, science has its uses and

157

the future is bright. Just as I was reaching for the dustpan, he assured me:

"Dad, you know that even at this very moment scientists are working out how to grow a computer so that it can perform all the tasks of today's machines better and faster and cheaper. They're even trying to figure out if they can make little baby computers, so that they can create a whole new generation of computers."

The very idea shocked me.

"My God – computers having sex. Whatever next?"

That wasn't the half of it, though, according to our computer genius. Apparently these machines will be able to detect whatever is in their path, not in the crude manner of today's machines, but in a sophisticated way that will allow them to 'see' even the most obscure objects. Some scientists reckon they will even display many of the characteristics of living beings, like personalities, for instance. To begin with, and just to make us feel comfy with these new generation of cyborgs, scientists propose to invest their latest creation with emotion.

Just imagine: a Hoover that breaks down crying every time it does its business and sees that the kids couldn't give a toss and make just as big a mess within ten minutes.

"Oh dear, no matter what I do, it's always the same. That lad's bedroom looks as if a bomb hit it and I only cleaned it an hour ago. As for the living room, you'd think I hadn't touched it for a month. The girl's bedroom isn't much better. Abandoned toys all over the place and I am sure she's spilled ink on the carpet. I hope they don't seriously imagine I can cope with that. I think I need to go and have a little lie down; it's all getting too much for me."

Or how about the laughing lawnmower, chatting with

the rake and giggling like a schoolgirl at your efforts to mow around that tree that should never have been planted in the middle of the garden?

"Will you look at that bloody idiot? If he thinks I'm going to circle that Magnolia one more time, he's even dumber than he looks."

You might even have an angry oven. "How many times do I have to tell you that small cakes should be put on at 220, not 180? You never listen to a thing I say. In any case, the mix is terrible. A child of ten could do better. I am not cooking that, no way."

Or how about a sarcastic washing machine? "And I suppose you think I can perform miracles with those so-called rugby whites, do you? That's not just mud on those shorts, you know; that's half the bloody pitch."

I've always suspected that so-called inanimate objects have a mind of their own. Why, for instance, does the plastic curtain like to wrap itself round you when you take a shower? It took a Professor of Physics, David Schmidt, of the University of Massachusetts, to conclude that it's all to do with having low pressure on the inside of the plastic and high pressure on the outside. The force of the spray of water from the showerhead causes a draught and reduces the pressure inside the area enclosed by the curtain. Thus the curtain is sucked into the area by the low pressure and it clings. The same principle works for the *Boeing 747* – or so the Prof says. The next thing they'll be telling you is that these machines with personalities they're building will become the most natural thing in the world. I wouldn't mind a cranky oven, or even a smart-assed washing machine but I'll be damned if I allow the kettle to continue being so heedless. It still refuses to turn itself on and appears to have gone on

159

strike. Don't anyone tell me it's a faulty plug or a burned-out element. Like any other guy with three kids, I know perfectly well when I'm being ignored.

If only I could programme either the kids or the appliances to do exactly what I wanted or at least help me recognise my own limitations. At the start of my house-husbandry days I tried to do everything right and that was my undoing. I ended up getting most things wrong.

It all started well enough, though. I ensured that the school lunches were made and neatly packed in tinfoil, bundled snacks and kids into the car; made the school run without a hitch; did a bit of hoovering around the place; attempted a bit of fake dusting here and there – so far, so good. My mistake was deciding to invite every kid on the block over for the afternoon and imagining I could stun them into submission by my culinary expertise while, at the same time, doing the ironing to the tune of *Sitting On the Dock Of the Bay*.

I knew that most of them were used to burgers but I wanted this to be more wholesome and nutritious – no chicken flamers and oven chips – and I consulted a few cookbooks for inspiration. Big mistake. The trouble is they make fascinating reading and before I knew where I was I had, much to the detriment of the basmati rice, become engrossed in an entrée to *Mrs Beeton's Book of Household Management*. This is an ever-popular Victorian treatise on domestic affairs with advice on everything from catching grouse to the duties of the upstairs chambermaid. Check this one out for starters:

USEFUL RECIPES FOR HOUSEMAIDS

To clean Marble

'Mix with a quarter pint of soap lees, a half gill of turpentine, sufficient pipe-clay and bullock's gall to make the whole into rather a thick paste. Apply it to the marble with a soft brush and, after a day or two, when quite dry, rub it off with a soft rag. Apply this a second or third time till the marble is quite clean.'

I must say I have to concur with Mrs Beeton when she says that breaking glass and china, '... is about the most disagreeable thing that can happen in a family and it is probably a greater annoyance to a right-minded servant than to the mistress.'

Do not despair, however. Mrs B knows how to repair a broken tumbler.

'Dissolve an ounce of gum mastic in a quantity of highly-rectified spirits of wine; then soften an ounce of isinglass in warm water and dissolve it in rum or brandy till it forms a thick jelly. Apply to the broken shards.'

From what I could see, though, she didn't seem to have any solution to a pot blackened by burnt rice so all I could do was steep it in bleach and hope for the best.

Two nights later the pot was as black as ever when Mick and Jim dropped by to see if there was any chance I might come to my senses anytime soon. I showed them Mrs Beeton's household hints book.

"Fascinating," said Mick, "but I think using rum and brandy to fix a broken glass is an awful waste. I have a better idea. Why not give up all this nonsense, say 'to hell with it' and polish off the rum and brandy? It mightn't fix glass but it should fix that brain of yours. "

Jim was equally unsupportive. "I have yet to find a solution to a pot ruined by burnt rice but I am sure Mrs Beeton has an answer. I would not be at all surprised if it recommended the use of boric acid and a sheep's gallbladder. Of course, you could always come down to the pub with us for a dram or two. That has been known to solve lots of problems over the centuries."

"I'm sorry, guys, if you see my new-found talents as nothing but an opportunity to make fun of me. I'm serious about all this and, if you'll excuse, me I am about to prepare a selection of dishes from that wonderful cookbook, *Last Dinner on the Titanic*. It contains the menus and recipes from the great liner. The last supper in the first class dining room was a lavish affair, consisting of something in the order of twelve courses."

"No wonder it sank so quickly," said Jim, before I showed both of them the door (with the gleaming brass knocker).

They had me rattled though and, two hours later, I hadn't a thing done and knew that the *Titanic* recipes would take far too long. So, in a mad panic, I tossed meat, carrots, onions and goodness knows what else into a big pot and boiled it to ribbons before presenting it to a shocked ensemble as 'real Irish Stew'.

The kids arrived home from school to a well-dressed table and silver service. It made no difference. They hated every scrap of the stew and were not in the least bit shy about letting me know, either.

Fiona tried to feed it to the dog, who was lying under the table waiting, as usual, for little tidbits. "Look Dad," said Fiona, "even Spenser won't eat it."

I thought a little redemption was called for and produced my 'surprise' from the oven with a flourish, but the sorrowful looking brown bread that emerged was greeted with unremitting hilarity.

Still, Luke had the perfect solution. "It will make a great Frisbee."

Maybe I should just stick to barbecues or packing picnic hampers. Even for this simple culinary expedition Mrs Beeton has some sage advice, especially when it comes to beverages for picnics.

For a large family picnic, she suggests:

> '3 doz quart bottles of ale, packed in hampers, ginger-beer, soda water and lemonade, of each 2 doz bottles; 6 bottles of sherry, 6 bottles of claret, and any other light wine the may be preferred. 2 bottles of brandy.

Sensibly, she writes: 'water can usually be obtained so it is useless to take it.'

I suggested to Lorraine that perhaps we could take a leaf out of Mrs Beeton's book when packing for our next picnic. She had other ideas.

"That would be fine if, say, we had two weeks to plan a picnic and a battalion of helpers to carry all the stuff. Get real."

The kids were more enthusiastic. Although Luke was a bit disappointed when I told him that ginger beer wasn't alcoholic. "Damn. I'll have to stick to the Budweiser."

As a homemaker in training, I was no Mrs Beeton and I marvelled at how women (for it is still nearly always

163

women) manage to cope with the complexities of running a household. Not just the cleaning, washing and ironing but all that endless shopping, food preparation and cooking. I found that one of the toughest jobs was trying to run a household budget. That meant tackling the family finances, despite the fact that I could hardly handle my own finances and I never know what I have in my pocket. I chose the wrong time of year – February – to tackle that one, though. I am not normally superstitious but there is something about February that makes me all a-quiver. It is the time when bills come crashing through the letterbox hell bent on causing domestic mayhem. Those little brown envelopes with the built-in windows may look innocent enough but they weigh more than other mail. Other letters tend to float gently to the floor, smile up at you and usually bring glad tidings but bills crash to the floor like unexploded missiles and are just as deadly.

Continentals are luckier than we are. They don't have letterboxes built into their front doors. They have them at the end of their driveways. They don't have to tread warily downstairs and endure the awesome sight of those insidious brown envelopes staring up at them. Bills are social by nature. They hunt in packs and take no prisoners. Whole swathes of them, battalions, arrive on the mat without so much as a by-your-leave. It cannot surely be mere coincidence that they all arrive together. No sooner has the phone company sent a gentle reminder, 'perhaps you may have overlooked…', then the gas company follows up with a 'despite previous reminders…' in the company of a sidewinder from the credit card crowd that has the word 'final' on it.

Credit cards are of course the deadliest enemy of the household budget. I read somewhere that the average

European owes €3,500 in credit card bills. Then, using all kinds of charts and formulas, the article went on to show that if the original debt were paid off using only the minimum payment due each month, it would take more than thirty years and incur €16,000 in interest charges before it was completely cleared. In other words, that pair of curtains you bought for €100 in the sale would really end up costing you €2,500.

Spending with plastic is just too easy these days. It used to be that the whole transaction took half a day and involved little blue slips of carbon paper, a call to get the credit card checked and the occasional prayer to the gods of finance to ensure that the machine didn't jam. Now, it's plastic everywhere. In my wallet there are two credit cards, an electronic library card, a medical drugs payment scheme card, a swimming club card, two value club cards, a video store card, three hole-in-the-wall cards from different banks and a very bedraggled looking Press card which hasn't been renewed since 1989.

Martin has even more than that. I started going on about cards one day and it was a case of 'I'll show you mine if you show me yours'.

"Look," he'd said. "My bulge is bigger than yours – in more ways than one."

He was right of course – about the wallet. He had scores of store cards, petrol cards, travel bonus cards, airline cards and even clothes boutique cards.

When it comes to plastic, size matters. Size particularly matters if you happen to have spent a fortune with the credit card and your household budget looks like its about to go under for the third time. I totted up income and expenditure and, to my horror, found that I had also spent next week's budget.

165

Having a good financial brain matters too, particularly if you're broke. I once knew a loveable chancer who, in his early days, had been very successful at his job and made a lot of money. However, not being the saving kind, he soon blew it all on fast cars and faster women. Somewhere along the line his luck changed for the worst. His marriage broke up, he took to the drink in a big way and he began to lose seriously on the gee-gees. He ended up borrowing fairly substantial sums from a dozen or so banks around town, none of which he ever bothered to pay back. Finally the penny dropped, so to speak, with the banks and the whole lot of them told him where to take his business.

"Glorified loansharks," he'd explained to me one night, as he tapped me for a loan while, at the same time (displaying a deft sense of the world of finance) paying me back half the money he had borrowed the week before.

This had been going on for a while and was something I could ill afford at the time. I was down a small fortune and the future looked none too rosy.

At last I'd decided to cut my losses. It was the day after payday, and my friend was on the prowl. For once I saw him coming.

"Here's the tenner I owe you," he'd said, holding out a crisp new note that, no doubt, he had borrowed from some other likely sucker.

I'd taken a deep breath, steeled myself and said: "No thanks. You can keep it. I don't want it back. In fact, you might as well hang onto the whole lot of it. I don't want any of it back."

He had been, unusually for him, momentarily shaken, but he soon regained his composure. Raising a pair of devilish eyes upwards, he'd let out a big roar of laughter.

"I don't care what they say about you, boy. You're not as dumb as you look."

That was easy for him to say. He'd gone to his grave not too long after that and any hope I might have had of seeing the money went with him. Judging from the murmurs in the pub after his funeral, I hadn't been the only one who had bankrolled him, either.

His way of getting out of a financial fix had a certain attraction to it and when the proverbial hit the fan on the household budget front I thought of getting another half dozen or so credit cards and taking a leaf out of his bad books: pay off one with the other and so on. Even if it didn't work, I felt the old chancer would have been proud. Not that I dare mention it to Lorraine though, because she might have a fit and, anyway I didn't want to burden her with our household budgetary woes.

The trouble was that it wasn't just the household budget that was overspent. My own finances were in an equally sorry state and demanded immediate attention. Everywhere there were bills, bills, bills and there seemed no end in sight. I wrote out a list of possible solutions to my own straitened circumstances, thinking that they might also help solve the household dilemma:

1. Bite the bullet and pay at once. This shows a certain lack of imagination.
2. Ignore all demands and make a nice bonfire in the back garden.
3. Open everything, gasp in horror, shove everything into a drawer and head for the pub.
4. Throw yourself on the mercy of the bank and respond to the invitation from the manager to 'drop in for a little chat'. That sounds fine and dandy, but the trouble with those 'little chats' is

167

the way they have of turning into an interrogation. I didn't do any of those things. Instead, I decided to put pen to paper to the guy causing most of my woes.

"**Dear Bank Manager,**

I know it's been a long time since my last confession and that you must be on the verge of utter despair, wondering why on earth I haven't been responding to all those lovely letters you've been sending me for the past few months. Perhaps you thought I'd gone to live on a houseboat somewhere, joined a commune of ageing hippies, skipped the country altogether or, God forbid, transferred my overdraft to another bank. In fact, I'm still where I've always been, keeping body and soul together, slogging away, feeding the dog, paying the mortgage (with a little help from your good self, of course) and you'll be glad to know that all your correspondence is neatly tied with a red ribbon and marked 'urgent'.

I normally don't like the look of those envelopes with windows on them that somehow find their way into the letterbox. I usually only open letters marked 'Private and Confidential' if they are meant for someone else, but your letters are a source of inspiration. You certainly have a way with words. I particularly liked your first letter where you, ever so gently, suggested: 'Perhaps, it may have escaped your notice.... ' It hadn't, but it showed you cared.

I was quite taken with the second letter where you cut to the chase straight away: 'We would like to draw your attention... '. I didn't even mind so much being reminded that 'despite previous correspondence' I had carried on regardless. 'Unless we hear from you immediately we will have no option… ' is bad-tempered, but I'm a forgiving kind of guy and I have a proposition for you.

Don't look at me as a problem. Look at me as an opportunity and let me join your Bad Debt League. It's the hottest ticket in town. I know that any bank manager worth the name has to have a quota of bad debts.

Yours sincerely,
Overdraft Dan

P.S. If that's asking too much, perhaps you could see your way to throwing me a few Euro on account. I'm not going to invest in shares or anything reckless like that, but there's a sure thing running in the 2.30 on Monday and, according to my horoscope, it's my lucky day. You can send the cheque to my new pad on the Cayman Islands.'

I waited in vain for a reply but none came. I heard later that the bank manager had retired.

My financial problems weren't going to go away though, so I found myself having to go for my first option of biting the bullet and instituting a period of cutbacks. It worked remarkably well and after a couple of weeks things were back on a more even keel financially. But there were other unforeseen difficulties to keep me busy.

One particular problem was trying to figure out where things were kept and why they were put in inexplicable place. Why was the vacuum cleaner under the stairs? Surely the shoe polish must be somewhere? Where were the light bulbs? Why was the furniture polish kept under the sink? It made me realise why men get themselves into such trouble even at corporate level. Men always seem to be the last to find out about the things that really matter. Any time you hear of some huge financial scandal it transpires that the bosses did not really know what was going on under their noses in their own companies. None of the scandals would have happened if the companies had been run by women. That's because women always know where things are, why they are there or where they should go; while men, if asked to find something around the house, couldn't do it if their lives depended on it.

Even men in the highest of high places often don't have a clue what is happening around them. The President of the United States can send in the Marines but I bet he would be hard pushed to find the sliced bread in the White House kitchen. He can jet off on a round of shuttle diplomacy but he never gets to pack his own suitcase. Neither need he worry about whether he's locked all the doors and windows and turned the gas off and he doesn't have to find a kindly neighbour to look after the dog while he's away on business. He'd probably be better off if that was the case.

Living in the White House, with all its attendant privileges, must be a surreal experience. Look at Dwight Eisenhower: when he went back home after the presidency, he tried to make a phone call. The only trouble was he hadn't placed a call for a long time. When he'd heard a buzzing sound in his ear, he'd had no idea what it was and he hung up. He didn't know that switchboard operators had been replaced by dial tones. The President never has to concern himself with passports, visas and the like or get in a tizz about missing his flight. Air Force

One is at his beck and call and the minute his bum hits the seat, the plane takes off. I can't imagine a woman president allowing other people to take such control of her life.

It mightn't do the American President any harm if he had to become a househusband for a while. Just imagine his State of the Union address: "My fellow Americans. Our forefathers. . . ."

I am unlikely ever to be president and I don't run a company, and my family is not yet completely bankrupt, although we do have three children, so it is not beyond the bounds of possibility. But I have to admit, even after my attempts to be househusband of the year, that there are still certain areas of my household that remain a mystery to me. I am probably not alone in this and I imagine that there are many 21st century men who are equally oblivious to the inner workings of their own homes. Sometimes I have nightmares just thinking about it and I can just imagine the scene if I am ever called to testify about the state of affairs at home.

After I am sworn in at the Domestic Scandals Tribunal, the grilling begins.

"Where," asks Killer Shark SC for the Tribunal, "do the cereal bowls go?"

As a man with nothing to hide, I answer honestly: "I'm not exactly sure."

"You're not sure?" he asks with well-practised incredulity. "This is your own house we are talking about, Mr Buckley. How could you not know where they are kept?"

"The kids keep moving them," I reply.

"Maybe you don't do the dishes often enough," interrupts the tribunal chairman.

"Well, I often do the washing up so I don't have to put the stuff away. It's a kind of *quid pro quo*," I respond, not very convincingly, hoping that the little bit of Latin might impress them.

Not a chance.

"How very noble of you," she says, sarcastically.

Luke is called as a witness. Mr Shark treats him gently but he gets the answers he wants.

"Tell me, young man, does your father ever do the shopping? Does he bring home food?"

Luke is too young to lie in court.

"He sometimes gets beer in the supermarket and brings home pizzas or a Chinese on Fridays."

"But have you ever known your father to arrive home with a car full of groceries?"

Luke looks over at me, not wanting to say anything that would hurt me. The question is repeated and I know, as the man who continually taught him to tell the truth, what the answer will be. My heart sinks when he responds but I am also proud of his honesty.

"No. I suppose not."

Luke steps down and, armed with his testimony, Mr Shark puts me through the mill again.

"Tell us, Mr Buckley how much did you spend in the supermarket last week?"

"Nothing," I say. "My wife did the shopping last week."

"The week before?"

"I'm not sure. I think that was the same situation. But I did get some shoe polish in the supermarket the week before that."

"Shoe polish? You can't eat shoe polish, can you Mr Buckley?

He doesn't even bother to let me answer that one.

Then he begins to twist the knife.

"You eat, don't you, Mr Buckley?"

"Yes, three times a day, usually a bit more."

"And you wash and bathe and enjoy all the comforts of home, do you not?"

"Certainly I wash, once a month – if absolutely necessary," I say with a chuckle, trying to lighten things up.

No one is amused.

Killer Shark spots another opening. "What is your bank account number, Mr Buckley?"

"Er, em. I should have it written down somewhere. I'm not much good at remembering numbers."

He goes for the jugular. "So what do you spend your time doing when you should be shopping or banking or looking after household chores?"

He has me on the run and he knows it. "I spend a lot of time on the computer."

"The computer," he says with a theatrical flourish. "The computer doesn't boil the kettle, does it, Mr Buckley, or do the cleaning or put out the rubbish, does it?"

The chairman tries to come to my rescue.

"I'm sure Mr Buckley puts out the rubbish", she says kindly, as if she feels I have had enough torture.

I nod in appreciation, unable to stutter further.

But then Mr Shark gives the knife one final twist. "I think you're not fit to run a family," he says.

A broken man, I can only whisper: "So what should I do?"

"Try becoming a househusband for a few weeks. At least it should help you find your way around the house."

With that, I woke up and the realisation dawned on me that maybe Mick and Gerry were right and homemaking just wasn't my thing. I decided there and then to give up my attempts to be Homemaker of the Year – my overnight finish was just as quick as my overnight start. It began with a rapid return to my more natural condition of slovenliness, much to the relief of my poker pals.

Anyway the kids hadn't really been too happy with an apron-clad Dad. I'm sure that they preferred seeing me wielding a hammer rather than a spatula. Lorraine was relieved, too, but for other reasons. My lamentable attempts at cooking and baking had been producing an unexpected result, mostly because I ended up eating everything left behind.

"I hate to say this now, but you have been putting on weight. I know you hate to see food being wasted but you're not a human dustbin. You'll have to cut down or you'll never get a handle on it."

In my attempts to do it all, I ended up doing nothing right. I simply wasn't tough enough for the hardest job in the world. It was time for the New Man within to emerge in other ways. Instead of trying to improve things around the house, I decided to improve myself.

ELEVEN

Eat Your Heart Out

There's only one thing worse than being on a diet and that's having to listen to someone constantly sniping at you for not being on a diet, or suggesting the kind of diet you should be on or, worse still, telling you of all the diets they and their whole family have been on. Everyone, it seems, has something to say on the subject. Lorraine, though, apart from one comment on my expanding middrift, kept her thoughts to herself and the kids didn't seem to notice that there was more of their dad around than there used to be.

Some of the worst comments, believe it or not, came during one particular poker night shortly after I had finally abandoned all pretensions of being a househusband. I was the host but that didn't stop any of the poker guys having a go at me.

"Lorraine is right," said Martin, as I cracked open a beer before dealing. "I hope you don't mind me saying this, but you are getting tubby, Dan, and it doesn't suit you. You should cut down on the beer or try changing to something like Vodka and cranberry juice. It has far fewer calories and you can still get high as a kite."

"First of all, of course I mind what you're saying about me getting fat and, as for vodka and cranberry, that's only for hookers. I'd rather drink leprechaun's piss, Martin, or give up the booze altogether, not that I've any intention of doing that."

For once, Jim was being conciliatory.

"He's only trying to help, Dan. All he's saying is that you cannot take your health for granted. You are over forty and you have to realise that if you don't do something about your weight now, it will be much harder later on. Going on a diet may not be such a bad idea. You should also go to the gym a couple of days a week. It worked wonders for me."

"Give me a break, Jim. The only reason you started pumping iron in the first place was because you and Darina were having constant fights and it was a way of getting out of the house."

Mick slammed his cards down on the table. Mind you, they weren't face up. He was angry but not stupid.

"That's out of order, Dan, and you know it. Anyway, it's your own business. I really don't care if you get as fat as a fool."

"Sorry Jim. Mick is right. That was out of order. But would you all please drop the subject?"

Gerry had been about to say something equally cutting to the rest of them but he thought better of it. "I don't get all this obsession with dieting. I don't think you're overweight Dan, but of course you have to watch yourself like we all do."

That was the end of dieting talk for that night and for the rest of the game we either played in silence or made small talk. However, it preyed on my mind for the next few days and I began to feel I should be doing something about my weight. My experience in the chipper when I had walked out in fear now seemed like eons ago. Despite all those promises I had made to myself about getting more exercise, I had done absolutely nothing about it. This time, though, I was determined to change and make some kind of substantial improvement, so off I went in search of some way of reinstalling my waistline.

I thought I was being handed a diet to die for. Actually, it was more like a diet to live for. At least that's what I was told by my GP who informed me that my cholesterol, at seven-point something, was seriously off the Richter scale.

"Let me put it this way: if you were Los Angeles you'd be having an earthquake right this minute."

It was all very well for him. He looked slim and fit and the only thing overweight about him was his wallet. He was a bit mischievous, though. I could sense a certain glee when he put a colour-coded sheet full of dos and don'ts on what I should and should not be eating into my hand. It was a product of the British Hypertension Society. I wouldn't have thought the British would need a hypertension society as I've always found them to be a very calm and collected lot, but apparently I was wrong. Perhaps what gave them palpitations in the first place was this diet that I was expected to take seriously. Some of the suggested meals from the 'good for you' group would hardly feed an undersized gnat.

Naturally, anything remotely tasty was on the Avoid Eating panel.

No croissants (merde), no chips or roast potatoes, 'unless cooked in rape seed oil' –whatever that is. No sausages, salami, paté, milk or 'margarine of unknown origin' and, worst of all, no fudge (damn).

What was there left to live for? How about tofu, curd (I never dared find out what that was) porridge, brown rice, untoasted sugar-free muesli? If that didn't float my boat I could always pig out on rice cakes, soya milk, cottage cheese, low sugar jelly and mineral water.

177

There had to be a better way. I spent days scouring the bookshops for a copy of a book called *Non-Mainstream Diets* that I was told came packaged with six Crunchies and a Mars Bar. Mind you, the person who told me this was a certain fourteen-year-old called Luke who spends much of his life playing practical jokes at other people's expense. Still, in desperation, I tried to find it. None of the local bookshops had heard of it. I tried to order it on the web but it said nothing about Crunchies or Mars Bars so I had to give it up as a bad job. Unfortunately, all that exertion made me hungry and, as my mind was full of Crunchies I had to run down to the shop for one (all right, three).

After that I figured it was time to get serious, but I didn't know how. I was passing Gerry's place one beautiful spring afternoon when he called me over. He always seems to have a conspiratorial way about him, a sideways slant of the head that suggests he is about to impart the real secret of Fatima or something equally compelling. Actually, he can be a crashing bore at times, not least because he's a bit of a know-all. Naturally, he had the answer to my problem.

"Like I was saying last week I really don't get all this obsession with dieting. You need to forget all those fancy diets. The only thing for it is to stop eating. Just starve yourself for a week. Drink plenty of water. It's simple, clinical, clear and it works."

"It doesn't, Gerry. I tried doing that to the grass, hoping that if I starved it of nutrients it would stop growing and I wouldn't have to go to the bother of mowing it. All I ended up with was half an acre of very brown, very long grass which I then was forced to cut with a shears before having to mow it anyway. My next-door neighbour's grass

178

was naturally perfect. That's because twice a week he feeds it lovingly with fistfuls of horseshit and shaves it shorter than pubic hair."

"Well, you could always try eating horseshit. It might keep you quiet, anyway."

That was the smartest thing he had said since we met.

Gerry's wife, Fionnuala, a disgustingly healthy, cycling, jogging, step-aerobicing kinda gal, overheard our conversation.

"I hear you've started a diet, Dan. I hope you keep it up."

"No, Fionnuala. That's just a nasty rumour dreamed up by some guys who should have known better."

"Still, you are piling it on, you know and you need to be careful with putting on too much more weight. The best thing for you might be to try eating bean salad and wild rice. It works for me."

She might as well have suggested I get a sex change. Even before I started piling on the weight, she was always on about healthy food. When we all went on a picnic together once she was so horrified when she saw our selection of granny's cream cakes that she nearly threw up. Although, come to think of it, I don't know if she would ever have anything in her stomach to throw up. Fionnuala is always either on a diet, beginning one or just finishing one. If she lay down on the grass she could easily disappear among the dandelions in my lawn.

All this talk about my weight was getting to me so I made some excuse about being late to collect one of the kids and walked off for fear I might say something I would later regret. Gerry is neurotic enough but Fionnuala is far worse, particularly when it comes to the subject of healthy eating. By contrast, I have never once heard Mick's wife Laura talk about dieting and, considering she was once a beauty queen, that is some achievement. She certainly isn't skinny like Fionnuala, but she never looks fat, either, particularly when she's standing next to Mick's twenty-two stone.

My problem is that I have a tooth so sweet that it needs constant nourishing. Certain times of the year are particularly problematic. Christmas can be bad, with all those cakes and puddings but Easter is the worst. It's a tough time for chocoholics – more chocolate, more temptation, more anxiety. It's bit like throwing a drunk into a vat of whiskey and expecting him to swim straight to shore. I can't make like an Easter bunny any more because of my expanding midriff, puny pectorals and an innate inability to resist temptation. For that you can blame those chocolate eggs that nest in the fridge for weeks just begging to be picked at when no-one is looking. I am a self-confessed chocoholic. I can sniff out a box of Smarties at fifty yards, consume an Aero bar at warp speed, down a Snickers before it's even paid for and, as for Yorkie Bars, they just can't seem to make them fast enough. I have been in denial for years, convincing myself that the Chocolate Flake I crumble into my cereal at breakfast is full of iron, vitamins, and other essentials for proper bodily function and that the Fruit and Nut bar I just happened to come across in the supermarket was really a lettuce in disguise. But the truth is I'm hooked, a chocolate bar junkie and now my body's beginning to pay the price.

Very few men will admit it, but most guys fantasise about having the perfect body. It doesn't really matter what age they are or if they happen to be tall and slim or small and fat – they all want to look like a Greek God.

180

Some men are more concerned about their bodies than others, of course. In fact, body obsession among men and boys is now recognised as a growing problem of the 21st century. Trying everything from compulsive weight lifting to steroids, more and more men are taking the quest for physical perfection beyond the bounds of normal behaviour. The condition even has a name. It is called The Adonis Complex. There is already a book out in America also called, appropriately enough, *The Adonis Complex*, which is aimed at helping men affected by this new condition. It's become a huge bestseller.

For the rest of us, there is the occasional desire to have the perfect physique but it doesn't often go beyond thinking about it. Usually, just like most men, women fantasise about having the ideal body for a few seconds, decide it's impossible and revert back to slouching on the couch, eating ice-cream. But women are subject to far more pressures than men in this regard. Most women's magazines feature photographs of razor-thin stars on their front-covers. It looks to me like they seem to promising ordinary women that they can also possess a star-like body. Unfortunately many otherwise sensible women will be tempted to find out how the celebrities achieve their stick thin (sorry, ethereal) figures and might even try the regimes listed. One look at some of the diets and exercise plans the stars follow, however, will probably be enough to make them want to accept their more normal curves after all.

Perhaps, comparing yourself to a particular film star is (and I know I risk torture for this) a woman thing. Although I have never known Lorraine to compare herself to any celebrity, there are many women who do. Fionnuala is one of them and she regards it as the most natural thing in the world.

It has always baffled me so when we were at her house for the weekly game I asked her straight out. I was two weeks into my own diet regime and obsessing about the world of weight loss.

"What woman wouldn't like a stomach just like the lean, toned one belonging to Geri Halliwell? Most women would die for Jennifer Aniston's slinky legs or Julia Roberts' arms. If you could put them all together you'd have the perfect figure."

Still, it had to take more than avoiding the odd cream bun to achieve celebrity-like perfection. I wanted to find out and, sure enough, Fionnuala knew all about celebrity diets. I was particularly curious to find out how the pop star Geri Halliwell went from being a slightly rounded, but still perfectly acceptable, Spice Girl to a size eight, seven-and-a-half stone pixie.

"She did it by cutting out meat, animal fat, eggs, poultry, dairy products, including milk and cheese, tropical fruits and juices, caffeinated drinks, chemically-treated foods and anything spiced or aromatically stimulating like alcohol."

Was there anything left? Not much. Apparently, twice a week she lets herself go really wild and gorges on fish but for the rest of the time she eats mostly rice. Mahatma Gandhi used to eat more than that, I thought. Still, I decided to ask Fionnuala for her collection of celebrity diets – if it works for Jennifer Aniston it might even work for me.

The first one I decided to try out was Haliwell's diet and I confined myself to experimenting with it for one day only. It was just as well because I didn't make it beyond mid-afternoon. All that brown rice gave me gas and by three o'clock I was so hungry I found myself watching Spenser with envy as he tucked into his tinned rabbit.

I took a look at the section on Jennifer Aniston next. She had slimmed down by using a high protein diet that involved using a calculator to work out what she could eat. Under this regime, food such as rice, bread and bananas are out. I had a go at it for a couple of days but, with my head for figures, I was miscalculating all the quantities and found that 5000 grams of desiccated coconut wasn't the best for my stomach.

Some of the celebrities on Fionnuala's list follow diets set according to blood type. If, for instance, you happen to be Group A that means munching lots of vegetables, eating a limited amount of seafood and cutting down on dairy products is for you. I like this idea a bit more than the rest. It set me wondering if people with certain blood groups are attracted to certain food and drink. A session in the pub with a few work mates seemed one way to find out and I asked Jim to join in the experiment for fun. For the purposes of research, I would require a fair bit of consumption but they weren't complaining. From what we could gather, most Guinness drinkers are O-Positive while Heineken slurpers tend to be B-Positive. There were only two O-Negatives among us, including myself, and we were both imbibers of Carlsberg. It didn't take us long to decide that O-Negative was probably the best blood in the world.

None of the research was doing my waistline any good, though, and despite a transfusion of lager, it looks like it is getting no smaller. In fact, if anything it is growing larger by the hour.

"A little bit of extra weight was something that never

bothered men in my father's day," said Mick as he shifted his ample buttocks into a more comfortable position while he dealt the hand.

We were back in his place for another session and we'd just filled the guys in on our Diet by Blood research.

"Back then it was okay just to look okay," agreed Gerry.

It was the same with my own father. I could never have imagined him or his cronies worrying about a bit of a beer belly or wondering whether to splash out on Lynx or Calvin Klein aftershave. I'd once bought him Armani cologne for his birthday and he'd turned his nose up at it.

"It smells like a piss-pot or a bordello, I'm not sure which. Thanks for the thought, but I think I'll stick to plain soap and water. That's the only cologne I have ever needed and I'm not about to change."

But not too long after that I'd caught him red-handed splashing on the Armani when I called to visit.

"I caught you rotten, Dad. And to think I fell for all that bullshit about sticking to soap and water."

With a look of mischief about him, he'd put his finger to his lips and whispered: "That's only so your mother won't smell the whiskey off my breath."

He had certainly looked like he'd had a drink or two but perhaps the whiskey was just an excuse and he hadn't wanted his son to think he was a wimp. But maybe he had succumbed to the lure of aftershave after all. He was not alone. Nowadays men, just like women, are besieged with images of unattainably beautiful bodies and the irony is that, while many women are being encouraged to ignore the images the media throws at them, men are wallowing in them. Perhaps the rise of feminism has caused men to focus on their bodies as the defining feature of masculinity. The lengths some guys will go to for attaining the perfect body have to be seen to be believed.

"There's a guy I know down at the gym," said Martin, as he raised his bet. "He has muscles on his muscles but he thinks he's fat and he is forever on some kind of diet. He is never happy with his appearance and he always seems to be copying the diet regime of some Hollywood actor or other. He seems to have this strange notion that if he does that he will actually get to look like them. Recently, he told me that he wanted to look like Denzel Washington but I had to point out the obvious that he might have a problem because Denzel is black and this guy is white."

Maybe Hollywood isn't the answer but it seems like everyone is on, or has tried, some kind of weird weight loss programme recommended by the stars. They are even called strange names, like the Atkins Diet, Carbohydrate Addicts or, scariest of all, The Zone. Eat more fat, cries one guru; no, just cut the complex carbohydrates, says another. One diet advises you to buy specially prepared diet meals and drinks and eat grapefruit every morning. That can be a problem if, like me, you happen to have a weak stomach. I ended up with diarrhoea for two days. Of course, that in itself caused me to lose weight and maybe that was the idea all along.

Like Sherlock Holmes on a case, I had even started to research magazines, scour book shops, and trawl through the internet, to find out more about diets – something I was dying to tell the lads about. I had soon learned that the Big Bang of Universe Diet was Weight Watchers and that they are still the heavyweights of the weight loss industry. Then came SlimFast, the Nutri-System, and so on. I had looked them all up to see if I could find the perfect diet for me.

185

In doing so, I had finally come across that diet book that Luke had been telling me about. It was listed on the internet and I hadn't found it before because I had the title wrong. It was called the *International Encyclopedia of Non-Mainstream Diet Plans*, and came with a hefty price tag of $49.95. It also came packaged, not with Crunchies but with six Nestles Crunch bars. I'd had a sneak preview and found that it featured a variety of little-known, but apparently effective, diets.

The one that had caught my eye was the Visualization Diet. The theory is simple: whenever you feel the urge to indulge in forbidden food, you simply visualise your head superimposed on a well-known person whose body you admire. I'd visualised myself with Sylvester Stallone's body. To add realism, I'd slurred my speech, started referring to myself as "Sly," and made a vow to date a different model, half my age, every three months. For a while I'd nearly lost my taste for chocolate but it didn't last.

Under pain of death (or at least the disapproval of my doctor) I'd tried every diet possible except the Drink Your Own Pee Diet and the Brocelli For Breakfast Diet. There are some things I just can't stomach. The most successful diet was called Eat Your Heart Out. Despite its scary sounding title, all it really involved was eating lots of fish, fruit and vegatables and, for a while it worked. But after a couple of weeks I'd started to drift back into old habits and had put back on all those pounds I had lost.

"Do you know what lads? At the end of it all, I realise that the only way to win the dieting game is to invent one myself," I said concluding my lecture on diets of the 21st century. "Diet plans have become so amazingly successful, that everyone with a vision of how to combine celery and cottage cheese, must have asked themselves: 'Hey, why don't I start my own diet plan, make a fortune, and quit my job?' Maybe I could make enough to retire to the Bahamas and pig out forever on Lobster and Chablis."

With the help of my skinny son Adrian, resident computer expert, and Mick, resident expert from Overeaters Unanimous, I'd devised a series of do-it-yourself diets. "It's about the only DIY thing you have tackled that might have a chance of working," Mick had commented and I couldn't argue with that.

To the amazement of the other poker lads, who looked a bit shellshocked, I pulled the DIY diet results out of my back pocket and started to read them out.

"The Stone Age Diet: You must grow or kill everything you eat. There is also a New Age version of this diet: All food must be consumed in the nude, during a rainstorm, while covered in mud. Adrian thought this one would be 'cool', particularly if he could wear a leopard skin and carry a spear while having dinner.

The Yoga Diet: While seated in the Lotus Position, you repeat your healthy food word mantra until you become disorientated, start mumbling nonsense and lose your appetite. Lorraine didn't think much of this one. According to her, if I drink all night in the pub I also start mumbling nonsense but I still have a beer belly.

The CIA diet: You arrest anyone who looks like they may be hiding a hamburger. You then steal their food and boast about it."

"Laura was not impressed when I mentioned that one," Mick chipped-in but I wasn't going to be distracted.

The Politician's Diet: You grab your anorak, dash to a fancy restaurant and ask for, "Ti food wit chips".

Since nobody understands what you're saying, you get nothing to eat.

Jim saw a flaw in this one. "You could be tempted to hire two hundred advisers to get the message across and then you would put all the weight back on."

The Lawyer's Diet: The best food available served on a silver platter. But it costs two thousand a day, and there's no guarantee that you will lose any weight.

"You could also call it the Fat Cats' Diet", Martin advised, winking at Jim.

The John Wayne Bobbitt Diet: You can eat anything you want, but your loved one must prepare it with a huge carving knife, while you sleep."

Lorraine had found that one intriguing but she'd seen a problem. "You might lose weight in the one area you don't want to."

I wasn't about to repeat that comment to the guys so I just carried on reading.

"**The Bono Diet**: Each time you get the urge to cheat, a representative of the Navajo Indian Tribe comes over and gives you a cold stare until you release your death-grip on the chocolate chip cookie."

"That would never work," commented Gerry.

He'd once lived with some Navajos while on his travels so I thought I better listen to him. "The Navajos wouldn't give a damn about the white man's cookie."

I wasn't going to start arguing about that one so I carried on.

"**The Boy Band diet**: All food has to be regurgitated by their manager and must be consumed in front of 10,000 screaming kids who have to pay for the privilege of watching you eat."

That one had upset Fiona who'd screamed: "If you're

talking about Westlife I think you're horrible. They're my favourite band."

All this talk of diets was making us all hungry so there was a sigh of relief all round when Fionnuala produced some scones.

"Don't worry," she said. "They're made with low-fat margarine and a sugar-free sweetener. They won't put on any weight; in fact, they might even help you lose some."

That seemed a bit crazy and it was a bit strange to be eating diet scones that were supposed to make you thin. It reminded me of the list of famous people who ate strange stuff that Adrian and I had picked up on the web when we were trawling for weird diets. We'd been sharing a plate of curry and chips at the time. I wondered what the lads might have to say about diets of yesteryear. Undercover, I pulled out another piece of paper and starting reading it out.

Voltaire, French philosopher, 1694 – 1778
Foods: None. Drank seventy-two cups of coffee a day, black.
Weight at death: Unknown, body still in motion.

"He should have been drinking decaf," said Fionnuala.

Diego Rivera, Mexican muralist, 1886 – 1957
Foods: Once lived on a cannibal diet for two months. "I liked to eat the legs and breasts of women," he wrote.
Weight at death: 15 stone.

"I wonder," said Jim, "how much of it was his own?"

Adolf Hitler, 1889 – 1945
Foods: Vegetarian, but ate a bullet at time of death

189

Weight at death: 12 stone.

Martin couldn't resist a wicked comment on that one: "Did that include his lederhosen?"

Elvis Presley, Trucker turned entertainer, 1935 – 1977
Foods: Peanut-butter and banana on white bread, deep fried.
Weight at death (which occurred while sitting on the loo): One ton, and still decomposing.

"The pity of it was," said Gerry, "He died with more roll than rock."

Mama Cass, singer, 1941 – 1974
Foods: Half-swallowed ham sandwich.
Weight at death: two ton.

Mick couldn't take any more of this.

"Enough of all this talk about diets. Let's finish the game; it's getting late."

Despite shovelling back three of Fionnuala's scones, the minute I got home after the session I headed straight for the fridge and devoured a chicken leg, a half pint of milk, some leftover coleslaw and a doughnut that looked like it had been hiding there for a month.

That, of course, made me feel guilty the following day and I went back on the QuickSlim plan I had been on for a few weeks. But after another fortnight of breakfasting on what Lorraine said looked like bird droppings covered in yoghurt, I'd had enough. I decided it was time to put the diet to the test. I climbed onto the new scales I had bought. The trouble is, these are electronic, unlike the old scales. There is no little counter wheel to fiddle with so you can cheat.

There had been a marked change, all right. After all those days of starving myself; after trying every celebrity plan from the Matt Perry Weight Loss Regime to Keanu Reeve's No Sweat Diet Plan; after gathering a library full of information and advice on losing weight, I found that things had indeed changed – I had gained half a stone.

"Maybe you could try eating your own words," said Mick when I rang him up to moan about it. "If nothing else, it might shut you up talking about dieting." He then had an even better idea. "You could always try bulimia. You always throw up after eight or nine pints anyway."

In the end, though, I decided that even if the numbers of men on diets were about to outstrip the figures for women, even in the celebrity stakes, dieting wasn't going to work for me. The only way of getting a body to die for was either to starve myself to death or to go and sweat it out in the gym.

TWELVE

The Body Beautiful

Just like diets, it's hard to avoid getting advice, usually without asking for it, on the subject of physical exercise. The amount of advice you get is often in inverse proportion to the fitness level of those bending your ear. Therefore, Martin, the fittest poker player of us all, stays fairly silent on the subject, except for giving us the odd exhortation to go to the gym.

"Of course, Martin, your main reason for pumping all that iron is to spot the talent and ogle those sweating torsos. You're as fit as a fiddle already anyway," I said to him one Wednesday night as our weekly game got under way at Mick's place.

"I know, but it doesn't do my pectorals any harm, either."

Jim and Gerry also looked trim. In Jim's case, that was partly the result of stress brought about by the divorce.

"I actually lost too much weight," he said. "It was all the hassle with Darina. I'm getting back to normal now though."

Gerry's fit shape was deserved. He had always been very sporty and had been running at least three miles every day for as long as I could remember. "I wouldn't feel right if I didn't have my run every day," he said.

Mick, on the other hand, had more spare tyres than you'd find on a bonfire but that didn't stop him from wagging his little fat finger at me on the subject of losing some weight and getting fit.

"Look, Dan, your so-called diets were all unmitigated disasters, but, as you still seem to be obsessed about the body beautiful, the only thing left is to get out and exercise more. Anyway as I've said before it's your own business so just deal and let's get on with the game."

He was right, of course, but I wasn't about to admit it. In fact, my doctor had pretty much told me the same thing. "You'll have to stop burning the candle at both ends and take up some regular exercise or go and work out in the gym."

In case I failed to get the message, he was quick to point out evidence of a bender or two, a few minor scrapes, a rear end that has seen better days and a couple of over inflated tyres. He even suggested I might consider laying off the high-octane fuel for a bit – pointing to my Carlsberg elbow as evidence of over enthusiasm in that department.

"You don't know what you're talking about, Mick," I commented, starting to deal. "In fact, I have just been wheeled out after my first ever medical overhaul and I am delighted to tell you that, despite a teensy bit of a cholesterol problem, a bit of high mileage, signs of some bumpy rides along the way, and a few hard roads travelled in the early years, I am, as the doc put it, 'good for another 100,000 miles'. At least, that's what I think he said."

Just at that moment rescue came in the form of Laura who had come in carrying a plate of freshly baked cookies. She had overheard our conversation.

"Come on guys, leave Dan alone. He isn't really overweight. He's just pleasantly plump. Here, Dan, have a cookie or, if you'd prefer to wait, your favourite apple and rhubarb pie is in the oven."

What the hell, I thought. I'll have both. Martin just shook his head as he watched me tuck into the cookies.

"Okay, tell you what, Martin. The next time you're going to the gym, I'll come along and you can show me the ropes."

The poker game turned out to be a fairly lacklustre affair with nobody either winning or losing much – even rookie me. There were no great hands played, no brilliant strategies, no great bluffs so we decided to pack it in early.

Martin was driving the 'car pool' so before he dropped me off, we arranged to meet at his gym the following night. He came to pick me up in his car just in case I chickened out. "You're not getting out of this one, Dan. You can just start easy and work your way up from there. It's a mixed club. Men and women sweat it out together. It will be no bother to you."

It wasn't quite the walkover that Martin suggested. Joining a gym class isn't easy. The Weighing In initiation rite is more traumatic for your body than a triple bypass or having twins without an epidural. All the classes are conducted in full view of an enormous glass screen, all the better to see yourself sweating it out and pretending you are enjoying the humiliation of letting it all hang out in the company of willowy figures. The shapes are absurdly uniform; lithe, hairless and glistening like street lamps on a foggy night. The women don't look half-bad, either. This is followed by a short but deeply meaningful sermon on the ecstasy of healthy eating, delivered with zeal in the manner of those monks who once travelled the length and breadth of the country, peddling Catholic guilt and warning horny young men of the dangers inherent in 'going too far'.

The first couple of nights at the gym were fine. I was mesmerised by all the equipment and looking forward to trying each one out. But then I found out that I had to join the aerobics class first before I would get to use all that lovely gear. I tried it twice but I couldn't stand the constant jumping about. I decided to employ my own personal trainer instead, just to get me started. She is so slim, fit and full of the joys that she'd land on Mars if she sneezed. She is also a real sergeant major. "Come along, Dan, time for a bracing run around the track outside. Don't worry about the rain. It will keep you cool. Then come back inside and give me thirty push-ups. That should get you started. I'll have you fit in no time."

I finally gave the whole gym business up after I found myself hiding Twix bars in my track-suit and wincing every time I saw my personal slave-driver. Instead I went home and dusted down a few of Lorraine's old Jane Fonda Workout tapes by way of cranking up those abs and pecs. Keeping an upcoming car test in mind, I reckoned that even if the banger outside the door hadn't a hope of passing at least the one inside should be given a fighting chance. I hate to think that all there is to look forward to in life is turbo-charged false teeth, free travel, bifocals, corns, bunions, irregular bowel movements and dementia. Sometimes I feel that if I look hard enough I will discover a Best Before date implanted in my nether region. My chin has already spawned a twin, those little love handles have become lifebelts and there are already signs of snow on my roof.

Unfortunately the Jane Fonda Workout didn't work out at all. The tapes are so old that they kept sticking in the video machine and the only exercise I got was dashing over to the recorder to give it a whack. Eventually, I broke the damn thing and had to run (well, walk) out and buy a new one.

After that I decided to give jogging a try. I invested in a pair of running shoes recommended by Luke. They cost a fortune but I did manage to give them one or two airings before I started making up excuses not to go out.

Of course, according to Lorraine, there was an alternative.

"Plenty of exercise can be had by having one more go at unblocking the drain in the yard. Even a DIY man of your talents should be able to handle that. It's been stinking up the place for months and you have done bugger all about it. That should keep you going for a while."

I declined the offer; I wasn't quite ready for martyrdom and, just to escape, I donned the track-suit and runners once more and went out for a run. It didn't take me long to get to The Corner House. Sitting on a stool was Mick and he looked the worse for wear. He was, as they say, tired and emotional, and he greeted me with a bear-hug that bordered on violence.

"I'm sorry for saying anything about the exercise thing."

"That's okay, Mick. You were right. I have to get some kind of exercise regime going."

To my surprise, he seemed to have changed his mind and, drunk and all though he was, he had the solution. "You've got it all wrong. The trouble is you're too sober to think straight."

There was, he had decided, a third way, one that would help with the vigorous demands of my new get-fit regime and, at the same time, allow a little fun. Being a well-practised debaucher himself, I had to take what he was saying seriously.

"Have a look at the poster on the wall there. It is a

map, as you know, of the pub trail associated with our annual October jamboree known as the Guinness Jazz Festival. If you care to look closely, you will see that it shows enough hostelries to make a wino weep. Now all you have to do is plot your route and have your own early festival."

There are two things you can do if you happen to live in a city that hosts an annual jazz festival. The first is to get out of town quick before you receive a call from that plonker of a cousin up the country who always rings at the same time of year on the lookout for free lodgings. The second is to embrace the whole shebang and try to get in as many as possible of the city's 400 licensed premises. If you are still upstanding on Monday you can always join the aficionados for lunch-time jazz and regale them with tales of having met good old Billy Bob, the one-armed trumpet player from way down in Louisiana who came for the jazz festival ten years ago and never left. You never know, by that stage, you might even know a bit about jazz.

I got Mick's point. All I had to do was pretend that it was Guinness Jazz time and jog along the trail laid out on the poster, calling into each pub along the way, standing only whenever I decided to quench my thirst and never staying too long in any one establishment.

"It's a new take on the pub crawl," said Mick.

"It's a pub marathon," I shouted back but I figured, what the hell?

Before long, Mick and I had a route worked out. I had to start at The Corner House in MacCurtain Street, head straight for the Metropole Hotel and Dan Lowry's, sweep back around Harley Street Hill, over the main bridge towards Le Chateau and on to Cashman's in Academy

Street. That would, he reckoned take me up to lunch-time.

After that, it would be a quick jog towards Clancy's in Princes Street, and straight down from there to The Long Valley for tea-time. Then we thought a restful sojourn in the Hi-B across the road would be called for.

It started fine in The Corner House but I dilly-dallied there and by the time I got over the bridge I reckoned I was in need of a real rest so I headed straight for the Hi-B. That was my undoing. Outside festival time it is a jazz free zone and, therefore, a good place to get a proper pint and enjoy a good amount of bad company. Of all the strange looking characters inside, one stood out. He was a big, grey-haired black man wearing Plus Fours and a pair of suspenders.

"Hi," he said. "My name's Billy Bob."

I still don't know what happened after that but I woke up the next day with a raging headache and with a mouth feeling like the bottom of a birdcage. I gave the Doc a call, telling him I was either on the brink of death or else I had some kind of rare virus. He was a bit miffed at being called to the house.

"So what's new about that?" he said. "Don't you know that there are people a lot sicker than you, that hospitals look like refugee camps and that half the country is in bed with some ailment or other while the other half is in recovery? All you have is a virus. You'll be up and running in no time. Now I have to go a look after patients who are really sick."

To make matters worse, I managed to pass whatever bug I'd caught along to everyone at home. They fell likes flies, either sick or about to be sick. Naturally, I didn't get much sympathy. Despite entreaties for a little hot whiskey or a currant bun, my beloved met me with stony silence, a stare and said:

"Don't push it or you'll feel a lot sicker. If you had kept up your gym or your jogging you might not have caught any bug. I just don't get it. You buy all the gear, you join the gym then pay a fortune for a personal trainer and you end up exercising your elbow with Mick."

The trouble was I had to be fit and able for the School Sports Day and, at the rate I was going, I would be lucky to win the 100 metres crawl. I had gotten nowhere the year before and I was determined to do better this time. I became obsessed with the idea of winning something, just to show my offspring what a cool dad I could be.

Obsession is often the name of the game, when it comes to any sport or physical challenge. It reminded me of a television programme called *The Fear Factor*. In it, contestants go through all sorts of trial by ordeal – wrestling alligators, eating live tapeworms, bungee jumping over the Grand Canyon, meeting the mother-in-law – whatever. The worst I saw was a group forced to stick their heads in an upturned goldfish bowl while dozens of deadly tarantulas crawled over their eyes, ears and mouths.

The Fear Factor makes the school sports look like a picnic, but they're not. My own overwhelming desire to win something at it was bordering on the neurotic. One morning I found myself hunched over the stove staring into a pot of boiling water with an egg in one hand and a stopwatch in the other. It had nothing to do with my puny attempts at a culinary Renaissance and, in any case, the egg in question was not for eating. It was all about winning the egg and spoon race. Luke had, unasked, taken on the role of my personal trainer. I preferred the first one.

199

"You've got to get in training, Dad, and make sure all your equipment is in order. The egg has to be cooked just right. Too lightly boiled and it will flop around like jelly; too hard and it will roll off the spoon."

Three tries and I still hadn't quite got it right. Choosing the spoon was no easier. I discarded the usual stainless steel contraptions, snorted with derision at the precious silver before finally settling on a delightful old nickel soup-spoon with the dimensions of the Superbowl.

Unfortunately, proceedings were being monitored and I was chastened to hear Fiona's horror struck voice whisper: "We can't use that, dad. It would be cheating".

I didn't care. I had to win some kind of contest. I was also entered in the 500 yards dads' race and, since my get-fit regime had become a get-fat regime, I didn't think much of my chances.

The great day dawned and I was as nervous as a virgin bride.

"Don't worry, Dad, you'll be fine," said Luke, reassuringly.

I wasn't too sure. In fact, I was convinced I would be anything but fine and I even tried to think up excuses on the way there for not taking part. I knew that would not be easy. Woe betide anyone who does not attend sports day – even if all they have to look forward to is a few hours left languishing on the sidelines, grasping soggy sandwiches and trying not to look too miserable.

By the time I arrived at the venue I had become so nervous that I felt there was no way I could do it and I looked for somewhere to hide and keep the head down. It was not to be. Just as I was slinking away to find a quiet corner, a strapping young cleric bounded up, panting like a springer spaniel. He was beaming with unreserved delight, as if he had just had an apparition. Smiling broadly, he slapped me a friendly thump on the back.

"I suppose you'll be hoping to take the 100 metres dash, or are you more of a long distance man yourself?"

For a minute I thought I had taken a wrong turning and ended up in an old episode of *Father Ted*. I began to explain that I had no running gear with me but he had obviously heard that one before.

"Don't worry about that. You'll always find a pair of shorts in the clubhouse. Running shoes aren't a problem either. People are forever leaving them behind. Some have been there for years."

There was nothing for it but to bite the bullet. Luke gave me a pat on the shoulder and repeated his reassuring words. "You'll be great, Dad, honest."

It was as if our roles had become reversed and I was the son. Despite the bad weather, there were a couple of hundred onlookers and they must have enjoyed the spectacle. There is something that is both amusing and ridiculous about the sight of a middle-aged man, clutching baggy shorts and dragging at least two extra stone, panting around a running track on what is supposed to be a fine summer's day. The rain was by now pelting down, a few stragglers were braving the elements but most sensible folk had chosen exile in the nearest pub or were at home enjoying their lunch.

With Luke's words still ringing in my ears, I perked up a bit and decided that I might have a chance after all, In fact, when I spied the opposition I became downright confident. After all, I thought, how difficult could it be?

I was about to find out the hard way as I sized up the opposition, haughtily dismissing the rest of the field as out of condition office workers who couldn't run to catch a train if their lives depended on it. I knew I could handle the giant if I managed to stay down wind long enough to sneak up on the inside. The little whippet with the crew-cut could surely be taken on the corners and the other two, though fit enough looking, didn't seem to have the stamina for the long haul.

I hadn't counted on two late entries, though. One was a short, stout, balding man whose absence of cover on top was more than compensated for by a rainforest of jet-black matting on his chest and legs. At a distance, he looked like he was wearing fur boots. The other latecomer was a different animal entirely – tall, lean and built like a racehorse. I knew instinctively that he was the one to beat.

Things began well enough: off the starting blocks with a skip, round the first bend at a canter and into the straight ahead of the posse. The next time round it got a bit hairier and the rest of the pack was closing in fact, but I was still holding my own and confident of staying the pace. It must have been the rain or the result of too many early mornings but, all of a sudden, the knees buckled and all I could see as I kissed the tarmac was Beckham bounding away towards the finishing line. Led by the guy with the woolly legs, the rest of the pack raced by in a blur. Even the monster lumbered past.

As I staggered to the sideline towards my only consolation – the drop of whiskey left in my flask I found that Adrian had mistaken it for red lemonade and, after an initial shock, had proceeded to drain its contents with what looked oddly like lip-smacking relish.

The racehorse, meanwhile, went on to score a hat-trick, taking the relay and the long jump as well. If they had had synchronised swimming, he would probably have won that, too. Like all good sports used to winning against considerably lesser talent, he was sickeningly magnanimous in victory, suggesting, that we all meet up, like old friends, the following week to watch the rugby on the giant screen he had just installed at home.

"I converted the garage into an entertainment room. It's brilliant. The garage was too small for my new Range Rover, anyway."

Naturally, no other dad could stand him, but most were too polite to refuse. I decided to give it a skip, though, saying I hated the thought of missing the panel discussion but I had to get in some training for the next school sports' day.

After the sports debacle, I began to have serious doubts about the wisdom of ever trying to become a new, improved, version of myself again. Some guys don't bother and it doesn't seem to do them any harm, either. Mick, for instance, is about as far from being a 21st century man as it is possible to get and remain on the same planet. Yet he manages to get away it, thanks to his own laid-back attitude and Laura's compliance.

My decision to abandon my exercise regime coincided, strangely enough, with the return of a recurring back problem. It started acting up but things got really serious when I found I could barely sit up straight on the bar stool. The back kept getting worse and worse and it got to the stage when I couldn't even play poker because it was agony to sit in a chair for anything more than about ten minutes. I missed three sessions in a row and I was getting thoroughly fed up. I tried everything for the back: the GP, who prescribed enough pills to fill a large spittoon, the physiotherapist, with the touch of an angel and the soul of a devil, the 'specialist' whose speciality was robbing patients blind, and the chiropractor whose contortions had me so befuddled I didn't know which way to turn.

As usual, there was no shortage of advice from all quarters. When I briefly returned to the poker game I found that everyone around the table was an expert on the subject of a bad back.

"Acupuncture is the only answer," said Martin, "or else you could try jogging three miles a day barefoot on wet grass. There's a tribe in Kenya that does that."

And, from Mick, came the most bizarre advice of all but the most useful: "Always drink with your left hand with the right shoulder slightly raised. That will do the trick."

I was getting increasingly desperate, hobbling around like Quasimodo and seriously contemplating travelling to France where I heard there was a medium who could put you in touch with a psychic healer from 'the other side'. That was until I was introduced to The Yank, an aging hippie who had given up the high life Stateside for the good life in the wilds of West Cork.

The Yank had once been a lifeguard in California where he enjoyed the kind of Hollywood lifestyle you see in the movies. He progressed from bay watching to the corporate world and was for a time, as the Americans say, 'in advertising', doodling on bits of paper and dreaming up cutesy phrases that would help sell everything from *Playboy* to cures for varicose veins. The hippie in him won out, however, and he eventually chucked it in, leaving behind a company credit card, large fancy car, medical plan and the kind of corporate benefits usually associated with a cradle-to-the-grave welfare state. He also threw out the company suit, literally. As he was leaving the office for the last time, he'd stripped to his underwear and flung the suit in the bin by the front door.

At our first session he told me his life story and what worried me the most was the fact that I was actually paying to listen to him tell me about it.

"I dumped it in the trash, man. It was, like, crazy, you know, the freest thing I ever did. Everyone around just stared but I was, like, shedding my company skin. They probably thought I was a Communist or something."

They probably thought he was a pervert or something, if the story is true, but I have my doubts. We're not talking dangerous revolutionary here. He doesn't seem capable of doing anything more subversive than running a red light at three in the morning. If he does, it will be on his Raleigh bicycle, vintage 1966, which he now cycles everywhere in deference to fossil fuels, the ozone layer and "all our futures, man". He is a committed disciple of the Dalai Lama and a living saint, if ever there was one. He did the trick with the back and he used nothing more hi-tech than a wire coat hanger and a few strange incantations. He promised me that within a month I would be well up to dancing at the crossroads and raising hell at high water. He was as good as his word.

"It works just as well with animals," he said and, as if to prove the point, outside in his little waiting room sat a tiny woman with a huge snarling dog that looked like a cross between a Great Dane and a werewolf. In no time at all, he had the dog licking his hand.

"It's all about relating to the inner animal, Man. It's about respecting the animal and their rights."

He then handed me a leaflet setting out new animal rights legislation in Europe and the US. "It's great. Owners of everything from horses to gerbils can now be fined if they fail to give their pets adequate food and water or enough space and companionship. It's about time."

I had never heard of it and I reckoned I could be in big trouble for harbouring the felon who slew Sylvester the goldfish. If I were living in the US that would probably get me a least a month in the lock-up where I would be lucky to be given the kind of space now demanded for pets by animal welfare groups. If Spenser could talk, he would probably have something to say about that.

It was our last session and The Yank was on a roll.

"In America a chimpanzee has won the right to legal representation."

I read in the leaflet how Simba, a retired funfair chimp, was given a lawyer by an animal rights group fighting to prevent him being sold for experimentation.

"They are now going to give rights to budgies and goldfish as well. The family budgie will have to be put in a large aviary. It's only right. Budgies enjoy the company of other budgies in a stimulating environment."

"But what about the traditional goldfish bowl?"

"Oh my god, no. That's so cruel. Happy, well-adjusted goldfish require a stone to shelter under, the company of playmates, clean, filtered water and shade. You have to keep animals stimulated; otherwise they can get depressed and may need therapy. It's the same with people. We all need to be more cheerful. It will help us live longer and fuller lives."

I reckoned The Yank had a point about the importance of good cheer but I couldn't share his view about how wonderful it was that a chimp had its own lawyer. Surely being forced to share a room with a lawyer was cruelty to animals and would make them thoroughly miserable.

He's right about the importance of being good-humoured, though. I was certainly very cheerful after the

206

school sports' day race, even though I didn't win. I was proud of myself for having taken part and that was 'win' enough for anything.

I am also full of good cheer about my new scheme to get myself a bit of breathing space every morning. I'm pretending to Lorraine that I am doing forty lengths in the pool of our local leisure centre at seven o'clock everyday. In fact, I buy the newspapers in the garage nearby and bring them into the steam room to read. This, in itself, is a kind of race against time because after about ten minutes or so the paper goes all soggy.

In the end, I was found out when a nosey neighbour passed some remark, in Lorraine's vicinity, about how flushed I looked in the steam room each day. My sentence for such a serious transgression is severe.

Lorraine, with an excess of cheer, devised what she saw as the perfect solution to the problem of an overweight husband and an overweight dog.

"Forget all this gym business and your early morning 'swimming'. From now on you can take Spenser for a two mile walk every morning. At least one of you might have some chance of getting fitter."

THIRTEEN

Cheers

As any doctor will tell you, being of good cheer is a medicine in itself. Mick is always cheerful, even when he is playing a losing hand. In fact, according to Jim, the bigger Mick's grin, the worse his hand.

"You can always tell when Mick is bluffing," said Jim one night during a session at Mick's place. He was careful to wait to say this until Mick went into the kitchen to get some beer.

"You're dead wrong, Jim," said Martin. "The reason he can't wipe the smile off his face is that he just kicked your ass with that pair he played. He caught you out and you never even saw it coming. That must have hurt."

It certainly did because Jim fancied himself as the king of bluffers and, to be fair, he did have the perfect poker face: blank, expressionless with just a hint of underlying menace. He loved to bluff and the worse his hand the more brazen he would become with his bluffing. Gerry rarely bluffed a hand. He always preferred to play things straight down the middle. If he had a good hand, he would bet and raise; if not, he would invariably fold. He was a pretty conventional player. He always seemed to be waiting for that perfect hand of high pairs or suited high cards. I, on the other hand, never quite knew when to do either and, in a funny kind of way, that gave me an advantage.

As Martin remarked: "the trouble with playing against

someone like Dan – that is to say an 'improver' – is that you never know what he is going to do next. That means he can take a game from under our noses without even trying."

Mick agreed: "That's right. In fact, my real reason for coaching you, Dan, is so I'll be able to work out what moves you're going to make and can start beating your ass."

That was a typical Mick-style remark and it made us all smile, even Jim. Mick always seems to be in good form and his good humour is infectious because people like being around him. He is fun to be with.

It was the same with my Uncle Joe and I often thought it must have been the reason he lived for so long, despite an array of ailments. He was one of the happiest men I ever knew. We all spent years trying to work out his secret. He wasn't particularly rich, or an Adonis, although in his younger days he did cut a bit of a dash. He was never particularly healthy, either. Three packs a day put paid to that, despite the care and attention of a loving family and a platoon of sturdy nurses. Stamina and sheer bloody-mindedness might have had something to do with his good humour, of course, or more likely roguery, but that can't be the whole of it. He was good-natured up to the last and in the end I put it down to the fact that he must have been born with the Happy Gene. As a result, he was the cheeriest, happiest, jolliest, most gregarious guy imaginable right up until the day he died.

It's a lesson to us all. Being of good cheer isn't just good for others on the receiving end; it won't do you any harm either. Even Jim, never the jolliest of people, cannot help but be good humoured in Mick's company. Jim was still smiling at Mick's latest observation.

"You know, I think this poker face business is over-rated. Look at the games going on in the internet. With an online game, everyone has a poker face."

Another thing Mick loves to do is to exercise the dealer's right to 'call' the game. That means announcing out loud what is happening in the course of the game. More than once a spouse has wandered in while we are playing to hear Mick bellowing something like "Pair of bullets", "The three gets another three", and "Nothing going on in that hand". To the uninitiated this sounds like gibberish. But, daft and all though it may seem, it helps to keep everybody's interest in the game and ensures the night doesn't become too dull.

One thing I have learned from Joe and now Mick is how to turn good cheer to your advantage, even in the face of adversity. I found the secret out a while back when I was still a teenager and Joe was merely middle-aged. I'd put it to good use during one hellish six months working in a hotel in France. Everyone there had been friendly and helpful except for the horror who'd run things, a five foot nothing bag of wind built like a Sumo wrestler and twice as mean. She had been evil incarnate although she'd often looked comical, with her Heidi-like pigtails and her blood-red lipstick. I can't reveal her name because she might still be around or at least rising at midnight to stalk unsuspecting prey; in any case, everyone had called her Madame. She'd struck terror into the kindest of hearts and nobody had ever got the better of her in any kind of verbal joust. But she'd had one major weakness, an Achilles' Heel that I'd discovered accidentally and thereafter exploited whenever I'd got the opportunity – considering her temper, that had been almost every day of the week.

210

Madame had disliked whistling. In fact, she'd hated whistling. She couldn't stick it even for a nanosecond and would stand transfixed like a rabbit caught in headlights at the faintest sound. Even the suggestion of a whistle had made her flush a deep mauve and cower. I was never much of a whistler; I was rarely able to expel so much as a burglar's whisper and could never quite manage that confederation of breath and pursed lips required to produce the pure falsetto of the true practitioner. But, with a little practice and a lot of motivation, I had managed to master it sufficiently to cause at least a modicum of distress.

Thereafter, a greeting like, "Aren't you finished that yet?" would be met with a piercing rendition of *Moon River*. "Can't you do anything right?" had demanded at least half a dozen verses of *The Mexican Whistler*. Even on the day she fired me I'd managed to whistle Dixie as I was being shown the door.

There is even a kind of metaphorical whistle that I find can be put to good use in all kinds of situations. Say your neighbour is complaining about your untidy garden, all you have to do is smile and remark how the view is so much better from your end. Difficult relatives? Buy them a garden gnome and say how the minute you saw it, you knew they'd love it. Go visit your worst enemy in hospital. With a bit of luck, it might bring on a relapse. Whatever happens, you'll have a laugh. Forget about wealth; the greatest gift there is has to be the Happy Gene.

Faced with a school or workplace bully, there is no greater sword than the judicious employment of polite good humour to counter the aggressive nature of the socially or managerially challenged. I particularly recommend it if you happen to have a teacher, boss or

211

supervisor whose notion of making things happen is to roar, bitch, moan and generally put everyone around them down while making sure that all subalterns are kept constantly aware just how brilliant and indispensable he/she is. Put on a winning smile, say "sure, no problem", saunter away with a jaunty gait and watch your nemesis squirm like a hooked mackerel and turn puce in the face with unrelieved fury. If you manage to do it early enough in the morning, it's enough to put you in a good mood for the rest of the day.

I'd even observed the Happy Gene in a politician during local elections not too many weeks ago when he wound his weary way up my steep driveway and practically collapsed at the front door. Wheezing and gasping, he had made several attempts to reach the bell but fatigue got the better of him. He'd finally stuck his snout through the letterbox and bellowed: "Is this the Last Chance Saloon?"

That had got my attention.

Here, I thought, was one of that breed of local representative fast disappearing, the kind untouched by spindoctors or minders and whose only acquaintance with handlers was at the dog track. If there was a pothole to be mended he'd have it seen to in jig time; if the local authority was remiss in collecting the rubbish he wouldn't be long sorting it out and if the electric company were dragging their heels on fixing the lamp at the end of the street he'd light a bonfire under them.

"I suppose you're cadging for number one," I'd said, a bit on the snooty side.

His response had been novel, to say the least.

"To hell with your vote, give me a cup of tea quick. I'm parched."

212

He'd then proceeded to outline what he called his DIY Manifesto.

"Everyone expects politicians to do this, that and the other for them as if we had nothing better to be doing. People are lazy as sin. My answer to them is Do It Yourself. That's my philosophy."

"But what about taxes?"

"Just be grateful you can afford to pay them."

"What about the state of the roads?"

"There's nobody stopping you putting pen to paper and writing to the council."

"What about the traffic?"

"More people should walk to work. We'd be a fitter nation for it."

I'd tried a different tack.

"What about those parents who have to send their kids away to college to get a university education? It costs them a fortune."

"It's a foolish conceit. Every parent from Cork to Cairo want their son or daughter to be a doctor, a lawyer or an engineer. Most of them would be better off being plumbers, electricians and carpenters. They'd make plenty of money and it would save the state a fortune."

The poker guys thought I was making all that up but it turned out that most of us had voted for him.

"I gave him my number one vote," said Martin, "although I found his relentless good humour a bit hard to take."

Jim could relate to that. "Some people make a career out of looking on the bright side. They're the kind of people who see a grumble as a symphony of complaint and who, at the slightest provocation, like to indulge in a little homespun philosophy of the uplifting kind. They

213

seem to think its their sacred mission to brighten the dingiest cubbyholes of all our lives by pointing out that, though things might indeed look bad, they could be so much worse."

Jim was on a roll and not about to stop.

"They're the kind of people I avoid at all costs but even then I always seem to come across members of the cheery brigade at the worst possible moment. It's all I can do not to go directly for the jugular when they say something stupid like: 'It's lucky for you that you only broke your left hand in three places. At least you can still write'."

The worst encounter I ever had with the hellishly cheerful occurred when I sauntered home one spring day full of the joys to find that Armageddon was waiting for me. A storm had ripped the garage door of its hinges, the chutes at the side of the house were dangling fore and aft like some drunken acrobat, Spenser still hadn't returned home from his night on the tiles and, as a kind of pièce de résistance, the new extension was leaking. Not to mention the fact that the heating was on the blink and the lights had taken on a peculiar habit of dimming whenever the downstairs loo was flushed.

I should have known someone would manage to look on the bright side, even when there clearly wasn't any. Sure enough, the ambassador of cheer had come in the shape of a door-to-door salesmen who had clearly been evangelical in his calling. Naturally he had to hammer on the door because, wouldn't you know it, the doorbell had decided to go on strike in sympathy with the heating and the lights. The world's last salesman was dressed Jehovah-style in a sensible blue suit and carried what looked like a ton of bricks but turned out to be a selection of heavily

214

embossed books the size of a cupboard door. He had been an eternal optimist to imagine that he could manage to shift a couple of ton of hardback encyclopaedias in the days of computers, CD-ROMs and DVDs. He might have been a bit thick but he hadn't been blind. He could clearly see the destruction all around, yet he'd chosen to ignore it all in favour of his sales pitch, which he'd recited like a record stuck in a groove.

"You can be the proud owner of these beautiful books, fully bound in calf leather, a real family heirloom for the future, something to hand down to your grandchildren, the envy of your friends... blah, blah, blah."

He'd lost me in two seconds, as I hadn't really cared if they had been rolled on a virgin's thighs. In an effort to disturb his sales pitch, I'd begun recounting my tale of woe, explaining how I had sprained my ankle after stepping in dog pee on the floor while transfixed by the dangling chutes that were bashing against the outside of the kitchen window.

"You're lucky you didn't break it," he'd said, cheerfully. "A break in the ankle can be very painful. I had an aunt once who broke her ankle in three places .... "

Jesus, if he hadn't set off again.

I'd pointed to the garage door. He'd had an answer for that, too.

"It's just as well the car wasn't parked next to it. It could have been badly damaged."

Even the leaking roof hadn't fazed him.

"You're lucky the storm came, all the same. If there hadn't been driving rain from the east you mightn't have found out about the leaks for another few months."

As for the heating, "at least it isn't cold for this time of year."

I'd eventually managed to put the run on him and he'd looked thoroughly dejected as he shuffled off with a boxful of books under both arms. I know it was mean but I hadn't been able to resist a little dig: "It's lucky for you the rain has stopped," I'd called, gleefully.

As I said good night to the guys, thoughts of the Spring Armageddon had jerked me back to reality and more current problems awaiting me at home. Things were not in quite so sorry a state on this occasion, yet there were more than a few matters to attend to. The garage door, which had never been properly fixed after the previous incident, (it wasn't me) had now totally departed its hinges. It occurred to me that it might be no bad thing to run away. I suggested as much to Lorraine when I got home in what I considered to be a cheerful fashion.

"Let's invest in a Bedouin tent. I hear they are warm and cosy, never need painting, varnishing or anything like that and can be carted off and set up on the highest and most inhospitable mountain top, safe in the knowledge that they will never, ever let in the rain."

She wasn't amused but that may have been because the garage door had swung out and bashed against the side of her new car. It looked like the car had come off worst in the encounter. There were also a few other little matters to be attended to. The kitchen sink was blocked again, the bank had sent a hat-trick of warnings about the overdraft and the telephone people seemed to be very cross about something or other. However, the cable company was happy enough; their bill had, for once, been paid on time.

And why wouldn't it? I had made a unilateral decision to accept the cable company's 'unbeatable all-channel offer', which included six film channels, fours sports channels

216

and about two hundred various other ones. I hadn't known there were that many television channels in the world so it didn't take them long to persuade me to take them up on their 'once in a lifetime offer'. Naturally, as Luke was quick to point out, what was the point in having all those lovely channels if all we had to watch them on was a miserable 20" screen? Of course, I knew he had his eye on the 20" for his bedroom, but he was right – the bigger the better. When it comes to televisions, size matters. I had been beginning to feel a kind of locker-room inadequacy, having encountered some king-size examples of cathode ray efforts among friends and colleagues while listening to their boasts about wraparound wide-screens and picture-in-picture special effects. To hear some of them talk, you'd swear they had discovered a cure for cancer.

For once I couldn't wait to go shopping. So off I went in search of TV heaven, full of good cheer, anxious to spend my money and happy in the knowledge that it isn't every day you get any type of excuse to invest in a television the width of a soccer pitch. This was the kind of shopping that men were made for. I knew, however, that I was fooling no-one, least of all Lorraine, by pretending that the big TV was really so the kids could get to watch educational programmes on the Discovery Channel. I also knew Gerry had a big one (TV that is) and, being an engineer, I thought he might know more than most. He met me at the shop and we browsed around together.

"Now, Dan, let me get one thing clear. I don't know any more about TVs than you do. I'm a civil engineer, not an electrical engineer, but I'll have a look at them with you."

That winded me a bit but I was too cheerful to be put

off and, anyway, I had already become mesmerised by a huge screen bigger than our front door. There was a UEFA cup match on and the picture quality was stunning. A young salesman ambled over.

"See, it doesn't matter what angle you look at it, the picture is never distorted, you can see a corner kick going right across the screen. It's the same no matter whether it's at night or the sun is shining right on the screen. The picture is always perfect."

It certainly looked the business.

"Aren't those Spanish players absolutely huge?" I said, awestruck at some of their forward line.

"Not at all. That's because we are on the 1:1 format. That's the real beauty of this little baby. It's one of the few machines that have it. Of course, you have to pay extra, but it's worth it. If we were only on full wide-screen, they would look much smaller."

Gerry could see I was fully convinced but he was not about to let the salesman get away with that load of bull.

"If that's the case, how come the Celtic players don't look any bigger than usual?"

The salesman slinked away to deal with someone more compliant.

I was furious with Gerry. It doesn't do to fail to be awestruck in the sight of such majestic technology, particularly when you are being granted a rare audience. "Why did you have to go and do that? Now they won't give us the time of day."

That didn't seem to bother him. "That guy was full of crap and you were falling for it. What would you have me do: lie to him and pretend I agreed with all that bullshit?"

"Of course you should have lied because, when it comes

218

to telling lies, size matters, too. And, anyway, I might have actually found out how to work the bloody thing. Now he's gone off in a huff and I wanted him to show me the other one with the built-in DVD player."

We left the shop empty handed, which was just as well in the end because when I got home Lorraine had gotten wind of the shopping project and immediately put her size fives down.

"What's this I hear about a 46" TV? That's like a bloody cinema. I'm not having something the size of a holiday home in the sitting room, particularly when it costs more than a small car. What's wrong with the one we already have anyway? It's still working perfectly."

I was about to suggest that she might not have noticed that it had been giving a bit of trouble lately but I thought better of it. Lorraine's lie detector radar is second to none and she would have seen through that little ruse in a nanosecond. Still, a pouting male lip can sometimes work wonders and we managed a happy compromise with a middle-of-the-road Sony 36" flat wide-screen with on-board DVD and fast-text. Before long I was back to my old self and, as we all stretched out on the sitting-room floor to give the new TV its first outing, couldn't help but recall all those wonderful, cheerful lies that guys sometimes come up with when they are trying to get their own way.

I remember at work on the day of a Premiership showdown between Liverpool and Manchester United, the whoppers told were nothing short of brilliant and inventive. My favourites included:

"I'm dying, must have been that fish I had in the canteen on Tuesday. You should get something done about that. There are at least a dozen of the lads from stores out sick today."

"I slipped on a wet artichoke, boss, must have been the Caesar salad."

"Granny's new boyfriend got his lip caught in a can of Carlsberg and I had to take him to the hospital." (That's probably a bit over the top; he drinks Heineken).

There are, as they say, lies, damn lies and statistics – like the ones you can get from the Central Statistics Office that solemnly declare that the average family has three-and-a-half children. It's a bit like saying that if you put your head in the fridge and your feet in the oven, on average you'll be perfectly comfortable. Worst of all, there are deceptions, like the comical notion of constructing mobile phone masts to make them look like trees. Or the latest, most insidious deception of all: go trawling in your local food store and you are likely to land the latest in designer fish fingers. Some marketing guy in Findusland has decided that we should all be eating fish fingers in the shape of – wait for it – fish. I hope his bonus is frozen.

If you must be economical with the truth, make it a double whopper. Never, ever blame traffic if you're late for work. Instead, explain how you were stung by a wasp taking a shortcut through the fields and, wouldn't you know it, it turns out you're allergic to wasp stings and if it hadn't been for the quick thinking of your favourite barman in dousing it with gin, you wouldn't be here to tell the tale. If you arrive home late of a Friday smelling like a brewery, swear blind you only had the one with lunch and that the aroma is from the bad company you were keeping.

The same goes for the nice cop who stops you for speeding and gets the smell of drink. Explain how you haven't touched a drop since you were twelve-years-old and that the odour was from the hitch-hiker you discarded a mile back the road. Little details matter, too, and make sure you do not strike a sour note. Good cheer also has its uses when you are telling massive porkies. Even if you are not believed, the chances are that a good-humoured liar will get into less trouble than a miserable one.

It is no harm to be a well organised liar, either. If you're ringing work to say you have to go to a funeral, remember that you've already buried Auntie Nora twice, you have had two hip replacements since Christmas and after your week in Bali to get over your sex change operation wanting more time off will not cut much ice with the powers that be. Don't forget that you have used up that toothache excuse long ago and a week on a fat farm has its limits. Bosses are inclined to remember that sort of thing.

Whatever you do, don't get all tied up in knots with a convoluted story that even your mother wouldn't believe. Consider the case of the three British tourists in New York who were collared by the NYPD boys when they falsely reported that they had been mugged in Central Park, hoping to collect on their travel insurance. What they failed to realise is that the Big Apple has cleaned up its act and that Central Park is now a crime free oasis. Reports of robberies and muggings there are now so rare that they are investigated thoroughly and with startling efficiency. The visitors, who had clearly been watching too many cops and robbers movies at home, had made the mistake of embellishing their tale of woe with Hollywood dialogue uncharacteristic of the local muggers. Far from having their holidays paid for by the insurance companies, the tourists had missed their flights and had to pay a hefty fine.

There is no harm, though, in introducing a touch of exotica into the proceedings. I should have thought of that when I was trying to get the jumbo-sized TV. Suggesting that the old one was crocked would never have worked. I might have got away with it if I had said something like how someone had discovered that older, smaller TVs gave off dangerous radiation and that the only way to counteract it was to sit for at least three hours a day in front of a giant wide-screen. I even told Lorraine my thoughts in this regard, thinking she might find it amusing. She did in a way but the laugh was on me.

"That's far too convoluted. It would never have worked. It's just like that plan you had to pretend you'd called someone to hang the garage door and unblock the sink. I knew well you were going to try to fix things yourself. But look at it this way: by buying the smaller TV we have saved oodles, more than enough for a handyman and a plumber. Now isn't that something to be cheerful about? Anyway, you really are a lousy liar. You're better off telling the truth, like George Washington."

I don't know much about American history but I do remember learning in Primary school that the founding father and first President was not alone noble and brave, but truthful as well and an example to us all. The evidence for this lay in the fact that, as a child, he'd once confessed to his father that he had committed a grave no-no. According to the legendary tale, which is still told to American children whenever they can be separated from the TV, young George committed the unpardonable sin of chopping down his father's favourite cherry tree.

When his father had enquired as to who had chopped

222

down the tree, young George had the cheek to reply: "Father, I cannot tell a lie. It was I who chopped down the cherry tree."

The fact is that he was caught red-handed, axe in hand, with the tree on the ground. Owning up to something only because you have been caught rotten is hardly an example of upright behaviour. This morality tale has sustained Americans ever since in their quest for a sense of values or universal code that they can pass onto their children. What I cannot understand is how those succeeding generations of American parents are still duped into believing that George Jnr is a worthwhile role model for their kids.

Our own two cherry trees had not yet bitten the dust – though not for the want of trying by a twelve-year-old whom I suspected was using them as handy goalposts. I have yet to catch Adrian red-handed, but I live in hope.

However, I was unable to pursue that plan because I had other things to worry about that had nothing to do with either soccer hooliganism or telling fibs. A serious crime has occurred – a grave and heinous crime affecting a stash of, what I thought had been, well-hidden chocolates. I had secreted a box of Cadbury's Roses in the shoebox under the stairs so that I could have my 'fix' whenever I needed it. I felt sure they were safe there because the only one in the family who ever bothers to polish their shoes is Lorraine and she is too honest and too mature to go around nicking my chocs.

There is, so far, only circumstantial evidence that a crime had been committed: to wit, one carefully opened box, one tab on top of the box resealed to suggest it had not been disturbed and, most damning of all, tiny fragments of chocolate barely visible to the naked eye.

But the most distressing thing for me is that all the caramels and toffees are gone and the sole mouth watering hazlenut chocolate has been half-chewed and replaced in its wrapper. All that I am left with is a motley array of Strawberry Delights and Coffee Supremes, the kind of selection that most people attack in January when all the real Christmas chocolates are long gone.

Since Inspector Morse had long since retired, and I had no actual witness, there was nothing for it but to convene a court of the Star Chamber. The charge sheet was read out to the effect that:

"He/she did, with felonious intent, rob, steal, or otherwise nick sweets from one box of chocolates and did consume, eat, or alternatively, demolish most of said sweets."

The culprit, or culprits, were in denial but counter-charges were flying, ranging from, "it wasn't me", to "I bet it was the mouse", to a cheerful "it must have been Granny". Blaming Granny was, in itself, a hanging offence, but, following a number of mistrials, I had to finally record a Scottish verdict and admit to myself that whatever lies children tell, they learn the craft of artful dodging from adults.

FOURTEEN

Play Mates

Considering that poker is such a sedentary preoccupation, it is surprising how men who play it, even very ordinary players, tend to attract the attention of members of the opposite sex. Maybe it has something to do with all those old cowboy movies that always seemed to have at least one poker scene where the most flamboyant player, unless he was shot dead for cheating, usually got the gal. But it is one thing to play seven card stud, it is another to be what that name suggests. Jim reckons the attraction has something to do with the sense of danger involved, as he explained one night when we were playing at his place.

"In big games for big money, particularly in the States, there is always an audience of groupies, stunning girls drawn by the tension, the excitement, and, of course, the money. The hotels even hire girls sometimes to flirt with the guys at the tables and to make sure they keep playing. It's good for business. In Florida you can even take a river cruise where the passengers do nothing except eat, drink and play poker. There are always groupies on those boats."

He should know because he's played in America himself and that is why he is such a good player. He's probably even better than Mick, although Jim is not such a good teacher.

"Even in the ordinary games when guys were playing for small bucks there were always lots of gorgeous girls around. Unless you were a total loser – and I don't mean at playing poker – you just couldn't go wrong. You could have a different girl every night if you wanted to and most guys did."

It sounded like a macho boast but I believed him, particularly when he explained how such obvious attractions nearly got him hooked on the game in America.

"I gave it up after a few weeks. I was lucky in a way because I learned a valuable lesson early on when I nearly got taken to the cleaners one night. I was in second year law in college and I had gone to the States to work for the summer. I was in Atlantic City working in a big hotel where they had regular poker games going on. It was amazing to watch the really good players and I learned a lot just seeing how they played. They know when to raise, when to fold, how to bluff even against very good opponents. I got my chance to play there one night. The table consisted of a drunk, a maniac and a cast member from a show downtown called *Boylesque*. He was 6'1" in full make-up with a red wig on. We were playing a game called Texas Hold 'em that I had just about heard of but never actually played before. It was obvious too. I was slow; I didn't understand the fixed betting structures and I had to ask each time how much I could bet or raise. It was embarrassing. I lost $300 in about an hour. I was getting creamed with straights, flushes and full houses but by a miracle I somehow managed to get it all back.

Then an old guy joins us. For about an hour he doesn't play a hand and then finally he raises his bet – I said to myself he must have something so I fold. This old guy goes nuts on me: "You've played every hand since I've been here and I raise and you fold." He keeps muttering and then leaves the table. If I hadn't been watching the

226

regulars play in the hotel I wouldn't have recognised that he was a professional on the prowl for easy pickings. That was my last attempt to keep up with the big boys."

There are women poker players too, of course, but, even in the 21st century, it still seems to be a predominantly male preoccupation, a bit like Mick's great passion, fishing. Mick is not alone in his obsession. During the summer months a strange spectacle greets the unwary in the form of a dozen or so people standing on the riverbank staring blankly into the water's rippling surface. Like little garden gnomes, they wait, slack-jawed for something to happen, looking suspiciously like the enraptured crowds who flock to Lourdes to see the statue of the Virgin Mary. The fields near our house are nothing much to look at as they stretch along the south-western flank of the river on the southside of town. The sole item of any great interest is a rather strange sculpture in the shape of a dinosaur that only comes into its own during the winter floods when it is half under water and looks vaguely menacing as it begins to rust. But every summer the fishermen flock to our area. They are certainly far less animated than the statue and I have often felt that if they did the same thing all winter they might begin to rust just like the hulking dinosaur.

They are, of course, predominantly fishermen. Always men. And the proof of this is that I have never once heard even the most strident feminist insist they be called fisherpersons. This is because river angling is a mental condition that almost exclusively affects men. This obsession with swishing a line across a river has always been something I could never quite understand. What's the big deal about sitting by a riverbank from dawn to dusk in the hope of catching something you could buy at a fish stall for half nothing? As leisure sports go, it is hardly exciting, adventurous or particularly challenging.

In fact, river angling is not really a sport at all. The word sport implies the utilisation of some kind of skill like strength or speed or stamina. At the very least a sport should involve jumping over something, running very quickly for some reasonable distance or having to get an object from one side of a vast area to another while other people – often with strange haircuts – are trying to stop you. Rugby, for example is a sport, perhaps the greatest of all sports. It requires not only speed and stamina but also nerves of titanium and a very thick skull. Even synchronised swimming is more of a sport than river fishing.

Sea fishing, on the other hand, is different. It is not hard to appreciate why thousands (again, mostly men, but not exclusively so) venture into the deep blue yonder to do battle with an unsuspecting shark or a mackerel. I can appreciate it even more when they bring plenty of six-packs along for ballast. I even indulge in this adventure myself for a few weeks in the summer. At least there is an element of derring-do and danger in fishing off a boat. There are tides to be considered, shoals to be searched for, wind and sea conditions to be taken into account and there is the little matter of having to ensure that your boat is seaworthy and that you can make it to shore if it begins to blow up a storm.

River angling by comparison has always been a foreign country to me, apart from a brief flirtation with my late grandfather's split cane rod that I soon abandoned to the attic. For the most part, if asked I would have to say hand on heart that I believe that all the river angler has to worry about is getting his feet wet and making sure that

228

those bundles of feather, fur and sparkly things he makes into flies work their magic. At least that was what I'd always thought until Mick started hassling me into giving it a go. He kept telling me I had no idea what I was missing

Mick finally persuaded me to join him by promising to give me a few extra poker lessons for free. The prospect of ambushing the other guys with my new-found skills had proved irresistible. As Jim was telling us about his adventures in America, the thought of beating him in particular was uppermost in my mind. I did not want to rely on beginner's luck, either. I wanted to win on pure skill and nerve and a day on the riverbank was a small price to pay. But when I told the others about our planned excursion for the following Saturday, Gerry shook his head in wonder and gave a loud guffaw.

"You're crazy, Mick. Dan will frighten all the fish away. He can't keep still for five minutes and his powers of concentration are zero."

Mick gave me a friendly pat. "Don't worry, Dan. It's not rocket science. You'll soon get the hang of it and you might even enjoy the tranquillity of it all."

Martin got a dig in, too, just as we packed up for the night. "That's right and you might even enjoy wearing enough rubber to make a fetish artist swoon."

I had forgotten about the gear I might need and it had never occurred to me that I might have to get my feet wet.

"Don't worry about it," said Mick. "All you need is a pair of waders and rubber boots. I have spare waders you can borrow although they might be a bit big."

Mick had a spare rod as well so on the way home after the game as I was driving the car pool I stopped at his house so he could kit me out. He showed me the waders first.

"Jesus, Mick. I'd get lost in those and, anyway, I have no intention of wading waist deep through freezing water. I think I'll just sit on the bank. I have a pair of Wellingtons so I should be OK. I'll borrow the rod, though, if you don't mind."

He also gave me some hooks and a book on angling as I left the house.

The following Saturday the riverbank was tranquil and serene when we arrived. Mick quickly got down to business, whipping the line across the river with the lazy confidence of a true artist and, believe it or not, hooking a lively adversary almost immediately. Whatever he had on the end of his line flashed like a Christmas light as it rose and vanished beneath the surface. Mick was ecstatic. I could swear his pupils were dilated when he finally landed what looked like a sorrowful specimen to me. It was no bigger than a pencil but he had a look of unbridled joy on his face. Now Mick can be a quiet enough guy and will sometimes sit for hours and say nothing but when he does decide to open his mouth he usually has something worthwhile to say. The day on the riverbank was no exception.

"Fishing is better than sex," he said, which was strange considering he was the one who had hooked a beauty queen.

"Don't let Laura hear you say that. I don't think she'd like to hear that you would prefer to look at a trout rather than her."

Mick roared with laughter. "Just kidding, Dan, and don't you dream of saying what I said to Laura. But, still, fishing has a lot to recommend it. Even when I'm past my prime in the romance department I will always be able to land a few big ones."

Just to prove the point, he suddenly hooked something big and, whatever it was, it was bucking and trashing like mad in the water. He played it for all it was worth, reeling it in and letting it out, until it finally gave up out of sheer exhaustion. This time it was a fish worth catching, a beautiful brown trout.

As luck would have it, I soon followed suit after a few false starts and finally landed my first catch, again a brown trout and, although not quite as big as Mick's beauty, it looked wonderful to me. Mick was right. I was enjoying myself. I felt so elated that I lit up a reefer by way of celebrating.

What I failed to realise is that there is an unspoken etiquette to this fishing lark. It's not written down in any rule book that I know of but if you happen to venture offside you'll never hear the end of it.

"Put that out at once," said Mick, turning momentarily angry.

I was obviously in the presence of a politically correct fish. My little faux pas must have put him off his stride because Mick failed to get another bite. In order to invest the proceedings with a more cheerful note, I proposed a radical strategy.

"We could always wire up some kind of stun gun and electrocute the little bastards."

The look of disgust I received could not have been more pronounced had I exposed myself there and then on the riverbank.

"That," Mick said, "is the most disgraceful remark I have ever heard. I don't think you're cut out to be an angler, Dan."

Maybe he was right, I thought, but, then I could never be as single minded as him. He has no interest in anything remotely controversial and he couldn't care less about the state of the nation. Despite being an active partner in the production of five children, he is unburdened by any inkling of what he calls 'women's affairs'. He was not present at the birth of any of his children and he scoffs at the very notion.

I tried to get a rise out of him. "Stop being so cranky, Mick. It doesn't suit you. Where's that famous good humour gone? Anyway, you're not exactly Mr Perfect yourself."

He gave me a quizzical look.

"What do you mean?"

"I mean that while you spend most of your time catching fish Laura is at home being Housewife Of The Year."

"That's the way she likes it," he said, and she didn't mind that he hadn't attended any of the kids' births. "She's an old fashioned girl."

She would want to be. He doesn't take any interest in housework, rearing kids or anything that sparks of the New Man. Nevertheless, he is beloved of this earth; adored, minded and coddled like no one else I have ever met. Laura makes sure of that.

I tried one last go at getting a rise out of him.

"I suppose you think the placenta is a Spanish singer?"

He didn't take the bait. Instead, he started packing up all the gear and we headed off back to his house. When we finally arrived, dripping wet, flushed from the exertions of sitting on our rears all day, Mick was treated like a member of one of the lost tribes of Israel. Despite having nothing to show for the day but a few fish, he was greeted by his beloved as if he had spent the day wrestling with a savage coyote.

"Oh you poor thing, look at the state of you; you must be frozen solid. Sit down there by the fire; I've made you a tasty lasagna. Would you like a drink to warm you up?"

I, on the other hand, was all but ignored. "I suppose he was showing you the ropes. That must have been what kept the pair of you. I wouldn't mind but he's just got over a nasty dose of the flu."

The lasagna smelt wonderful and, just for a second or two, I envied him this cosy domesticity although I knew in my heart of hearts I would find it all too claustrophobic. Sent on his way by a fond kiss, Mick went off to change and put the gear away. I have always been puzzled by the great attraction between Mick and Laura. I would never have dreamed of saying anything about it to Laura but suddenly, and I don't know what possessed me, I heard myself asking her straight out: "What do you see in him, Laura? I know he's a great guy and he is my best buddy, but what's the attraction for the former Miss North Carolina?" It must have been the influence of the fish.

Laura thankfully didn't get offended. She looked at me a little wistfully. "It's like this, Dan. He's safe, he's dependable and above all, he's here with me, where I want him. He's not about to go running off with some bimbo when I start showing my age. He wouldn't dream of going somewhere without telling me and I know that he would never, ever stay out all night. I can trust him and he's all mine. I've been with the other kind of guys, the cowboy studs, the neurotic Wall Street traders, the Hollywood types, and Mick is worth ten of any of them. He mightn't be the most exciting man in the world but he makes me happy. Anyway, I've been around the block too many times and all I want now is a bit of peace and quiet and a guy who loves me to death."

Maybe that's it. Maybe that's why Mick, with his pipe, his gumboots, his fishing tackle and his little leather pouch full of neatly tied flies, still manages to excite the passions of the former beauty queen. Maybe there's something in his lumbering countenance that women find attractive in a reassuring way. Maybe it is guys like him and not the Adonis types who have real sex appeal.

I asked Lorraine her opinion when I got home. As per usual, she had very definite views. "Despite what the magazines and the movies might have to say on the subject, most people choose their mates for reasons other than pure animal passion. Physical attraction is important initially of course but you couldn't spend a lifetime with someone if that was all there was too it. It's true what they say, beauty is in the eye of the beholder. So is sex appeal and, as far as Laura is concerned, Mick has plenty of it."

As she spoke, I thought she was right. In fact, one of the sexiest people I know is Gerry's older sister and, in a way, she doesn't really need it. That's because his sister is a Sister, that is to say a nun of holy orders who, unlike many of her calling, believes in living in the real world. Sister Mary Francis – MF to her friends – is a devout, committed and valued member of her Order and a zealous defender of her faith and mission, but she sees no contradiction in being holy and wholesome at the same time.

"Some lay people think we're all sexless, one-dimensional clones of Julia Andrews in the convent. That makes me mad. There are more fascinating, marvellous, truly alive people inside these walls than you'll meet outside

234

in a month of Sundays."

MF also harbours the kind of passion for horseracing normally associated with those dog-eared punters you'd see sidling out of the betting office at lunchtime of a Friday, full of hope but with years of disappointment etched on every face. True to her vows and her own nature, she never gambles for real, hasn't attended a race meeting since she was a child and rarely gets the chance to watch her favourite sport on television, though that's not for the want of trying. Although there isn't much demand for racing in the convent, she's managed to convert the new curate who says mass there every Sunday.

In the style of a true champion, she has overcome all hurdles and has acquired an encyclopaedic knowledge of racing. MF knows the height, weight and past successes of every jockey worth bothering about, either here or in Britain, and could give a rundown of the form of any top horse with the kind of assurance that would put a professional tipster to shame.

Naturally, I always make a point of asking her for a tip for Cheltenham. There are some defining moments in the short journey from the cradle to the grave when you discover you have crossed some kind of invisible threshold; like cutting your first tooth or experiencing that first seriously passionate fumble in the front seat of a Fiesta with the windows steaming and the car in second gear. Then, there are other milestones, like the realisation that you are no longer considered the coolest kid on the block, the discovery of a tiny bald patch, or, if you happen to be one of life's lucky punters, enjoying the fruits of your first win at Cheltenham. I have yet to make a penny out of all my years of investing in the world's greatest racing festival but I am saving hard for the next outing in the knowledge that those minor deprivations currently being suffered by the kids will bear fruit one day when I hit the jackpot. I also believe that my time has come, thanks to a little faith in the man above and the nod from my favourite racing tipster.

MF is also super-cool, which I once discovered to my consternation while having a drink with Lorraine in one of those ultra modern pubs that like to play host to the young and restless. We'd arrived after spending a couple of hours in an art-house cinema. It came as no surprise that most of the movie audience naturally graduated to the arty pub up the road, the kind of place where the barmen wear all black and the barmaids have spiked orange hair and permanent scowls. Two couples had been perched on high stools, within spitting distance. One of the girls had her arms around the two men and was busily giving one a very wet and supposedly passionate kiss. She had then turned to her right and done the same with the other. That seemed to set the two guys off because, seconds later, they were mauling each other and it'd looked like nothing was going to stop them until MF had waltzed in the door, togged out in full ceremonials. She had come to find me to give me her tip for the three o'clock in Newmarket the following day – a rank outsider that she'd felt could do the business if the ground conditions were right (I'd won a small fortune on him). She'd swaggered up to the two men who seemed to be in some kind of suspended animation, and said: "Thanks, fellas, you just made my day."

The little sideshow hadn't taken a feather out of MF but Lorraine had been riveted to the spot and nearly gave herself whiplash trying to follow the proceedings without turning around completely.

"For God's sake, don't stare," I'd whispered. "We're supposed to be cool."

Lorraine's mouth had looked like it was going to drop below ground level. "I know. Those two guys don't bother me in the least but I just can't get over MF. She looks like Clint Eastwood in drag. In fact, I am convinced that's the only reason she was let inside the door; the staff probably think she's a transvestite. I bet people are expecting her to do a dance routine or a bit of karaoke. They probably think she's doing some kind of risqué *Sound of Music* cabaret act."

If that had been true, it didn't seem to have occurred to MF or, if it had, it didn't knock a feather out of her. She must have overheard me because she'd arrived over, put her hand on my shoulder, and whispered conspiratorially.

"I have news for you, both. I'm cooler than the two of you put together and that's saying something, considering I'm the one in the sackcloth and veil."

Then, pointing to another little drama going on in the corner of the bar, where two bodies of indeterminate gender had become entwined in a figure of eight, she'd blessed herself, given a loud guffaw and declared: "There but for the grace of God go I."

Bars and nuns don't really go together – even in the 21st century. The only other time I can remember seeing a nun in a bar was when members of the Sisters of Mercy would venture out of the safety of the convent once a year and go on a sort of pub crawl to collect money for the missions in Africa. In those days, the minute they came into the bar, rattling their collection boxes, there would be utter silence. They generally came in around closing time and I always figured they knew exactly what

237

they were doing. Many of the drinkers would be a bit tipsy and would have no bother putting their hands in their pockets. They always seemed to make plenty of money from the clientele who couldn't wait to see the back of them. MF, on the other hand, had sat at the bar and ordered a pint of Guinness and when it had seemed to take ages to arrive she hadn't been a bit slow in making her presence felt. The young barman hadn't known quite what to make of her and he'd looked petrified with fear when she'd hollered: "Hey, cutie, where's my drink or do I have to prostrate myself on the floor?" He'd served her the drink at once. I'd never dared mention the bar night to Gerry. I have a feeling he is a bit embarrassed by his sister and thinks she is a bit of a nutter.

Nutter or not, MF is right about one thing, though. Compared to most of us, she is as cool as it is possible to be. Some people can never be cool no matter what they do. I suppose there's nothing quite so pathetic as the old and the listless trying to behave like the young and the restless. There's no sadder sight than that of a middle-aged, middle spread man trying to look young and trim with the help of Nike runners, a new hair style, and trying to project an attitude robbed from the latest 'cool' movie release. Some people, like Sean Connery and professors of music, are perma-cool, born to it and never lose it. Others acquire coolness at a young age but let it slip away. People like accountants, young, old or middling, can never, ever be cool no matter how hard they try. It's next to impossible to disguise the image of the knitted cardigan or the three-piece boring suit bought in the January sales, shiny black brogues, cheap jockey shorts and chat-up lines like: "Wanna come up and see my balance sheet?"

Sister Mary Frances manages to be cool without even trying. She harbours a second secret passion that she has managed to keep under wraps from all but her closest friends. She is a closet Abba fan and has been for over two decades. She can sing *Dancing Queen* with the best of them and does a fair version of *Waterloo*. I have promised her that if she comes up trumps for Cheltenham, I'll take her to see one of those Abba musicals. She also wants to go back to the trendy pub and chat up the barman. She says she fancies her chances.

But before I'd even started to get my Cheltenham gear together Lorraine and I received a very unusual party invitation. It breezed through the letterbox and landed on the mat and, even from the outside, it looked intriguing. It was a bit like a wedding card but there were none of the usual little silver bells, twisted ribbons, garlands of peonies or other manifestations of imminent nuptials. It wasn't an anniversary card either, none of that stuff about twenty-one glorious years together; no hint of luvvie duvvie, smaltzy sentimentality. Instead, on the cover there was a charming black and white photo of a handsome, smiling couple resplendent in bridal gown and morning suit but with a jagged line drawn between them. I turned it over, looking with some trepidation at the back, peeked inside, held it to the light and gazed at this unsolicited missive every which way. Inside, in neat copperplate handwriting it said: "I have pleasure in inviting you to celebrate the divorce of.... "

It was from Jim and, for a minute my only thought was: 'he must be taking the piss.' He had finally got officially divorced from Darina. I knew it wasn't beyond the bounds of possibility that he might want to celebrate the fact but I wouldn't have thought he'd be in the mood for a big party. Getting divorced at the age of thirty-four can't be easy, especially when there's a kid involved. We all knew that Jim was crazy about Cian and was getting to see less and less of him so the notion of a divorce party came as a shock.

As I read on you could have knocked me over with a politician's promise. The invitation was actually from both of them. It appeared that having finally, and legally, had a parting of the ways, the two sparring partners had found something else to agree on for the first time in years. They had decided to share the glorious moment with their mutual friends. Would we go? Would we what! After the initial shock wore off, I thought it was a great idea and I had even managed to persuade Lorraine that it might be fun, so she agreed to go although she thought the whole thing somewhat bizarre.

There was only one problem, as Lorraine was quick to remind me when she looked at the invitation again a week later.

"Dan, have you seen the date of the party? It clashes with Cheltenham and we are already booked to go. I'd much rather go there. I know I agreed to go to the party but I still think the thought of celebrating someone's divorce seems is just a bit too weird for my liking. Sound Jim out and see if he would mind if we didn't go."

Shit! I had forgotten to tell her that I had, in fact, already noticed the clash of dates and had mentioned the problem to Jim at our most recent poker game, just as we were finishing up for the night. He was none too impressed at the thought that we might prefer to go racing.

"It's all right, Dan, if you and Lorraine want to go to Cheltenham instead. It's just that it has been so long since I have had anything worth celebrating that I thought

240

it would be nice to have all my buddies with me."

He then turned to Mick, Gerry and Martin. "Anyway, the rest of you are coming, aren't you?"

There wasn't a word out of the others but there were nodding heads all round. It looked like there was no way out of it.

"No, Jim you're right. We'll be there," I said as I left. "Don't worry about Cheltenham. Anyway, I'd probably just lose my shirt there. You'll actually be doing me a favour by saving me a fortune."

I thought the best thing to do was to confess to Lorraine immediately. She wasn't happy. It had taken the promise of a weekend away on our own in a five star hotel before she came around.

The next order of business was what to wear to such an unprecedented gathering. Lorraine decided to done her Cheltenham outfit but the only decent thing I had to wear was a suit I had bought for a fancy wedding in London. I thought that it would be ironic indeed to be wearing a suit meant for a wedding to a divorce party but what the hell. In any case, we never actually got the wedding invitation despite the fact that we knew many other people going, most of them horsey people we had met last year at the races. I had, of course, been upset at first, saddened and dismayed to the point of going off the drink, but I'd rallied. You like to be asked, even if it's only to refuse.

In any case, the divorce party was a fascinating alternative and, as it turned out, it was a great night. We all had a lovely meal in a nice hotel and there was dancing afterwards. There were about two dozen people at it, all of them old friends of Jim and Darina. They were in the best of form and they even danced together. MF had also been asked along but she hadn't managed to snaffle the barman. Instead she came along with another nun from the convent and they both wore evening dresses and took great pleasure in chatting up all the eligible men in sight. Everyone dressed up for the night, even Mick, and Laura looked particularly gorgeous. Mick had a new suit on but it didn't take him too long to discard the tie. As I looked over at him standing by the bar it occurred to me that he would probably much prefer to be wearing his waders.

FIFTEEN

Game of Love

When you consider the growing number of divorces, it is easy to despair about affairs of the heart so it is important to remember that romance can be fun. I was reminded of this one day in the most unexpected way. There I was, driving into work one Tuesday morning. I'd just gone onto the main road into town when a young guy, standing practically in the middle of the road, flagged me down. He had a rucksack on his back and his thumb in the air, clearly on the lookout for a lift. I screeched to a halt.

"What do you think you're doing? You could get yourself killed."

"Sorry, but I'm late for college. My first year exams start today. I stayed in bed too late and my bike is punctured."

He looked ashen-faced and jaded with that kind of haunted and hunted look of the perpetually weary who know that success and prosperity are within their grasp. He must have been laden with all manner of care and worries and I figured he had nobody to blame but himself. I admired his cheek, though, thumbing his way on what should have been one of the most important days of his life.

"Hop in. I'm passing the college gates and I can drop you there. You still have plenty of time."

That seemed to cheer him up and we started chatting. The conversation inevitably centred on the exams and his date with destiny. Despite a conspicuous lack of effort, he seemed to have it all worked out. He reckoned he would be all right in English Literature and Philosophy but he didn't hold out much hope for Psychology, and Medieval Poetry had him knackered. The reason was obvious: he had skipped too many classes, dodged too many of the grinds paid for by his parents and drunk too many pints of cider with his pals. In fact, he was repeating First Year.

Then, as if to put his worries on hold, he turned his attention to the car.

"Fine motor," he said, "plenty of room, but not in the same class as the Toyota Prius."

I was mildly put out by what I considered to be a breach of passenger etiquette and, in any case, I had never heard of the Prius. I was about to be enlightened – in more ways than one.

Apparently, the Toyota Prius, with its environmentally friendly petrol-electric hybrid engine, recipient of many awards, had been tried and tested by *Penthouse* which declared it the Mobile Love Hotel for the 21st century due to its '... free and open front-seat area... ' In other words, it was the best car to have sex in. No wonder he couldn't concentrate on Medieval Poetry. His source of information was the American *Automobile Magazine* which he had looked up on the internet on the computer he had conned his parents into buying him in a desperate and obviously futile attempt to improve his English. I was not convinced, however, considering the Mobile Love Hotel to be another latter-day myth like the so-called Mile High Club. I've always had my doubts about that one: you can't even light up on a 747 let alone get up to any kind of mischief. Still, I decided to play along.

"What about the Ford Focus?"

"It steams up too quickly."

"The Honda Civic?"

"Not enough legroom."

"The Renault Mégane Scenic?"

"Not exactly a passion wagon."

"The Volvo S40?"

"For geriatrics."

I was sure you could steam things up a bit in a Nissan Primera, but I was clearly out of my league.

"You might manage a bit of fun if it's an automatic but the manual is useless. You have to be in second gear."

As I dropped him at the college gates, I was suddenly inspired.

"Surely, the Chrysler Voyager?"

"Now you're talking. You could have a orgy in one of those."

I wished him luck, but considered it unlikely that Sex on Wheels would turn up in the English exam.

He had me thinking, though, about our most primitive instincts and what attracts men to women and visa versa. Naturally, I consulted the poker pals during a lull in a game of seven card stud the following Wednesday.

"OK, Gerry. You were once one of our nation's great womanisers. What's the secret of love?"

"You might as well ask what is the secret of life or the meaning of the universe. The real secret is there is no secret."

Martin, who was hosting, turned to Hollywood for inspiration and took down a video from the bookshelf. "Look guys. This is a movie called *What Women Want*. It's a few years old now but still popular. It stars Mel Gibson and, if his star rating is anything to go by, he knows more about women than most."

Gerry was not impressed. "I wouldn't give much for his star rating now, Martin. Up to that movie, that wide-eyed, snake-hipped, bubble-arsed $25m a movie star, never seemed to have any problem driving women wild but, as Fionnuala said after she saw *What Women Want* he drove them wild for all the wrong reasons. She thought it was a condescending load of crap."

Mick was puzzled. "I never heard of the film. Would someone please enlighten me?"

I duly obliged, explaining that the movie was billed as a romantic comedy in the mould of the films of Spencer Tracy and Katherine Hepburn. "Mel Gibson's character, Nick, manages to secure what men want by getting the inside track on women. To do so, he has to resort to a Boy's Own bit of supernatural cheating. During a cross-dressing session (in pursuit of manly research), Nick has a nasty mishap with a hair dryer in the bath. Falling unconscious after an electric shock, he wakes up in the morning to find that he can hear women's thoughts. The trouble is that, according to the film what they think about is none too glorious or profound."

Gerry butted in. "According to *What Women Want*, all that concentrates the minds of women is make-up and men. But it upset a lot of women film reviewers. They found it insulting, patronising and, like Fionnuala, condescending."

Martin wagged his finger. "In that case, you'd better take care, guys, if you think you can rely on Mel. The woman in your life is more likely to give you a piece of her mind rather than a place in her heart. You'd be better off consulting your horoscopes."

Jim gave him a look that said 'Here we go again –

Martin and his horoscopes'.

Martin warmed up to his favourite subject. He was still going on about horoscopes even as we finished our game, but this time I listened. I used to scoff at Martin's enthusiasm but he's actually managed to convert me to the Chinese variety. I'm still not overly interested in the usual starry designations like Pisces and Capricorn but the Chinese version divides the world into animals and is, therefore, far more fun. The Chinese New Year is an event celebrated by a quarter of the world's population and, as Confucius might say if he was around nowadays: one and a half billion people can't be wrong.

According to my own horoscope, it was going to be a tempestuous time – particularly since I happen to be a Horse. According to my chart, 'it will be a year of mixed blessings. There are stormy paths ahead and finances could be worse than expected.' No kidding? Yet I am told that I should embrace my kindly nature to make more friends and am warned: 'The Horse is prone to erratic behaviour and can be scatty.' As I looked around the table waiting for Jim to raise Gerry's bet, I wondered who else might be a Horse.

"I can't be the only horse around here, guys."

It was late and Martin was growing impatient waiting for Jim to make his play. He had just come back from a series of long overnight flights and wanted us to go so he could get to bed. "Come on Jim. Get a move on. I don't know what animal you are in Chinese terms but you're definitely no racehorse when it comes to playing poker."

Jim finally played his hand and glanced across at Gerry. "How about you? You used to shag like a rabbit. Maybe you are one or have you turned into an old goat?"

Gerry upped the ante in the betting stakes again. He

clearly had a good hand. "You're only half-right, Jim, as usual. I am a Goat. Unlike scatty Horses like Dan, Goats are sensitive and talented, though they tend to be eccentric."

Mick piped up. "An old Goat I used to know held an unshakeable belief that there was life hereafter and that he would return to terra firma, newly constituted and invigorated for another go on the merry-go-round. We would often joke about what his reincarnation would be. Would he be man or beast or would he be, as in his lifetime, a bit of both? Because he was an even bigger rake than Gerry, he favoured coming back as a rabbit."

It was down to the wire at this stage. Martin folded with a sigh. "It's getting too hot for me. I'm out."

I had already quit long ago and even Mick had thrown in his hand. Gerry and Jim faced off like a pair of rutting stags.

"What would you like to come back as, Jim? How about a monkey?"

Jim was playing his cards close to his chest. He flung down three Jacks, taking the wind out of Gerry's sails. "Now who's the jackass?"

Martin looked relieved to see the back of us and, as we trooped out the door, I thought that not even his Chinese horoscope could have forecast Jim's win.

I had plenty of time to be perusing my horoscope two days later because I suffered a relapse from my Jazz Trail syndrome. I was lying in bed feeling particularly sorry for myself because I happened to have a week off work at the same time. There's only one thing worse than being out sick from work and that's being sick on holiday. It's all very well to fall foul of the latest bug on company time; it's quite another matter to find yourself snorting, snuffling and sneezing when you should be snogging, surfing and snoozing, happy in the knowledge that someone else is paying for your pleasure.

Once again, everyone at home caught the bug. On this particular occasion, we had decided to take it in relays: first one went down, than another and another, like a pack of dominoes. Even the dog had his day sick and I bet if Sylvester the goldfish had still been around, he would have been looking pale and begging for breakfast in bed. The relay system had one advantage. It meant that while the rest of us were in bed at least one of us was partly recovered and could do the honours with the little errands that every sick person requires. I was the last to succumb, which meant that by the time Lorraine and the kids were back on their feet, I was still feeling sorry for myself in bed.

"Sorry darling but you know I'd get up if I could, don't you? It doesn't give me any pleasure lying in bed nursing a thundering headache without even the consolation of knowing that I must have had a good time the night before. Not only that, but I am aware that you are all sick of me being sick. It isn't that I want to be a burden or anything, but the toast was a little on the cold side and the kids, bless their hearts, are making a teensy bit of noise downstairs. Also, I don't want to be too much of a bother, but would you mind plumping up the pillows that have somehow managed to slip down behind my poor, aching back?"

My little complaints were met with what can only be described as a less than enthusiastic response. I suppose it was understandable in a way as I, being of temporarily unsound body, had to be waited on hand and foot. Not that that was what I wanted, mind you, but I couldn't

249

help it if Lorraine happened to be the one left standing. What cut me to the quick though, following a deathbed plea for a little more hot whiskey was being told firmly: "I'm off to work and to drop the children to school. You'll have to fend for yourself. You're looking much better anyway. Don't forget to put on the dinner before the kids come home."

Sick or not, being at home meant that I had to try and act the househusband again. It used to be otherwise in the glory days of the 1950s as Mick proved when he called over to see me later that morning. Despite my illness, I had managed to make my way downstairs to make a cup of tea. The minute I answered his knock on the door I could see that he had a mischievous look about him. He appeared to be holding something behind his back.

"What's that you're hiding there? You look like you're up to something."

He gave a kind of schoolboy giggle. "It's your get well present. It's an old school book from the States called *The Home Economics Guide*. Laura's mother studied it when she was a little girl going to school. In fact, Laura has the very copy her mother used. I happened to pick this copy up in a second-hand bookshop in North Carolina a couple of years back. I'd forgotten all about it until you started that housekeeping lark."

I had a quick look through it. "You know, Mick, this might make a nice present for Lorraine as a 'thank you' for looking after me or for Valentine's Day. That's only two weeks away."

Mick suddenly became paler than I was. He was horrified. "Have you completely lost your mind? Not only should you not give it to her, you should, if you

250

value your life, put it in the garage or somewhere she'll never find it. I won't be responsible for what might happen if she reads it. You think you're feeling sick now. I wouldn't risk it if I were you."

I was more intrigued than ever so, while Mick finished making a pot of fresh tea, I sat down and read it aloud.

The Good Wives' Guide
Have dinner ready. Plan ahead, even the night before, to have a delicious meal ready on time for your husband's return home from work. This is a way of letting him know that you have been thinking about him and are concerned about his needs.

"What do think of that, Mick? I bet Laura does that all the time for you."

He grinned. "She loves doing that. She's a 1950's kinda gal, anyway."

Prepare yourself. Take 15 minutes to rest so you will be refreshed when he arrives. Touch up your make up, put a ribbon in your hair and be fresh looking. He has just been with a lot of work weary people.

"Isn't that sweet, Mick?" He said nothing but just shook his head in wonder.

Be a little gay and a little more interesting for him. His boring day may need a lift and one of your duties is to provide it.

That one got him going. "I'm not too sure about that one, Dan. Laura has enough to do without worrying whether I'm bored. Anyway, being gay ain't what it used to be."

Clear away the clutter. Make one last trip through the main part of the house just before your husband arrives. Gather up schoolbooks, toys, papers, etc. and the run a dust

251

cloth over the tables.

Mick thought I was making this bit up. He obviously hadn't even bothered to read more than the first few lines of the book. "Laura wouldn't be much for dusting. She doesn't get obsessed about keeping things tidy. A messy house doesn't bother her as long as the kids and I are happy."

Minimise all noise. Try to encourage the children to be quiet. Be happy to see him. Greet him with a warm smile and show sincerity in your desire to please him.

A quiet house was something neither Mick nor I could ever get used to. Having five children meant Mick's place was even more manic than my own. "It's usually bedlam at home, Dan. I couldn't imagine life without the kids running around."

That last one I read out was the most incredible of all.

Don't complain if he's late home for dinner, or even stays out all night. Count this as minor compared to what he might have gone through that day. Speak in a low, soothing and pleasant voice.

"You know, Mick," I said, "the last time I stayed out most of the night all I got was abuse. I do not recall being greeted by a soothing and pleasant voice."

After Mick left, I continued to thumb through the *Good Wives' Guide* with increasing wonder. The more I read, the more unreal the guide seemed to be, even accounting for the fact that it was published in the 1950s. It certainly had no place in the 21st century. Mick was right, of course. It would hardly do the trick as any kind of present for Lorraine, even for a laugh next Valentine's Day.

Valentine's Day is a big scam, of course, but men forget it at their peril. It takes imagination to get through the Valentine nightmare. Don't bother to think that a potted geranium will do. It's going to take more than that, but the good news is that there are two main ways in which it can be achieved:

(a) In the bedroom if you're feeling frisky and want to see if you can still get from 0 to 60 in twenty seconds.

(b) Down in the tool shed if you want to show off your creative side by making that special gift with your own hands.

(a) The Bedroom: Not so fast, Romeo. So you think all you have to do is strut your stuff and she'll be like putty in your hands? Forget it. In any case, the average romantic man now faces more pressure than ever to perform. Someone has even invented an electronic orgasm machine for women. The person responsible is a doctor in the States (a man – will we never learn?). He was conducting a pain relief operation that involved implanting electrodes into a woman's spine. He positioned them incorrectly and the patient suddenly let out a yelp of pleasure and said: "You're going to have to teach my husband to do that." Eureka! a future for women in which men are a thing of the past. He has now patented it and is pretending that it is a therapeutic device. The thing about it is that women can have the time of their lives with it and nobody else needs to know. They don't even have to take their coats off. All they do is press a button. Mind you, as any hot-blooded woman will tell you, there is no substitute for the real thing and even a balding, overweight 20th century throwback of a man is better than the 21st century plug-in model. That,

253

of course, also puts it up to all those Lothrios out there who had better make sure they are able to outperform any cyborg devices beneath the sheets.

(b) The Tool Shed: If we can be so easily replaced by a button, there's nothing much left for the hunter-gatherers of the species but to dust down that drill and electric saw in the garage and set about making something artistic, like a heart-shaped coffee table, for instance. I decided to do it in the kitchen because it was too cold in the garage. Lorraine was out and I didn't want her to see what I was up to. As I felt I knew what I was doing I thought it wouldn't take too long. How hard could it be? The tools were readily available but any know-how I might have had must have taken a hike. I whipped out the electric jigsaw and proceeded to cut the piece of solid oak I had bought into the shape of a heart. The trouble was I also cut through the chair it was lying on. The drill was balancing on the draining board and slipped into the sink, causing the electric fuse to trip and creating a lake of water on the floor. The hammer then fell on the floor and cracked the tiles just as Spenser bounded in the back door. Just in case things were not bad enough, he immediately proceeded to do his usual trick of vomiting on the floor.

I was in the middle of trying to clear it all up when Lorraine arrived home. I did suggest later that one day we would laugh our heads off at this little incident but I'm still waiting.

In the end I bought a voucher for us to go hot-air ballooning. "You can go on your own," she said. "In fact, that wouldn't be a bad idea."

I was still contemplating the demands on 21st century man when the phone rang. It was Gerry. "I can't host the game next Wednesday, Dan. I'm putting in a new floor in the living room and it probably won't be ready by then. Can you do it?"

Him and his bloody DIY. Still, I said it would be no problem, provided I was fit and able. As it turned out, by the following Wednesday I was fully recovered and, as I was host, I thought I would get the guys to indulge me by chatting about the fate of the modern man and, in particular, how to be a Valentine's Day Superhero (There was always next year!).

Mick was surprisingly animated on the subject.

"If by any chance you happen to be living on a different planet and don't even know that February 14 is Valentine's Day that's your first problem. Your second problem is that you have to know what you want to get out of the day. I see Valentine's Day as a frenetic jamboree for the warm-hearted and hot-blooded but not everyone does. There's a type of bloke who would prefer to hang up their lederhosen, next to their Boy Scout outfit, slip on a pair of woolly slippers, iron their thermals and brew a nice cup of Bovril rather than get involved with Valentine's Day. They're not even worried that they'll be going to bed on their own. They'll never be a Superhero."

That seemed to say it all, but it occurred to me that if the thought of the day that's in it is enough to give a guy goose-pimples, he could do worse than consider how he might measure up in the amour stakes. Did I see myself as a natural born lover, full of the joys, rampant with ardour, a stud in a sweat-suit? If so, I was either a congenital liar or I was fantasising. More likely, I was not

255

unlike most men: shy and hesitant, a slow burner with a faulty fuse and unlikely to set too many hearts a-racing.

Martin turned to me.

"Dan, it's time for all of us to change our images and attitudes. Most guys haven't a hope of remaining a Casanova in middle age if they're wearing a gaberdine and hush-puppies."

He looked down at my feet and I was relieved that I was wearing leather boots.

Martin was on a roll and there was more to come.

"You can't expect to be Don Juan if the only thing that makes your blood boil is the electricity bill. You'll never make the top ten in the lover's hit parade if, when things are getting interesting, you keep wondering whether the back door is shut."

That was too close for comfort and there was no stopping him.

"You are hardly likely to make the earth move when a certain someone is nibbling your earlobe if all you can think about is whether Arsenal are still worth supporting."

I wasn't an Arsenal supporter but I thought it better to keep my mouth shut.

What he said made sense, though. Some guys would make you weep and wonder whether the male of the species is really worth preserving. Take Bionic Man, for instance. As I looked across the table at Gerry, it occurred to me that he is a perfect example of this type of male. He used to have more women than hot dinners. Now he reserves what little passion he has left for machines and other inanimate objects – no longer for him the joys of the boudoir now he answers to the call of the garage. He will gleefully, playfully caress the burgundy interior of his new BMW, wax and polish the bonnet until it shines like a star and gaze lovingly at its curvaceous contours without a thought for his nearest and dearest.

Then, there's Mister Nine-Iron, something of a misnomer. Mick, was at that very moment showing great dexterity by picking his nose and scratching his backside at the same time and I thought that he would not be a million miles away from this kind of character although the love of his live is fishing. Mister Nine-Iron's notion of Nirvana is dressing up in a dusty pink Pringle sweater, wearing funny shoes and chasing an oversized gobstopper for three hours in the pouring rain. Then he'll march manfully into the clubhouse to swap dirty jokes with the lads over a pint.

Macho Man is no better. Down in the gym where the mirrors are shining and the bodies glistening, he will pull, lift, squat and bully those pectorals into a frenzy but he won't work up much of a sweat at home. Martin, for all his talk about what we should and shouldn't do to become the perfect lover, is a perfect example of this. At least he can spot the talent while he's pumping iron.

After we had packed up and the guys had left, I got to thinking that it doesn't take any great magic for the average guy to become a superhero lover on Valentine's Day. You don't have to go to outrageous lengths to improve your prospects, either. You don't have to have a personality transplant, start buying sexy underwear, take up ballroom dancing or do anything like that. All you have to keep in mind is a few simple rules of engagement.

Don't, for instance, arrive home early brandishing a potted geranium and a box of chocolates and think it'll see your way to a night of unbridled passion. That would be sacrilege, like going to Lourdes for a dirty weekend. If you're lucky, the chocolates would be fed to the cat and the geranium would go straight over your head.

Don't go all Latin lover either. Don't say: "Darling, I could smother you with kisses. I want to feel your soft skin against mine, I want to hear our two hearts beating as one. I want to taste your lips and make passionate love all night." She'll think you've gone completely mad, or worse, suspect that you have been playing away from home with some floozy you met at a sales conference.

If you are really stuck, you could try learning off a few Valentine facts to excite and amaze. Mention something like it all started out as a pagan festival to the god of fertility Lupercus and didn't become Valentine's Day until AD 496. Learn the facts by heart and recite them as if they mean the world to you and you have given the whole Valentine business a great deal of thought. There's nothing sexier to a red-blooded woman than a bit of intelligent beefcake.

Whatever you do, don't make the mistake of taking your partner to see some skin flick. There's no greater turn-off nor anything so mind bogglingly boring as being subjected to the sight of a couple of celluloid high-enders making whoopee for two hours on the big screen. It would almost put you off the real thing.

But, above all, never, ever come home at two in the morning after a boozy lunch clutching a dozen wilting red roses in your hand and expect to be greeted with anything but abuse. It's amazing what your partner can say with flowers, particularly when they are being thrown at you.

SIXTEEN

Young and Old Fogies

I always get a bit nervous whenever Gerry starts a conversation with, "The trouble with you, Dan…. " It usually means he is going to go into his finger-wagging routine and impart some words of wisdom which I won't like hearing. This was no exception. We were in Gerry's house for our weekly game. I had been late arriving because I had to drop Luke off at rugby training. The minute I walked in the door I could sense an awkward silence and I got the distinct impression that I had been the subject of conversation. Most of the time that can be a sign of creeping megalomania and, for a moment, it struck me that maybe I was turning into a poor man's version of my tree-hugging neighbour, Mr Personality, but it turned out that I was right. They had been talking about me for some time. No sooner had I sat down to join in the game then they all ganged up on me, with Gerry leading the charge.

"Look, Dan, I'm only saying this as a friend and I don't want you to take offence. The trouble with you is that you're growing old before your time. You think you're cool and all that but, in fact, you're anything but. I know that occasionally you act like you're an eighteen-year-old when you're on the town but the rest of the time you behave like a bloody pensioner."

Martin agreed. "Gerry is right, Dan, and you know how it pains me to agree with him on anything. You're becoming set in your ways. You used to be lively and fun to be with. Now you've become morose and withdrawn and all you can talk about is your garden and, in particular, that bloody hedge you spend so much time cultivating. You've even started baking, for Christ sake."

I had always thought of myself as a reasonably cool kind of guy, one of the lads certainly, but fairly broadminded and forward thinking so this all came as a great shock to the system. I was particularly horrified when even Jim (hardly an example of modern man) joined in the attack.

"You're becoming an old fart," he said.

"I am not. I love new things and new experiences. I'm game for anything."

He shook his head vigorously.

"Martin and Gerry are right. You used to be up for anything, but you've changed. Only last month when I suggested we take the kids go-karting you said it was too dangerous and that they might hurt themselves and we would live to regret it. You suggested we go for a picnic instead. I mean how sad is that? I ended up bringing Cian on my own. We had a great time and neither of us suffered as much as a scratch."

I was shocked because I had always thought of Jim as a bit of an old fogey himself, early thirties going on early sixties to be exact. I turned to Mick. Surely Neanderthal man would come to my defence? He tried his best, but his heart wasn't in it.

"Look, Dan, I don't think you're an old fart; at least not entirely. I just think you're slowing down, that's all. Maybe you should go mad a bit. Take up hot air ballooning

260

or something different like that. You have become very chauvinistic, though, if you don't mind me saying so."

I couldn't believe my ears. Mick was accusing me of being chauvinistic. Talk about the kettle calling the pot black!

But before I could open my mouth Mick was in again like a shot. "This business of blue jobs and pink jobs at home is the most sexist thing I ever heard. Even Laura, who is not exactly a feminist, was shocked when I told her."

That put the dampeners on the evening for me and I was anxious for the session to be over. After about an hour listening to this abuse, I could take no more.

"I'm sorry guys, this old fart has to go. I have to pick up Luke from rugby. They are training under floodlights but I get nervous when it starts to get dark." That much was true but it didn't alter the fact that I couldn't wait to get out of there.

For days afterwards, what the lads had said stayed on my mind. I decided I needed to run it by someone from outside our usual circle so I went off to consult someone I call The Oracle. Her name is Masie and she is an old friend of the family. She is funny and wise and always seems to be in a good mood. She also has the energy of a dervish and lots to say about politics, the weather, what's on TV and the latest celebrity scandals. Masie is well into her eighties but she's full of fun. She is also a great listener and is never shy about imparting her words of wisdom even if her advice is occasionally off the wall. I didn't talk about myself at first but told her about Jim's older brother, Patrick, a teacher, who decided he needed two weeks sick leave just as he was due to go back to school. I knew she would have something to say about

261

that and I wanted to sound her out and see what her reaction would be to his dilemma.

At the age of thirty-nine, Patrick is healthy as a greyhound, always keeps himself fit, goes to the gym regularly and, unlike a lot of men approaching the big '40'. He has even managed to hang on to most of his hair. During the summer holidays he and his wife go off on brisk walking tours to far-flung and exotic places and whenever he comes in sight of the sea he is the first to take the plunge. But, come the autumn, when you would expect he would be fully refreshed and ready to stride purposefully into school to do battle in the classroom, he always finds he doesn't want to go back. Usually his wife, who is also a schoolteacher, manages to persuade him to go but on this occasion it hadn't worked. He just couldn't face it.

"The trouble with him", said Masie, "is that he has become old before his time. He is thirty-nine going on ninety-nine. If he hates his job that much he should quit, become a New Age traveller or something and forget all about those little brats at school."

I pointed out that his wife may not take too kindly to that suggestion and, anyway, his behaviour was already driving her demented.

"Well then," she said, with the wisdom of one who knows, "maybe it's time for more drastic measures. His real problem may not be anything to do with work. Maybe he has been neglecting his marital duties."

I could hardly wait for what was to come next.

"Tell him to go out and buy his wife a big bunch of flowers, take her in his arms and let them make passionate love every night for a month in every room in the house. After that, he'll be ready for anything, even those horrors in the classroom. That'll see him right."

She has some experience of affairs of the heart. She was once the mistress of a shipping millionaire and, according to herself, "I was dynamite". I bet she was, if any of the old photos I have seen of her are anything to go by. Her advice for Patrick is typical of the way she thinks. I love the way Masie manages to be practical without being altogether sensible. She has always been like that and she accounts for her longevity by way of a lifetime of roguery. I remember her once telling me how when she was, as she put it herself, 'a slip of thing – barely seventy', one day on a whim, she withdrew most of her savings from the post office and booked a cruise on the Nile.

"It was something I always wanted to do and I thought the money would be no good to me when I was dead. I also wanted to see if I could still attract a nice, handsome man. I wasn't looking for Mr Right. I wanted Mr Right Now," she said, roaring with laughter. "And I got him."

She might have grown old but she has never grown up. Masie never married (her only regret) but it wasn't for the want of trying. Her first beau, a handsome young farmer, was killed in the trenches during the First World War and I suspect it is something she has never got over. She still keeps his faded photograph on top of the piano in her sitting room and on occasions I have spied her giving it a wistful sideways glance. Still, you could hardly say she spent the rest of her life pining for what might have been.

I don't see her slowing down any time soon and asking her to take things easy is about as pointless as arguing religion with a Jehovah's Witness. I once found her hauling a barrow full of manure to plant a pair of conifers in the

263

garden. Naturally, being an eternal optimist, they were the slow growing variety. "Why would I want to take it easy? I'm not about to end my days sipping soup through a straw and praying for a happy death." I was relieved to hear that she thought Patrick could get over his difficulties by the simple expedient of a bit of 'nookie'. But Patrick's problem had just been a test run. I really wanted her advice for myself. I told her about my friends' comments and how I was afraid of becoming an old fogey.

"The best thing is not to worry about it or you will turn grey. Then you would be really old before your time. You need to do something silly occasionally. You don't always have to be so sensible. I think that's what your poker friends are getting at. It's like they are in mourning for the friend they used to know. They want their old lively buddy back. What have you been up to lately, anyway?"

I swallowed hard before I spoke. There is one thing about Masie that drives me to distraction. She is a voracious gossip and can never keep a confidence for more than two minutes, even if she has been sworn to secrecy. I knew I was taking a big chance by telling her about my new-found passion for matters culinary.

"I've taken up baking. Not just a few scones flung in the oven, either, or the proceeds of one of those 'just add water' affairs, but the Full Monty of fruit cakes, apple tarts, lemon pies and all that."

This had been thanks to dogged determination and an armful of advice from my mother. It wasn't that I was in any way ashamed of my latest pastime but it wasn't something I cared to broadcast except to those I hoped would have the good sense to keep the information to themselves. Masie wasn't exactly in that category.

Her immediate reaction was to roar with laughter, mutter darkly about how she'd be able to dine out on it for a month and what a laugh they would all have down at the bridge club where she has enjoyed a lifetime of cheating at cards. Then she gave me a nudge in the ribs and cut to the chase.

"I know what your problem is," she said. "You're wondering if the notion of a man up to his armpits in self-raising flour is a bit odd. Don't worry about it, darling. I can think of nothing sexier. I once had a passionate affair with a Belgian chef who could turn out the most exquisite soufflés, enough to melt any woman's heart. You can take it from me that his libido was never in question."

She then had the cheek to attempt to give me a few culinary tips.

"Baking is a bit like having sex, dear. You have to take your time, knead it well, keep the temperature up and let everything simmer away nicely."

Compared to Masie, I suppose I am an old fogey. She is the youngest old lady I know. Her male equivalent was Mick's Uncle Peter. His full name was Peter James but everyone called him PJ. It was a pity he and Masie never got to know one another. They would have got on like a house on fire and they might have even had a fling. The trouble was that PJ did a most unexpected thing. He upped and died without telling anyone. Naturally, all the poker guys were at the funeral and I remember that for the whole day none of us could stop laughing. It was not the drink that made us laugh, though there was plenty of it flowing till all hours, thanks to a kindly publican and a decent and understanding local sergeant. It wasn't the craic, though that was not in short supply either, both at the wake, the graveside and in the pub afterwards. It certainly wasn't the funeral service, because that was a sombre affair. The service was conducted in a manner totally out of sync with the subject matter of the proceedings. A Father Trendy type, who was practically salivating at the sight of an overflowing congregation, had seen us as a captive audience for his theological meanderings. As one member of the congregation said afterwards: "Jesus, I never thought that boy would shut up. It's a wonder PJ didn't rise up and choke him with his own collar."

What had us all in such good form was the memory of PJ's exploits.

"Do you remember the time he bought the greyhound?" said Mick. "It was the world's slowest dog and he swore he could run faster himself."

None of us would ever forget how he'd organised a race at the university running track between himself and the dog and had Mick taking bets on who would win.

"That was unbelievable," said Gerry. "Do you remember the big crowd that showed up? PJ won by a mile and got back the money the dog cost him."

In fact, we had all won money betting on him. None of us had ever doubted for a moment that PJ would win.

"I wonder what happened to the dog?" said Jim, trying to control his laughter.

Mick had a fair idea. "I'm not sure but he did say something about putting him in a stew. I wouldn't have put it past him."

Considering that we buried PJ at the fag end of a faded old churchyard on the day he was to have celebrated his sixtieth wedding anniversary, it may seem somewhat irreverent to say we were laughing as we put him six feet under, but that was the kind of guy he was. You couldn't think about him without smiling. That was the effect he had on people and the fact that he was dead didn't change that. PJ was a scream. He never planned, never saved and did the most outrageous things to the day he died. The pity of it is that he didn't live longer.

Oscar Wilde had it about right when he declared that youth is wasted on the young. He didn't have a particularly long or easy life himself, but he lived it to the full, passionately, sometimes outrageously. Contrast that zest for life with some of the deathless, heedless, gormless youth who grace our streets in their Hugo Boss suits with their designer mobile phones, rushing to God knows where without once stopping to look around them and enjoy the view. There's only one thing worse than an old fogey and that's a young one. Give me an old codger any day.

The difference between a young fogey and an old codger is that one thinks the world will never end while the other spends his whole life afraid that it might. The young fogey is a sight to behold: usually clean shaven but occasionally sporting a bit of a beard, he has all the appearance of having being a paid up member of the Young Conservatives since the age of seven. As a child he never wanted to be a fireman, astronaut or sailor. Instead, he dreamt of being a well-heeled solicitor, an accountant or some kind of civil servant. He never forgot to bring his jacket home after school and always kept his uniform spotless. He never complained about taking out the bins for his mother and did his homework without so much as a murmur of dissent. By the time he was twenty-years-old, he was going on sixty. By the time PJ was seventy he had barely reached puberty. When he turned eighty, he told his wife: "I think I might be getting teenage pimples." There is no doubt that, had he lived to ninety, he would still not have grown up.

We did right by old PJ. The thought of taking him to a funeral parlour with piped music, plastic flowers and nylon carpets never entered anyone's head. He was spruced up in his own home, laid out in his one decent suit on the bed and despite the absence of professional intervention PJ had looked the picture of health.

"He was a handsome old devil, all the same," sighed a spinster who looked like she might, with a little encouragement and the assistance of a brace of brandies, have a tale or two to tell. She made do with giving him a little peck on the forehead.

The rest of us told more tales, tall and true, of PJ's escapades, like the time he disappeared for three days with everyone worried sick and finally turned up out of nowhere. He had taken the boat to France to buy a strange brand of cigarettes that were not available here and he couldn't understand what all the fuss was about. Then there was the story of how, as a young man, he had proposed to three equally gorgeous girls on the one night and they had all accepted him. By all accounts he'd had to do some dirty dancing to get out of that one. He was always a ladies' man and, even up to the end, wasn't beyond spotting the talent. Mick told us about the last conversation he had with his uncle. Apparently PJ had the hots for a very pretty female television newscaster and had gladly explained the attraction: "She has a lisp, you know. Very sexy, I like that in a dame."

I once helped a search party look for him after he had gone off hill walking and failed to return overnight. We found him the following afternoon, half way up the mountain, stretched out on a grassy slope and listening to a soccer match on a transistor.

PJ never had it in him to become an old fogey simply because he was never a young fogey. He couldn't help growing old but thank God he had the good sense never to grow up. The last time we met, barely a week before he died, he was getting ready for his first parachute jump at the age of eighty-four, a birthday present from his grandchildren. I drove him up to the airport and helped him get his gear on, knowing it would have been less than useless to try telling him that what he was doing was madness. As he made for the plane, he turned around, beaming, gave me the thumbs up sign and, amid the scream of the plane's engines, shouted: "You're only young once, boy."

Whenever I fear the onset of premature ageing or becoming an old fogey, I am reminded of that moment. I don't need a lecture from my poker pals to remind me to stop being an old fart. All I need do is think about PJ and his zest for life. I wonder what he would say to me if I told him my fears about growing old before my time. He would probably say the same as Masie and tell me to stop worrying about it. "How old you are is really in your head. It's got nothing to do with chronological age. Stay away from old farts or you might become infected and become one yourself. A real old fogey is to be avoided at all costs."

That's easier said than done, particularly if you happen to be on a crowded train and there is only one seat left and you know, you just know, that the sweet, elderly lady sitting opposite you on the four hour journey is going to drive you crazy. It must be me. According to Mick, I have a sign on my forehead that says: "Please bore the pants off me." I figure he must be right because I cannot think of any other reason why I always get to hear the life story of all those flaky people you come across on trains.

I have met a few beauties but my worst encounter was with a nun. I didn't know she was one at first because she wasn't wearing the habit. I had no sooner planted myself down when she began to talk faster than most people breathe. If there were Oscars for talking (and I suppose in a way all Oscars are for talking) then the old dame with the twin-set would have swiped them all.

She was going to visit her sister who was feeling poorly and she was only wild with excitement at the joy and rapture her surprise visit would surely bring.

"I even bought her a large packet of Fox's Glacier Mints. She's a terror for the mints and they keep her regular."

It was now 9.06 am and the train had yet to slip its moorings and, for the sake of sanity, it was necessary to make a mental diversion. It occurred to me that if this was an Agatha Christie movie Madame Windbag would meet her maker somewhere in the dark recesses of the long, dank tunnel at the far end of the station. As the train emerged into sunlight her lifeless form would be found slumped in the seat, pierced in the jugular by a diamond-tipped hat pin, grey, lifeless eyes staring at the ceiling of the carriage, her mouth open in supplication but, for once, silent and unmoving. The passengers – at least those who failed to make a quick getaway in the tunnel – would feign shock and concern but be secretly thankful that some shadowy and sinister hand had saved them from a fate worse than death.

As the train hurtled ever onwards, the diminutive Hercule Poirot, greatest detective in all the world, would

270

emerge, moustache twirling, to pronounce: "Zis was a most devious crime, delicately executed but ze killer made one fatal mistake. He zought zat by employing a peculiarly female instrument of death zat it would be assumed ze crime was committed by a woman. But he reckoned wizout ze little grey cells of Hercule Poirot. He also left, how you say, his calling card in ze shape of ze hatpin which, if you examine it carefully, bears all ze hallmarks of a crest of ze minor royal House of Schlesweig Holstein. On his lapel, ze murderer wears a similar pin." As the other passengers gasp in amazement at this cerebral deduction, M Poirot delivers his final verdict. "Ze killer is none other zan ze train driver, known to his employers and colleagues as Paddy. In fact, his real name is Daniel Frederik Von Holstein III, grand-nephew of ze dead woman, Mrs Charlotte Winkler, a New York socialite who sided with the Nazis during ze war and whose husband, Henry Winkler tricked the Von Holsteins out of zeir inheritance."

I was trying to figure out how the driver could have managed to do the deed and still keep the train on the rails when I was startled into full consciousness by a lurch as the so-called express trundled into a station. Motor-mouth was still in full flight.

"And another thing, I always feed my irises an aspirin every day. It keeps them healthy, free from fungus and the blooms are only gorgeous. As my sister May always says, you can't go wrong with irises in spring, although I have a fondness for tulips myself. They have such delicate petals, don't you think? But you must always plant them in odd numbers – rows of three, five or seven. As I always say, there's nothing worse than an even number of tulips. They look all wrong."

It was now past eleven o'clock and I was not only going crazy but I was also starving. The breakfast trolley finally arrived and, with its arrival, I had hope of a temporary reprieve, but she was having none of it.

"I'm not a great lover of marmalade on toast. I don't mind it so much with homemade brown bread but there's nothing like a nice pot of strawberry jam, although those pips can be a terrible nuisance if you have false teeth, see."

Then, oh my God, she reaches a gnarled and liverish hand into her mouth and produces the most yellowish false teeth I have ever seen. She held them fondly in the palm of her hand like they were some kind of family heirloom or talisman.

I lost it.

"Put a sock in it, you old windbag. I've had just about enough of your ramblings. I've been listening to you for the last two hours. I've heard about your dog and his worms, your sister's elegant bowel movements, how the elastic on your khaki knickers is too tight, the story about the neighbour with the mad son who spends his day casting a fishing rod out his bedroom window, and how you make your bloody irises bloom with aspirin. I have even put up with your moaning about the marmalade but I'll be damned if I spend my breakfast gazing at your false teeth. I don't really give a tinker's curse if you have corns; I'm not interested in how much of a bargain you got in Marks and Spencer with that new gingham skirt, and I'm not in the least bit impressed by the fact that you perm and dye your own hair. In fact, it's easy to tell. It looks like a Brillo pad. All I can say is that your sister must be either stark raving mad or a living saint to put up with you and I feel sorry for her if the only bit of cheer in her sad life is the prospect of a scabby old biddie like you landing unannounced on her doorstep. And no wonder that poor boy spends his day fishing out the window. You probably drove him to it."

Actually, that's what I should have said. In fact, just like I did with that pilot all those years ago in Greece, I chickened out. Smiling sweetly I made an excuse about having to see someone at the other end of the train and, in what I consider to be an award-winning performance, hoped that her sister would be suitably enchanted by her presence. Then, I headed straight for the bar. As I arose, I noticed she had a hat on the seat beside her, skewered by an impressively large hatpin. The pity of it was that there wasn't a tunnel in sight.

Contemplating my recent encounter on the train and thinking about what PJ's advice might have been, it occurred to me that if close contact with an old fogey could be catching, perhaps the opposite was also true. Hanging out with someone eternally youthful might be equally contagious. With that in mind, I decided to go and visit an old codger by the name of Tony O'Reilly, not the media baron but a small farmer who herds a few cows barely ten miles from the edge of town. He is a fine example of advanced manhood and always manages to lift my spirits. I try to visit him as often as I can and make a point of bringing along a bottle of whiskey or some tasty morsel. I fool myself into thinking I am doing him a favour but, in fact, I probably get more out of the visit than he does. Whenever I call he is always in great form, sitting by the fire in the kitchen of his tiny cottage with a large glass of whiskey or out in his garage tinkering with his collection of old motorbikes. I usually call on Tuesday nights because it is the one evening I don't have to bring someone to Tae kwon do, rugby training, tennis, swimming or piano. I arrived to find him washing his oily hands along with the dishes in his kitchen sink. As I came in, he grabbed the tea-towel to dry his hands and ushered me out towards the garage, a converted cow shed far bigger than the cottage itself.

"You're just in time. I was about to take Betsy out for a spin." Betsy is what he calls his pride and joy, a Norton 900 bike and as I peered inside I could see the beautiful beast gleaming at the back of the garage. It was huge and made the rest of his collection look puny by comparison. "Isn't she a beauty?" he asks as he wipes the chrome handlebars with the tea-towel. "Fancy a ride?"

For a split second, the old fogey in me started to panic. I knew for certain that Tony never bothered to tax any of his bikes, was most unlikely to have insurance for the Norton 900 and certainly never bothered to wear a helmet. I took a deep breath.

"I'd love to," I said and, ignoring the fact that the jacket and trousers I was wearing were hardly suitable for the occasion, I jumped on the back of the bike as he revved it up and steered it out of the garage. Seconds later we were racing at ninety miles an hour along a country lane.

"Yahoo", I shouted as we sped along, thrilled to feel the wind in what was left of my hair and thinking that, with Tony's help, perhaps I would never become an old fogey after all. I remembered the admonishments from my poker buddies about my sedentary ways. I recalled, in particular, Gerry's words: "Dan, you're behaving like a bloody pensioner." As we raced on at breakneck speed, I thought, if this is how pensioners behave I'll have no problem ever becoming one.

SEVENTEEN

Toys for Big Boys

"Love the wheels."

Considering that he spends his time flying from one end of the world to the next, it isn't easy to impress Martin but my newly acquired Porsche 911, glistening under the lamplight in front of his apartment, seemed to have done the trick. He was hosting our weekly session and I had arrived in style. I wasn't about to give him the satisfaction of knowing it but it was partly his fault that I had bought the Porsche at all. In consort with the rest of the gang, he had continued to nag me for weeks.

"Seize the day," he had told me.

"Stop being such an old fart."

"Act your shoe size, not your age."

"Do something outrageous."

Well, I had done something outrageous. I had bought myself a classic sport's car, circa 1972, and I didn't give a toss if everyone thought it was a product of my middle age crisis. Lorraine, bless her, had tolerated my indulgence and her only worry was whether the Porsche had rear seat belts. It hadn't but that was soon fixed because I knew there was no way I would get away with bringing it home without those belts.

I'd parked the car directly outside Martin's apartment so he would have a bird's eye view. I'd thought it might have the dual advantage of making him envious and impressing his neighbours at the same time. It worked. I hadn't even got the chance to ring the main doorbell to the block of flats. He'd got to the front door before I did and, without so much as a greeting, had bounded over to the car and run his hand admiringly over the bonnet.

"Holy shit! You must be selling your body or something. What are you using for money? It's absolutely gorgeous. What's the colour, canary yellow? It's a bit over the top, but, still, I wouldn't say no."

I assured him that the only prospect I had of selling my body lay in the hands of the medical students in the university. Then, with a flourish, I opened the front door of the Porsche. He slid down into the driver's bucket leather seat and ran a knowing eye over the instrument panel on the dashboard.

"Wow! I've flown planes with fewer instruments than this has. This baby looks like it could really take off."

At that moment, everyone else arrived. Mick, Gerry and Jim were travelling together in Mick's car as part of the car pool arrangement. I had given it a skip so I could show off my new machine.

They all rushed over to examine my purchase. Gerry, being an engineer and a car lover himself, knew more about these classic machines than the rest of us put together. He stood back a few yards, dropped down on one knee and gazed at it knowingly, probably checking to see if it had ever been crashed. "Six cylinder job, is it? Very nice, although they say the turbo version was a better engine." Then he came over and popped open the bonnet. "It's an inline job, a straight six. She's capable of doing well over the ton at her ease, I'd say. Lovely, just lovely."

Mick and Jim were more interested in slinking down into the leather bucket seats and admiring the small racing car style steering wheel, the short, five-speed gear stick and the speedometer that showed a top speed of 150 miles an hour. Mick almost got stuck. The Porsche was built low on the ground and he was having difficulty extracting himself from the driver's seat. It took Martin and myself all our collective strength to haul him out.

"I don't think I'm built for that machine, Dan, but it's a beauty. Well wear."

Finally, we took our leave of the Porsche. I wondered if it would be safe or whether some scumbag would come along and rob it or vandalise it and I kept an eye on it from the sitting room window in Martin's flat. There wasn't much poker played anyway that evening. All the talk was of sports cars and other kinds of boys' toys.

"I think there's nothing to beat a Corvette," said Gerry. "It's the sexiest bit of steel on wheels. It can do nought to sixty in a heartbeat."

Jim loved the Audi Quattro he drove. "It is pure muscle, a real macho machine. In fact, sometimes it's a bit too hot to handle and the road holding can be crap. It would give your Porsche a run for its money, though, Dan."

I wouldn't have thought Mick would have been all that interested in fast cars, but he surprised me. "Usually, my only interest is in getting from A to B. My old Volvo 940 estate does that. She's a real workhorse and I've had her for years. But if you were to ask me for my favourite car of all time I would have to say it was the Mercedes 300SL Gullwing of the 1950s. It was a magnificent beast of a thing. Your Porsche is lovely, Dan, but it doesn't really compare. Anyway a Gullwing would set you back about a quarter of a million so, unless, you are planning to improve your poker game, I don't suppose you'll be buying one anytime soon."

How right he was, on all counts. Despite my efforts and his patient guidance, my abilities at poker still left a lot to be desired although I was improving. I now had a better idea when to see a bet, when to raise it and when to fold. I had even tried a bit of bluffing but, so far, I had failed miserably at that. The bluffing bit didn't bother me so much but what really got to me was not being able to win a game on skill alone. So far, anything I had won had been pure luck. Even Luke was streets ahead of me on account of all the time he spent playing with his buddies while travelling to rugby matches on the train.

When I was a youngster, I had never been very successful at any kind of sport or game, although it had not been for lack of trying. The only time I had ever been considered a winner at anything was when I was conkers champion for three years running at school.

Of all the contests I have ever encountered, playing conkers was the most hotly contested. There are certain tests of endurance, races, matches or sporting meetings that take on a gladiatorial aspect by their very nature. There's the Man versus Machine chess championship which can occasionally drive one of the participants to the brink of insanity and schoolboy boxing bouts will often generate more genuine thrills than the choreographed waltzes common among adult performers. But, for sheer viciousness in combat I have yet to see anything to beat a bout of conkers. I don't suppose my championship years are any particular cause for celebration – and they are not something I will ever contemplate telling my grandchildren – but even years later I was still obsessed enough to attend the World Conkers Championships.

The Championships were held in Chelmsford, a prissily neat town near London populated by insurance brokers, retired civil servants and remnants of Empire. The contest took place in a somewhat dilapidated exhibition centre that had all the charm of a 1950s Scout Hall. At the door had been a Sergeant Major type complete with florid cheeks and a pencil-thin moustache.

"This way, please. Keep your passes in view at all times. Ladies and children on left, gentlemen on right," he'd bellowed as if he was organising escape from the Blitz and wartime style segregation was the most natural thing in the world. Inside there had been even more segregation with competitors herded into a kind of enclosure at ground level and viewers forced up a side stairs to a mezzanine where they had to sit on hard benches in order to watch the proceedings. I'd managed to, as they say, 'access all areas' by flashing a press card. The Sergeant Major had looked none too happy at this but he'd been outranked by one of the organisers, a big, busty Jolly Hockey-sticks who happily let me in.

The hall had been an Aladdin's cave of Boy's Own wonders. All over the floor were stashed a staggering collection of old Hornby Railway sets, Matchbox toy cars – some still pristine in their original cardboard boxes – and a whole armoured division of painted tin soldiers which Jolly Hockey-sticks had severely informed me were actually made of lead and were known to cause brain damage among children. Looking at the collection of old boys milling around a particularly fine example of The Flying Scotsman that hadn't been too hard to believe. Most of them had looked like they'd been let out for the day. I'd been wistfully gazing in awe at a magnificent collection of Wellington's hussars when I'd felt a hand on my shoulder.

"Shelby, old man, how are you? It must be over twenty

years. You haven't changed a bit."

"Sorry?"

"I said you haven't changed a bit, the same scallywag you always were. A bit thicker around the waist, but aren't we all? How's Marjorie, or is it Helen? I can never remember."

I'd tried to explain that he was mistaken, I wasn't Shelby, there was no Marjorie and I had never even encountered a Helen but he'd been oblivious to all my protestations.

"Come on, surely you haven't forgotten me? It's Bertie, big old Bertie from Brighton, remember?"

He would have been hard to forget: 6'4", at least 18 stone, with more hair on his chin than his head. There'd been no stopping him.

"Remember the time we peed on the pink carnations at Chelsea Flower Show and were chased by a couple of battleaxes from the Women's Institute? Surely you can't have forgotten that?"

Just when I'd thought the only way out was to practise walking backwards, another hand on shoulder saved the day. It had been Jolly Hockey-sticks and, with a knowing wink in my direction, she'd propelled him towards the centre of the hall.

"Come along George, it's time to meet your next opponent. You made it into the second round."

George, Bertie or whatever his name happened to be, had turned out to be one of Conkers' elite. There had even been a kind of seeding arrangement in operation and he'd been seeded in the top ten. I'd figured he must have been dropped as a baby or had swallowed one too many chestnuts. It didn't seem to matter. Whatever about his mental abilities, he'd been in big demand as a chestnut master.

When it came down to it I had expected the Championships to be nothing more than a polite sideshow to the Matchbox models and Hornby railways. How wrong can you be! The Conkers' World Cup had been mean, rough, tough, noisy and raucous. The participants were nearly all crabby old men in shabby tweeds who, while affecting to exude an air of faded grandeur, had become positively gladiatorial in pursuit of victory. They had left any remnants of stoic endurance or British reserve with their walking canes at the front door. They were products of the English public school system. Many had probably endured frightful indignities at the hands of brutal teachers and house-masters, which had, no doubt, toughened them up enough to compete for the Conkers' Cup. Even the Christian Brothers would have found it hard to match the casual cruelties inflicted on public school pupils. Most of the competitors were Old Boys of Eton or Harrow, the latter a school that the old Etonians delighted in calling The Other Place.

I can't remember who won the conkers' championship, but I do recall him making a touching reference to his old nanny who had spent years perfecting the baking of chestnuts to a granite-like hardness on the kitchen range. I am told that it is no longer the done thing to do that. Cooking your conker is against the rules nowadays, equivalent to an athlete swallowing steroids.

I told the lads an edited version of my conkers story while trying to decide whether to chance bluffing my way and raise the stakes or stay as I was. Even with all the excitement about my Porsche, we did manage to play a few rounds but I was dealt lousy hands in each one. This round was no exception. Of course, I was so anxious to dispel any notion that, despite the mean machine on the street outside, I might have always been a closet old fogey that I wasn't concentrating properly. Just in case there were any 'conkers equals old fogey' comments I'd come up with an excuse for going to the thing in the first place: "I only attended the conkers' championships as an observer, you know, as a newspaper journalist."

I didn't know if they believed me or not but it was the best I could come up with in a hurry. I should have guessed that Jim wouldn't let me away with it.

"Sure you did. I can just imagine your editor paying for you to cover the World Conkers' Championships. Give us a break. I bet you had a great time playing soldiers with all those Old Etonians and the crowd from The Other Place."

"I know that place," said Martin. "I sometimes go to a club called The Other Place but mostly the only Old Boys who go there are ageing queens on the lookout for tender meat."

Mick gave a big guffaw and slapped Martin on the back.

"Good on you, boy. That'll teach him to try and bullshit us. The fact is Dan, you have tried to bluff us twice, once about your encounter with the Old Boys and now, from the way you are holding those cards, it is obvious you're hoping to bluff your way to that little pot of money on the table. You're not fooling anyone on either count. I know you haven't one decent card in your paw so I'm going to raise you and watch you squirm. By the way, Martin, I know somewhere called The Other Place as well. It's the clubhouse belonging to that GAA team that keeps beating my own crowd. In fact we call it The Other Fucking Place."

Mick, damn him, was right on both counts. He forced me to fold and take my beating on that round. As the others continued to play, I got to thinking about passions other than cars or conkers. It's amazing the trouble some guys will go to in order to indulge their passion, whether it's cars, boats, sport or even conkers.

Apart from fishing, Mick's passion was Gaelic games, particularly hurling and he would go to any length to get to a match. It's amazing what people obsessed with a particular team will do to get to that one crucial game.

"Do you remember that time you tried to buy that site Mick from the GAA mad farmer so you could build houses on it. Was he from the Other Fucking Place or your own crowd?"

Jim was looking blank: "What's he talking about?"

Mick flushed puce with rage even at the thought of it.

"It was over three years ago and I had only just gone out on my own in the building trade. I spotted this field near town that was being rezoned for housing. I wanted to build about twenty houses on it and I knew there wouldn't be any trouble with planning. I approached the farmer and it was all very straightforward at first. We had everything sorted and we reached an agreement on the money. But then he threw a spanner in the works. He said the only way he would seal the deal was if I came up with a pair of stand tickets for the All Ireland Hurling Final. It was a bit like the movie *Indecent Proposal* – you know where Robert Redford tries to buy off Demi Moore and her new husband. He offers the husband $1million in exchange for a night of passion with his wife. Some people think everything is for sale."

Mick is obviously made of sterner stuff than that husband because he turned the farmer down flat.

"I said no way. I only had two tickets myself and I was damned if I was giving him those. I told him where to shove his site."

Gerry was impressed. "There aren't too many guys who would give up a money making deal like that, even for something they loved. I'd say you would, though, Dan when it comes to your real passion, what you used to call the biggest boy-toy of all – space. You were so space mad as a kid. I bet you'd still sell your mother for a chance to hitch a ride on one of those shuttles."

He was right.

"Absolutely," I said, thinking back on all those years ago when I was an armchair space cadet, barely out of short pants but with an inexhaustible thirst for anything to do with space exploration. I couldn't get enough of it. I can still remember the inspiring words of that time:

"We choose to go to the moon in this decade and do the other things, not only because they are easy, but because they are hard."

The words are those of President John Fitzgerald Kennedy. The year is 1962. The place: Houston, Texas.

My memory of the night when that very dream came true is still crystal-clear:

"That's one small step for man, one giant leap for mankind."

The words are those of Neil Armstrong. The year is 1969. The place: 6 Wellington Terrace, Grattan Hill, Cork, Ireland, Earth.

It is almost 4 am and a boy of nine is sitting up in bed in striped pyjamas, transfixed by the ghostly flicker of the black and white television. He has to get up for school in a few hours and this is his fourth late night but, who cares? This is history in the making, the zenith of human technological achievement. It is also enormous fun.

He has been gazing at the screen for hours, occasionally adjusting the 'rabbit's ears' on top of the set and, silently cursing, banging the wooden casing to halt the wavy lines that occasionally block reception.

A bulky faded figure makes a hesitant descent down what looks like a makeshift ladder, the kind of thing his mother might use to help wallpaper her bedroom. He holds his breath and watches as the world changes forever.

At 10:56pm Easter Standard Time on July 20, 1969, Neil Armstrong became the first human to set foot on the Moon.

The journey had taken four days. The boy in the bed hadn't done his schoolwork but he had done his space homework. He felt sure that one day he, too, would watch the Earth rise over the lunar horizon. He had long ago worked out the enormous energy required to breach the Earth's gravity, knew the velocity in his head and, in his school notebook, where he should have been transcribing his long division, he had plotted the trajectory required to get to the moon. He had done all that with the help of his very own NASA penpals: one of them Armstrong, the other Edwin Aldrin, better known as 'Buzz'. The third man was named after an Irish revolutionary super-hero. His name was Michael Collins, commander of the lunar module.

Two years before, he had begun writing to them, asking for photographs, information, anything to sate a schoolboy's appetite for space exploration.

"Don't expect too much," his father had warned. "You could end up disappointed. They are very busy men and may not even get to see your letters. The big boys at NASA will probably get someone else to write back."

For once, Dad was wrong. The letters came flying back with amazing regularity. They were real letters, real responses, not just printed cards. The astronauts and I were soon on first name terms. The last communication before Apollo 11 included a request from Neil, Buzz and Michael: "Please keep us in your prayers."

I assured them I would.

In 1969, anything seemed possible. Even before the landing on the moon, the Apollo missions had heightened expectations and fired the imaginations of millions of people the world over. My attitude at the time was to hell with school work. I might have had a little trouble with long division but I could plot the trajectory of the Apollo 11 mission. Admittedly, there was a time when I thought Seville was in Sweden but I knew that beyond Earth and Mars lay the massive gas planets of Jupiter and Saturn. I could have told you that Venus was a very odd place because it is covered in a thin layer of carbon dioxide, which means that the surface temperature is something like 800 degrees centigrade. Only a little hotter than the headmaster had been when he'd discovered I had been dossing again.

I don't regret any of it.

I can also clearly remember learning the next day that the footprints left by Neil Armstrong, are likely to remain undisturbed on the moon for at least a million years. The reason for this is that, unlike the west face of the Matterhorn, Tornado Alley in Kansas and Inch Strand in County Kerry, the Sea of Tranquillity is as calm and as tranquil as its name suggests. Even the American Stars and Stripes raised by those first moonwalkers will never feel the flutter of a friendly south-westerly.

"There really were great moments, Gerry, during those

extraordinary days. I bet you all still remember the famous words: "The Eagle has landed... A small step for man... We came in peace for all mankind."

Gerry shook his head. "Not me, Dan. I was only barely three years old at the time so even if I had for some weird reason been up with my parents watching it I wouldn't remember it. I have to admire the science and engineering that went into that first moon landing, though. It took not only brains but amazing nerve as well. That first mission was really built on a wing and a prayer. Did you know that the whole computer power used to get them there and back was be far less than you would find on your average laptop nowadays? It was extraordinary. Mad, in a way, but extraordinary."

The tiny amount of computer power the astronauts had at their disposal was not news to me but Jim found it unbelievable.

"Wow! That's incredible. I wasn't even born then so the whole space thing has never meant all that much to me, but I have to admire their guts and their pioneering spirit. Their enterprise has never been equalled. Despite all the exploration that has gone on since 1969, they were still the first and no-one can take that away from them."

Martin also remembers being allowed up to watch the moon landing, on a television as dodgy as mine, but he was less evangelical than me about the great moment.

"I still think the whole thing was a bit of a waste. I mean it's strange to think that, even today, the most tangible legacy to the achievements of those space pioneers, not to mention the dreams of mankind and the billions of dollars spent by NASA, is a faded flag and the dusty imprint of an astronaut's boots."

Mick hadn't much interest in matters celestial but, as

he dealt the last hand of the night, he posed a question.

"Martin has a point. What has happened since? I thought Armstrong's small step for man was supposed to herald a giant leap, not only in space exploration but also in inter-planetary tourism. We were told that after a few years of lunar exploration – a decade at the outset – holiday trips on commercial rocket ships would be commonplace; exotic, yes, but no more so than a Kenyan safari or that once-in-a-lifetime trek to Tibet. Walt Disney was even said to be toying with the idea of building a theme park on our nearest celestial neighbour. Whatever happened to that plan?"

None of us had an answer for him but I had to admit that Mick was right. You would have thought that by now it would be no bother to pick up a holiday brochure and finger your way through the exotic goodies on offer away from terra firma. You would have thought that those who put a man on the moon could have found the wherewithal to build a Holiday Inn or two away from it all. Forget about camping in Brittany and take a rain check on Florida and just imagine what it might have been like:

'Don't forget to join us in our Moonraker hospitality suite. Meet our representative in the Mars Bar for zero gravity champagne. Dance the Night away to the sounds of The Lunatics and bring the little ones along to see the biggest bouncing castle this side of Uranus.'

It would beat the hell out of two weeks in a farmhouse in France. In the end of course, expediency put paid to such lofty ambitions, the world grew weary of the same-again space exploits and the Apollo missions foundered in a sea of indifference.

I had been dealt my only decent hand all night but I

288

couldn't concentrate. I was worried about the Porsche and anxious to get it safely home. Mick was on a roll and made off with the biggest haul of the night. I was glad to pack up fairly quickly after all that talk about boys' toys and space exploration and go rescue my Porsche.

That night I had a dream about Neil Armstrong. I suppose it must have been something to do with remembering back to 1969 and then Mick's comments on the 'future' of lunar tourism. Whatever the reason, I pictured him in his astronaut's outfit sprawled nonchalantly on an edge of moonrock in the Sea Of Tranquillity eating a slice of leftover turkey and trying to belch.

As I approached he began to speak and I had to try very hard to hear him. I wasn't wearing any spacesuit but, hey, this was my dream and I'll wear what I like. His words were somewhat less than profound: "Nobody can hear you fart in space."

By the looks of him, he has been spending hours trying to prove his theory. Like all memorable dreams, most of it doesn't make a lot of sense. Before you know it, we are cracking open a couple of beers and chatting about the great mysteries of the universe.

I still have my dreams, though, but, according to another good authority, who serves the best pint this side of Saturn, if and when holiday trips start to the moon, it will cost at least a cool million to book passage. That seems like a bargain to me. A million doesn't go quite as far as it used to, although it will still get you a few of life's little luxuries. You could, for instance, drive away in a brace of Ferraris, complete with six year anti-rust warranty, or try out a sixty-foot yacht for size, complete with onboard Jacuzzi and waterbed. A million big ones would probably even get you a deposit on a secondhand

289

twin-engined Lear jet, but what's all that compared to getting a suntan on the moon?

I have my hopes fixed on raising a brood of bloated capitalists who will have the good sense to get good university degrees and then become plumbers so they can afford to keep their dear old dad in comfort in his dotage. If they are feeling particularly generous they might even see their way to adding to my comfort with a toy for this old boy. Maybe Mick's idea of the Mercedes 300SL Gullwing would do the trick or, if they couldn't quite rise to that, I might make do with something in the order of Tony O'Reilly's Norton 900. But really I pray that they will invest their fortunes in something wiser than oil shares and have enough salted away for the future so that in thirty years time, long after Neil Armstrong's ashes have been cast throughout the Milky Way, they will be able to buy me a one-way ticket to the moon.

If it comes to pass, the first thing I'll do is take a flying leap, with the aid of lunar gravity of course, in the direction of Armstrong's famous footprints and raise a bit of a storm on the Sea of Tranquillity. There's nothing like kicking your heels up when you're on holidays and getting away from it all. It helps create a bit of an atmosphere. Perhaps the future of mankind really does lie in the stars.

EIGHTEEN

Back to the Future

There is a certain moment of utter stillness that comes occasionally in a small gathering of likeminded souls. It is when a lull appears in conversation, when quiet contemplation takes over, when moments of fun or hilarity are put to one side and sober reflection takes centre stage.

These are never awkward or tense moments if they happen among close friends. They are to be cherished. I have found that they seem to be occurring more and more during our poker games and, perhaps this is because, with each passing week, we are all getting older and maybe even a little wiser. I also feel, though, that they are a reflection of a growing sense of foreboding among men, a kind of silent terror that lurks in the male heart and makes him wonder as he gets older what the years will bring.

So what does the future hold for mankind, or at least for the men of mankind? That's a question that has been concentrating the minds of philosophers for years – and not just the bar stool philosophers either.

The long held belief that men were all the same or, at least, represented some kind of monolithic power block or homogenous grouping with fixed ideas and desires, was never more than a myth. Men are not all misogynists, or chauvinists or thoughtless, mindless, gormless prigs, though some may appear that way. Neither are all men big, brawny, brave and sure of themselves. Men of all ages, of all colours, creeds and political persuasion – single men, married men, fathers, sons, brothers, lovers, straight men, gay men and those in between – are as complex, as amazing and as fascinating as women.

One of those quiet moments came late one evening as I played host during a long poker session. I had actually been putting into practice all those hours of careful tutoring by Mick. It seemed to be finally paying off because, for once I was not only winning, I was winning well; that is to say deservedly and, although he was the biggest loser of the night, Mick was delighted.

"You have finally cracked it, Dan. That was a clever play last time when you raised me. I actually thought you had a flush or something. You fooled me good and proper. I'm proud of you."

With that, he got up from the table, came over to me and gave me a warm hug and a kiss on the cheek, something that took, not just me, but everyone else by surprise.

"Steady girls," said Martin. "I think I'm going to cry with all this male bonding going on."

Mick blushed, sat down and the game went on. Then, as if to break the ice, Jim spoke. "Have any of you guys heard of *The Vagina Monologues*? They are a collection of, well, monologues written by an American woman who went all over the world to get women to talk about their vaginas."

I had, in fact, seen a wonderful stage production of the Monologues but the others looked perplexed. Gerry, for all his travels, found the notion of women talking openly to another woman about their vaginas a bit disturbing. "I don't get it. You wouldn't, for instance, ever get men to sit around chatting about their penises. I

292

find the whole thing a bit off-putting, to be honest."

Martin was equally dumfounded by the whole thing. "I don't know about you, but I have never heard even gay guys talk in those kind of intimate terms. I suppose it's because of the 'mine-is-bigger-than-yours' thing that goes on between men. Women don't have that problem."

I suggested that maybe it wouldn't be any harm if men were prepared to talk openly about something so intimate although I could never imagine doing it myself. Then Mick, the guy we had always thought of as Mr Traditional, surprised us for the second time that night.

"I think the notion of, say, a woman of seventy being prepared to explore herself is bloody wonderful. It certainly wouldn't bother me and it wouldn't do men in general any harm. It might even ensure our survival. We are in peril, you know. For the first time in human evolution, men can be done without. The science of genetics has seen to that. Let's face it guys, men are finished. We've had our day. If we were to have the equivalent of *The Vagina Monologues* for men you'd have to call it *The Penis Epilogues*. "

Mick's speech stopped us all in our tracks. Another moment of silence descended like a mist over a mountain and we all thought the same thing – could he be right? There's a fair chance that he could. For the first time in human history, the future of mankind no longer depends on men. Males are now superfluous to requirements and the female of the species is poised for dominance, thanks to the latest in DIY insemination techniques employed by many lesbian couples. In fact, in Britain, there are a number of companies that will post male sperm to the home of lesbians who want a baby. Men, like lemmings, are even queuing up to supply it. To make matters worse, if women don't fancy artificial insemination they have another choice thanks to the invention of a Scottish sheep named Dolly. Who would ever have thought that a sheep could cause such international uproar? But she has and, as a result of her unorthodox beginnings, women can easily have children without men. They can just clone their ideal child. That, of course, takes the live, active female out of the equation as well.

Martin wasn't quite as pessimistic as Mick about the future of men.

"That's not the whole story. The women-only crusade in Britain is totally different to what has been happening Stateside. Look, I spend a lot of time flying in the States and I think that there has been a change of attitude there towards men. Bizarrely enough I think it could have something to do with the terrorist attacks in New York. There has been a restoration of traditional gender roles and a new appreciation of 'manly men' from watching the TV images of firemen and police officers coming to the rescue. After years of male-bashing, male heroism is cool again. "

Jim wasn't convinced. "Yea, I suppose that means that even if men are no longer needed in the bedroom, they can at least take some comfort from the fact that they still have their uses, if only to save the world for the mother race!"

Gerry, who had been remarkable quiet up to now, looked like he was about to say something, but Martin interrupted him

"Hey, lads, I've just had a thought. All this artificial insemination and cloning. It's really a gay plot. Just think about it: you straight guys have had your day. Your input, so to speak, is no longer necessary. We, on the other hand, can clone ourselves to kingdom come. Nellies of the world unite."

Gerry finally got his spoke in. "Whatever about Nellies, Martin is right about one thing: sexual reproduction between men and women is no longer necessary for the survival of the human race. Cloning is everywhere. In a few years time human cloning will be commonplace. You can't stop the march of technology. Look at that strange sect the Raelians. They've been around since the 1970s and they still believe aliens brought us to life. Raelians totally revere technology, which they say is the key to our advancement. They hope that through science we can eradicate disease and make life enjoyable for everyone. Cloning is their ultimate goal. They see it as the key to eternal life."

I had always assumed the Raelians were a group of small kooks with a big imagination but, according to Gerry, there is nothing small about them. They have 50,000 members worldwide and the money to complete their cloning project. It all sounded scary.

"Boiled down to the basics, their beliefs aren't that different from other religions: belief in a mysterious life-giving entity, a drive to improve the Earth for yourself and those around you, and the pursuit of some kind of afterlife. The difference is in the terms: their 'Gods' are aliens and their 'heaven' is cloning. There is one big bonus though: Raelians are big fans of sex and indulgence, as long as it doesn't hurt anyone. To the Raelians conventional religious beliefs are risible."

As I listened to Gerry, it occurred to me that, considering all those cults that tend to peddle only misery and self-denial, the Raelians were really a breath of fresh air and maybe they would be fun to join. Jim clearly thought they made some sense as well and, in particular, felt the Raelians had a fair point about religions like Christianity being a bit of a joke.

"More than 75% of the world's population believes in God yet no-one so far has managed to prove that he or she exists. Imagine if there was a CNN report about a big imaginary guy who claims to know everything and who says he'll judge whether you're good enough to go float on a cloud or bad enough to take the heat in hell, without a fire extinguisher, for all eternity. This supreme being then claims to have given his son a kamikaze mission but says it was okay because: 'Hey, he was resurrected and now I'll see some of ya all later in heaven.' It's enough to turn you into a devout atheist."

The Raelians also have a unique sense of humour. When their founder, a guy called Rael, dies, he wants his body coated in plastic and exposed at UFOland, the Raelian theme park in Canada. He wants to be "… naked, half-skinned with an erection, and in a seated meditation position."

I suggested that in view of all this talk about religion and cloning it might be a good idea to come up with a new Book of Genesis, especially the part where it says: 'In the beginning God created the heavens and the earth... And God said, Let there be light: and there was light.'

"How about this?" said Jim who was playing a blinder. He had been betting high for the last round which meant that he either had a really good hand, and was increasing the pot so he could win it, or he had a lousy hand and was bluffing, betting high to scare off the rest of us. It turned out he had been bluffing all along and he managed to scoop the pot with the kind of hand you normally wouldn't bother playing with.

As he gathered his winnings, he announced what he called The Revised Book of Genesis. "In the beginning, God created the heavens and the earth. Within the next six days came everything else: man, woman, light, dark, Riverdance, yoghurt. On the seventh day He rested. And on the eighth day, a group of alien-worshipping scientists told an epic tale of cloning intrigue, only to find that the world would rather believe that a pair of naked apes started the whole world turning by stealing apples."

They all left that night dwelling on the future of the world of men. It was the same for me but I decided to try and go one better than Jim and come up with a new, improved Ten Commandments. Just in case anyone has a notion that I am being deliberately sacrilegious or blasphemous, be assured that I have nothing against religion – organised or otherwise – and, in fact, I happen to be a big fan of Moses because, by some miracle, he fixed my laptop.

It happened like this: my computer keyboard was awash with the yellow residue of dribbled whiskey which begun to cascade onto the pinewood floor and was being lapped up by a precocious King Charles spaniel who should not have been hiding under my feet. This all came about because my efforts to grapple with a sticky mouse caused a cheerfully large glass of Black Bushmills to spill itself onto the keyboard, with the result that I could neither type nor drink and was reduced to swearing in a most unChristian manner. I was also prevented from enjoying the expedient of licking the keys clean by a combination of fear and trepidation; my curses might draw the wrath of the Almighty and the thought of being found electrocuted the next morning with my tongue stuck between 'Y' and 'U' was too much to handle. There was also the fact that my ranting might wake everyone up, it being the middle of the night and way past normal people's bedtime.

The upshot of it was that I lost every scrap of work so I took to musing quietly on the nature of Man and the universe. I took down a copy of the Bible from the bookshelf. It was dusty, having lain there for years. The book, being inordinately heavy, fell on top of the keyboard and – lo and behold – suddenly the computer came to life again. It was a real 21st century miracle.

While I waited for the computer to fully reboot (Adrian had finally got the term into my head), I glanced at the Bible and concluded that a few new commandments for the 21st century would be just what Moses might have ordered. Clearly, we're long overdue some updated Commandments more relevant to our current lives and times but the problem in seeking out new Commandments, is that all the grand, important subjects – those dealing with ethics and morality – have already been covered in the originals. What, then, remains? Now, I'm no Moses, but if I had to select some new and admittedly lesser Commandments – Ten Commandments which we would think about on a daily basis – I might suggest the following.

I.   THOU SHALT NOT COVET THY
     NEIGHBOUR'S NEW CAR
Particularly if it happens to be an all-singing, all-dancing, 3.8 litre Mercedes. As soon as you discover it berthed behind the hedge and growling like a Rottweiller, it is incumbent upon you to stride purposefully in the direction of next door and offer your heartiest congratulations that such an awesome beast has found a good home. Tell your neighbour how discreet is his choice of transport and

don't forget to mention that lime green is your favourite colour. Do not neglect to forewarn of any dangers.

Mind you, I must confess to being a trifle lax in that regard. My neighbour had a slate loose on his roof and it was perilously close to shifting, hanging like the sword of Damocles over his Merk. I kept thinking I would tell him next week but next week never came.

II. THOU SHALT NOT SNORT AT BILLIONAIRES

Thou shalt particularly not do so when it happens to be a young whippet who has made his fortune selling computer hardware and tells you he plans to retire at age thirty. Don't try to be a smart-ass, saying how you remember when hardware meant hatchets, clothes pegs and broom handles.

III. THOU SHALT LIVE WITH BALDNESS

Diverting attention from your bald patch by growing a beard or sprouting a moustache will not work any more than sweeping those remaining locks onwards and upwards. Beards are for diehard Socialists and monks; otherwise they look scruffy and take more maintenance than the front lawn. Moustaches look daft unless you're a commercial fisherman or you're gay.

IV. THOU SHALT EAT HEARTILY IF INVITED TO DINNER

In fact, scratch that it should be: THOU SHALT NOT TURN UP IF INVITED TO DINNER WHERE DECENT FARE IS NOT ON OFFER.

Alternatively, have it made clear that it's 'drinks only' and have a good plate of stew before going out. Some folk have a strange notion of what constitutes a civilised night out and it is not unknown for a famished invitee to have to endure a party where thirty guests are slobbering over one chilli dip. Don't end up going to a 'supper' with a hearty appetite to find that the only thing on offer is a cup of weak tea and a slice of apple pie.

V. THOU SHALT NOT BULLSHIT ABOUT WINES

Unless you happen to be to the manor born or the king of all bluffers, stay away from rattling on about wines. I still blush at the memory of refusing an offering of a glass from a bottle without a label, saying: "I'm sorry but I couldn't possibly drink home brew." It turned out that the gentleman in question produced wines of such startling perfection that his 'home brew' graced the tables of the finest salons in Paris and had a cult following among wine snobs in New York.

VI. THOU SHALT NOT WEAR TIGHT KNICKERS

This is particularly true if your most outstanding protuberance lies above the waistband. It is far better to hide your embarrassment in a pair of flannel drawers than to risk odium, ridicule and contempt in the clubhouse by donning a pair of leopard-skin knickers. Choose your underwear with care. Those with tent flaps are for wimps, trunks are gone with the wind and those brief numbers are only fit for bubble-arsed boys with little to hide. Neither shalt thou parade around in a Speedo at the beach if thou art more than two stone overweight. It's not sexy. It's not macho. If you really want to wear a thong without looking as if you are flossing your arse, you have to starve yourself, go to a gym, work out or get a bum-tuck. Otherwise, leave it to the sixteen-year-olds.

VII. THOU SHALT NOT CHOOSE THE EUROVISION AS YOUR SPECIALITY ON MASTERMIND.

That is, unless you can recall the colour of Vicky Leandros' dress or can recite the names of the two singers who won jointly with Lulu. You could, on the other hand, shock everyone by revealing that Sandy Shaw had an ingrown toenail when she sang *Puppet On a String* in her bare feet. I think that's worth about douze points.

VIII. THOU SHALT NOT GIVE THINE CHILDREN NAMES WHICH REQUIRE EXPLANATIONS FOR THE REST OF THEIR LIVES

Attention parents who name their kids Zoë, Brooklyn, Trixiebell or Dexter. This is a kind of child abuse. Boys should be Mick or John or – dare I say it – Dan. Girls are Mary, Susan, and occasionally Fiona.

IX. THOU SHALT NOT REVEAL TO THINE MECHANIC THAT THOU KNOWEST ABSOLUTELY NOTHING ABOUT CARS

Mechanics have special Idiot Detection Radar Devices built into their bodies. In fact, as you're expressing your complete ignorance about your car, if you look deeply into your mechanic's eyes, you can actually make out images of the Caribbean holiday he'll be taking with your money.

X. THOU SHALT NEVER, EVER FORGET THY LOVER'S BIRTHDAY

You'd better come up with a damn good excuse for breaking this commandment. May I suggest: "I was pistol-whipped while defending your honour." As a last resort, try: "I was in the hospital, donating a kidney to your mother." Of course, she'll never believe that one.

Here endeth the lesson.

The following week's poker session was to be our last for over a month as Jim and Gerry were each going on holidays and Martin was going to be busy flying in the States. That left Mick and myself – not exactly the makings of a poker school. I had brought along my Ten Commandments and was about to show each of the guys a copy but one look at Jim told me it wasn't the right time. He was hosting and he seemed to be even more agitated than usual.

"It's Cian. He's driving me crazy, sullen and cheeky and acting almost like a teenager. He has a thirteen-year-old cousin that he's seeing a lot of lately and I think Cian is picking up his bad habits. His cousin has just turned thirteen and he's aleady a pain-in-the butt sort of teenager. His parents say he's been driving them mad for the past twelve months. You'd better watch out, Dan. Luke is fourteen and he's not so bad but Adrian is about to turn thirteen. In a few short months, he'll think his brand new trainers are wildly uncool and consign them to the dustbin or, just for the hell of it, leave them on the sidelines after a match along with the new designer jacket or 'forget' to bring them home from a school tour. Then, down the road a bit, there will be demands for more 'hang time' with pals, just one of a bunch of kids loitering without

302

much intent down town and trying their best to look as surly as possible. After that, maybe a year or two further on, he will insist on dragging his grotty, ripped, trodden on, oversized jeans along to the underground clubs. He will be part of the in-crowd in the sort of hellhole where the guys stare gormlessly at the wall and the girls spend their time perfecting those lip-curling sneers that belong to popstars with attitude. The kind of place you dare not enter unless you have a pierced nipple and can prove it by flashing same and saying: 'So, how's it goin', dude?'"

The problem was, the more Jim went on about what was supposedly in store for me, the more I felt a sneaking suspicion that some of the more unruly behaviour he spoke about had a faint scent of familiarity about it. The greatest fear is not that your kids will do something you never thought of doing but will do exactly the kind of thing you used to do at their age. I hope, for instance, that when Luke gets older he will never even think of scooting about in a Volkswagen Beetle with ten other people because it seems like a good idea. I can only pray he will have more sense than to drive to the coast on a provisional licence after smoking too much home-grown weed and I can think of better ways of Adrian spending his time than sitting naked in the snow with a bunch of wanabee Buddhists waiting for the world to end. Neither can I recommend using gin as a mixer with Pernod on a camping trip in France no matter how desperate you are. Waking up in hospital while your head is being stitched after a night on the town is not kosher either, even if you are on the wrong side of forty, and it just happened to be an office party.

However, I decided to put all thoughts of future horror to rest and try to stay cool. Not too cool, though, I wasn't about to get my nipple pierced. I could try saying, "so, how's it goin' dude?" but that would be a monumental embarrassment all round. I know that, at the end of the day, no teenager worth his smelly socks would ever want a cool dad.

It was getting late, way past midnight and the game was winding down. Once again, I made to show my Ten Commandments but Martin got there ahead of me with his own list: **The Good Things About Being A Man**

Same work – more pay
"Not always, Martin", said Gerry. "Not if you happen to be something like the female editor of a newspaper, in which case you can laugh all the way to the powder room after showing the boys a thing or two about where you stand on the payroll.

A five-day holiday requires only one suitcase
Even Jim was amused at that one. "Well, I suppose you're the expert there Martin. After all you travel more than the lot of us put together. I never bring more than hand luggage no matter where I'm going."

You can leave the hotel bed undone
Martin was adamant about that one. "Leaving a mess is definitely a guy thing. My sister actually cleans up before her housekeeper arrives and I will never understand it. She, on the other hand, thinks men are disgusting creatures who would happily pick each other's noses if they got the chance.

You get extra credit for the slightest act of thoughtfulness
I had to agree with Martin on that. It is something that

no woman on earth can help feeling resentful about. Bring a small box of chocolate to Aunty Nora and she will think you are a latter-day saint. If your beloved does the same thing the chances are she will be met with an icy stare and an even more frigid comment: "Well, will you look at this: a little box of chocolates; I didn't know they made them so small. Anyway, we were never really chocolate people ourselves; bad for the complexion. Still, I suppose the children will pick at them."

You are not expected to know the names of more than five colours
In fact, according to Mick, you only need know three. "Black and white are both shades, not colours. Who in their right mind would want to paint their bathroom duck-egg azure anyway?"

Wrinkles add character
This is a real bitch as far as women are concerned. If in doubt, check out the likes of Michael Douglas, Sean Connery and Robert Redford. Even Paul Newman wouldn't be past attracting a hot babe or two. Their female equivalents are either dead, gone into permanent hibernation or have had more facelifts than the Brooklyn Bridge.

The world is your urinal
None of us could argue with that one.

"OK, who farted?"

"Gerry, for fuck sake. Will someone please open a window?" said Martin.

"Open it yourself. Anyway, wasn't me," says Gerry. It

was the end of our mammoth session and everyone was getting a bit tired. I had been out of the game for a while and had been thinking about where we might all be in years to come. I had never got around to showing my Ten Commandments but it didn't matter. Would we all still be alive in ten years' time or would one or two of us have died? Which one, if any, would have become super rich? Would we still be friends? Would we still be playing poker?

I looked at each of my friends in turn as the last hand was played.

"Hey guys, I have something to say."

They all looked at me, somewhat bewildered.

"I just want you all to know I think you're great, a fine example of manhood and the best reason in the world for the survival of the male. Most of all, though, I want you to know that I love you."

Each in turn said the same thing back to me. "I love you all too."

I laughed. If anyone overheard us, it would seem very strange indeed.

"You know what's really weird, guys? Here we are, five grown men telling each other how much we care for one another and we're not even completely pissed."

MORE GOOD THINGS ABOUT BEING A MAN OVERBOARD

You can open all your own jars

Phone conversations are over in thirty seconds

You can drop in on a friend without having to buy a little gift

You can kill your own food.